MW01088227

HELLBOY™

OTHER HELLBOY BOOKS FROM DARK HORSE BOOKS

Hellboy:

Seed of Destruction (with John Byrne)

Wake the Devil

The Chained Coffin and Others

The Right Hand of Doom

Conqueror Worm

Strange Places

The Troll Witch and Others

Darkness Calls

Hellboy: Weird Tales Vol. 1

Hellboy: Weird Tales Vol. 2

Hellboy Junior

Hellboy: Odd Jobs

Hellboy: Odder Jobs

Hellboy: Oddest Jobs

Hellboy: Emerald Hell

Hellboy II: The Golden Army

Hellboy: The All-Seeing Eye

B.P.R.D.:

Hollow Earth & Other Stories

The Soul of Venice & Other Stories

Plague of Frogs

The Dead

The Black Flame

The Universal Machine

The Garden of Souls

Killing Ground

The Warning

1946

The Art of Hellboy

The Hellboy Companion

Hellboy: The Art of the Movie

Hellboy II: The Golden Army—The Art of the Movie

The Fire Wolves

TIM LEBBON

Hellboy created by Mike Mignola

Dark Horse Books®
Milwaukie

Book design by Heidi Whitcomb
Cover design by Lia Ribacchi
Cover illustration by Duncan Fegredo
Front cover color by Dave Stewart

Published by Dark Horse Books
A division of Dark Horse Comics
10956 SE Main Street
Milwaukie, OR 97222

darkhorse.com

Library of Congress Cataloging-in-Publication Data

Lebbon, Tim.
Hellboy : the fire wolves / Tim Lebbon. -- 1st Dark Horse Books ed.
p. cm.
ISBN 978-1-59582-204-8
1. Hellboy (Fictitious character : Mignola)--Fiction. I. Title. II. Title: Fire wolves.
PS3612.E245H45 2009
813'.6--dc22

2008051086

First Dark Horse Books Edition: April 2009
ISBN 978-1-59582-204-8

Printed in the United States of America

10 9 8 7 6 5 4 3 2 1

This one's for my good friend Chris Golden,
who always goes above and beyond.

And a big thanks to Mike Mignola
for letting me play in his world.

"There was a fearful black cloud riven by darting tongues of flame, which then dissolved into long plumes of fire. We could hear the shrieks of women, the screams of children. Most were convinced that this must be the end of the world."

—Pliny the Younger, AD 79

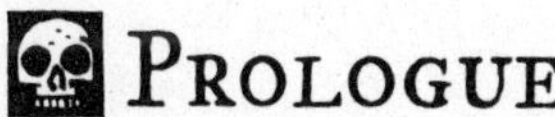

Prologue

AD 79
Pompeii

As the ashes landed in her hair, tears fell from her eyes. The old woman had already lived many lifetimes of suffering and grief, and she had started to believe that tears were only for younger people with much life still ahead of them. But she had been called once again by the spirits of light and the echoes of the silver cloud, urged up from her aged slouch to confront dark forces, and she felt that she could allow herself such a luxury.

She coughed, spluttering as a flake of gritty ash landed on her tongue. The air was heavy. Her lungs struggled, her vision swam, and soon the screams she had been hearing from outside for most of the day would start to fade away.

She had failed.

Dropping the shard of colored ceramic, the old woman put her hands to her face once again and wept. The tears cleared her eyes of dust, and that let her see the image that was forming clearer than before. But that sight only brought more tears, and she cursed the Fates who tortured her so.

Something landed on the roof of the small dwelling, sending shudders through the walls. Dust fell around her. The air, already heavy with ash and choking gases, felt thicker that ever, as if the space she occupied was shrinking. The woman—the old demon hunter, wraith catcher, and spell wielder—held her breath, waiting for the roof to cave in.

And it must, she thought. *That thing will not wish to leave even a trace of itself here. No memories, because almost everyone will be dead. No songs or legends, because they arise from twisted memories, and the dead don't remember. And if a few survivors* do *see it stalking the streets of Pompeii this night, it will burn out their eyes and char their brains in their heads.*

But the roof held, and she continued in her work.

She had never considered herself an artist, and it seemed ironic in the extreme that as the affluent town of Pompeii suffered beneath the wrath of Vesuvius, so she was channelling all her efforts into creating something such as this. The mosaic was simple but effective, and her vague hope was that it would warn those who came to rescue the town in the days to come. Perhaps they would find this and realize its significance, and then . . .

And then? She shook her head, trying to shed the doubts she carried, but like splinters of shattered ceramic peppering weak flesh, they only buried themselves deeper. *If I cannot defeat this thing, then who can? I know so much about it, and yet I don't have time to . . .* Sighing, the old woman used a cutting tool to etch out another thin sliver of shiny orange stone. Always oranges for this thing, and yellows, and reds. Lively colors for something so deadly.

Resting in her palm, the stone burned like fire.

Pompeii was dying, and thousands would die with it. The woman had tried warning them, but no one would listen, and now the city reaped the crop sown by its ignorance. Ash floated on the air, scalding to the touch, smothering. It landed all across Pompeii, quickly growing deeper, and the roofs of weaker structures collapsed under the weight, crushing to death anyone hiding inside. Poisonous gas drifted through the streets. Chunks of pumice rained down—some small as a finger, others the size of a horse—killing those fleeing the ash and gas, battering buildings, exploding as they struck and adding to the dust in the heavy air. If there had ever been a scene of damnation upon Earth, this was surely it.

Behind Pompeii, Vesuvius vented its fury at the darkened skies. A column of ash, smoke and gas rose five miles high from the ragged crater blown in its summit, and in that billowing mass lightning thrashed like something alive, and the glow of unthinkable explosions blinked down across the city.

Day was night, and before this long night was through, alive would be dead.

In the city, fires erupted in a hundred different places. With no one to fight them, they roared out of control, consuming whole buildings, streets and districts. Some were killed by the flames, but perhaps they were the lucky ones; in truth, luck was not looking down upon Pompeii this day.

Many had already fled, and even during the height of the eruption, a few more managed to escape. But thousands were dead, and many more were soon to join them. Survival on their mind, panic leading them, terrified citizens could hide from the ash, dodge the falling rocks, and perhaps even cover their mouths against the poisonous gases that flowed through the streets like groups of hunters stalking prey.

But there was worse yet to come.

And where most fires burned in place, perhaps spreading slightly at the whim of wind or the closeness of neighboring buildings, there was another. This fire moved rapidly through the city. It darted from cover to cover, leaving seeds of itself behind to blossom and bloom and add to the conflagration. When it realized that the furious breath of Vesuvius was closing on the city, it broke cover and poured headlong through the streets. Some people saw it and died from shock. Others drew in a breath to scream, and in doing so sucked flame into their lungs to roast them from the inside out. It ran, leaping across buildings and venting a fiery, ecstatic howl over that doomed place.

The old woman had met this thing three times over the past day, and three times she had failed to stop its progress. Charms and wards protected her skin, though her flesh and blood boiled from the anguish of seeing it pass her by. She had fought it as hard as she could, learning in the process. She had used every means at her disposal. But its victory was as inevitable as what followed it down the mountainside.

From the slopes of Vesuvius, the first of two pyroclastic flows poured in, ready to bury what was left of Pompeii and remove it from the world.

She could feel the ground shaking, and she knew the end was near.

It would be fleeing now. *It* would be gone, out into the world where it did not belong, and in its wake it left ten thousand sad stories that should have never been told.

She had failed, yes. It had been much stronger than she had feared, and perhaps pride had hobbled her, preventing her from calling for help she knew she needed. But she had to dry her tears and do her utmost to make amends. This was one service she could yet perform, and time was running short.

The old woman carved, scored and cracked the fine mosaics, setting them in the wet plaster on the wall before her, slowly building a picture that chilled her to the core. When they came to Pompeii in the days, weeks or months that followed, someone would find her in here and see what she had done. They would view the image. And she prayed to the spirits of light that they would understand.

The roar from outside became unbearable. She could no longer breathe, yet she worked on. Her skin had blistered and bubbled, her eyes had shrivelled in her skull from the heat, but she could still see with other sight. She placed the final splinter of stone and sat back, considering what she had done.

It was simple, but it told the whole story—the volcano and the fire wolf.

Curling into a fetal position on the floor as though preparing to be born again, the old demon hunter waited to be buried alive.

HELLBOY™

CHAPTER I

Amalfi

Carlotta Esposito was beautiful, intelligent, almost eighteen years old, and terrified that she was going to die. She felt eyes upon her everywhere she went. She sensed the attention of dangerous people focused on the back of her neck when she walked past the cathedral steps, along the sea front, or up the gently sloping coastal road towards the old Saracen watchtower that now housed a hotel restaurant. She knew they were dangerous because their stares burned her skin. Sometimes she would turn to try and catch whoever was watching, but they were clever. If they had been strangers, they would have been just other faces in the crowd. But she feared that they were not strangers at all, and if that *were* the case, then they were hiding well.

Not strangers at all, she thought, though a family member or friend who would conspire to see her dead was surely less known to her than someone on another continent, another world.

She had left the family home, La Casa Fredda, early that morning. Wandering the busy streets of Amalfi, she had met with friends for coffee, then bought an ice cream and sat on her own down at the harbor, watching a tourist boat set sail for Capri. The ice cream had dripped onto her blouse, but she did not mind. She needed to appear casual.

Out in the bay, an expensive-looking yacht was moored, all dark timber and bright white sails. She watched someone in swimming shorts jump from the deck and start to swim in toward the harbor, his head occasionally lost to the gentle swells. She stood to get a better view. He paused halfway between the boat and harbor, treading water as though examining the ancient buildings along the coastline. Then he turned and swam back to the yacht. He looked fit, tanned and strong as he climbed the ladder, and someone was there to hand him a towel.

A rich sailor, Carlotta thought. *That's what I need. One that won't be put off from swimming all the way in, and who will take me back with him to his boat.* It was a romantic dream born of fear and desperation, but it was also something that she knew could never happen. She was an Esposito, one of the oldest families in Amalfi, and with money and social standing came certain responsibilities.

If she ran away, she would do her family great harm. But that didn't mean she could not leave for just a little while.

She popped the end of the ice cream cone into her mouth and stood, darting across the road to one of the framed tourist maps of the town. *You are here*, the words above the little red arrow said, but its certainty did nothing to make her feel any safer. She looked past her reflection, trying to scan the shop fronts and pavement behind her for anyone who might be watching. *Is it just me?* she thought. She had told no one about her fears—how could she?—but now that the time had come to change that, she was more nervous than she'd ever been before.

She knew for certain that she was right about the curse. What she didn't know was how much danger revealing her knowledge would put her in. Would they call her a fool? Would they accuse her of tainting her family name? After all, not *every* young Esposito vanished without a trace.

She saw the Naples bus turn around the bend of the Luna Convento Hotel, making its way carefully down the coastal road towards the harbor.

Carlotta sighed and ran a hand through her hair. She was sweating, a mixture of trepidation and excitement at what she was about to do increasing her heartbeat. It was a fine, hot Amalfi day, and she pulled her blouse away from her damp skin and turned casually around.

At a pavement café fifty yards along the front, a man lifted a newspaper in front of his face.

Carlotta dashed across the road, ignoring the admiring glances from a couple of rich, pale tourists in a Mercedes convertible. She darted between parked cars in the small parking circle, glancing back at the café and seeing the man still apparently reading his paper. *Him, yes*, she thought, but she knew that there would be others.

She looked at the Mercedes and caught the passenger's eye. He smiled. She glanced away again, wishing she had the nerve to flirt her way into their car and away to Naples.

The bus approached, horns honked, and the Mercedes powered away from the harbor.

The man in the café lowered the newspaper and looked around, frowning. She had not seen him before, but that meant little. When it came to reach, she knew that when the occasion called for it, the Esposito Elders had very long arms.

Carlotta ducked down between two parked cars, watching through the windows of one as the bus drew closer. More horns honked, and she heard the metallic scrape of a parked car losing its wing mirror. So it went in Amalfi.

"Have you lost something?" an old woman asked. She was leaning on a cane, swaying slightly as she stood before one of the parked cars.

"Bus fare," Carlotta said. "Dropped it."

"Well hurry, girl, because it's here. I'll ask the driver to wait for you."

Carlotta grinned, knowing that she had a dazzling smile. "Thank you."

The woman smiled back, perhaps thinking of her own lost youth, and when she moved on Carlotta stood and followed her onto the bus. It was full of locals going from one town to the next and tourists exploring the scenic coastal route with wide eyes and pink faces. Several men looked at her as she swayed along the bus, but the only eyes she felt, like a burn mark on her skin, were those of the man in the café. As she took her seat and looked through the window, he glanced away again, pretending to fan his face with the newspaper. He was already talking into his mobile phone.

Carlotta took out her own phone and switched it off. She could do without the Elders trying to coax her back. *Stay here with us,* Adamo would say. *If you really think there's danger, the best place to be is with your family*. She could already see his calm, demeaning smile . . .

But this was *her* time. And though it would only last for the rest of the day before she knew she had to return, she was determined to make the most of it.

Carlotta closed her eyes, and thought of her cousin who had escaped.

Naples

Franca Esposito waited for the bus that was bringing a blast from her past. She had kept the family name, true, but releasing herself from its grasp had been the making of her. It had been difficult—they had not wished her to leave, and the Elders had expressly forbidden it—but though controlling and sometimes even dominating, the Espositos were a good family. She'd upset them by coming here to Naples, and for a time relations between her and the rest of the Espositos had been strained. But none of them would ever see a family member shut out entirely, and slowly but surely things had started to mellow. And her parents, though still disapproving, had remained in contact.

The Elders, however, still regarded what she had done as betrayal. But she had always said that they clung to the past, and Franca was ever the modern girl.

She'd been quite confident that most of the family would come around to accepting what she had done. And if they *had* cut her off completely, she was just as certain that she would have returned to Amalfi. It had been a daring risk, and it had paid off. She loved her life now, mostly because it was all hers.

Franca stubbed out her cigarette and lit another. It was part nervousness, and partly because it was rare that she sat at a pavement café doing nothing. Usually she was studying, preparing research materials for a local dig or, lately, spending more and more time away from her studies, and staying in bed with Alex instead. Damn him for making her fall for a hot American, but fall she had, and she was plummeting further every day.

And Alex didn't like smoking.

She dragged deep, feeling the smoke caressing her throat, looking around at the bustling street through the shade of her sunglasses. They looked expensive but were cheap. One thing she'd had to leave behind at La Casa Fredda was her entitlement to any family money.

Naples was packed with tourists at this time of year, skinny and fat, pale and sunburnt and dark, but all of them distinguishable from the locals by the way they walked, talked and seemed to exist in another world. Franca spent much of her life looking back in time, digging down through layers of silt, mud and rock to unearth the truth about what had once existed in a certain place, and who had breathed its purer air hundreds or thousands of years ago. She was comfortable with the past, at home with the dead, and Alex had only recently jested that it was because they could not answer her back. She thought perhaps it was a defense mechanism against the tightness of the family she'd grown up in, but she was a strong-minded individual whenever an argument or discussion raised its head.

Yet she was also fascinated with the living. Though not especially garrulous—she did not suffer fools gladly, and perhaps it was another defense mechanism that made her consider most people fools—she loved to watch and ruminate, constructing hidden histories for people from the way they dressed and spoke, the look in their eyes, the cast of their shadows. It was something else she had little time to indulge in nowadays, so she was relishing this hour sitting at the café and watching the world go by.

Another such rare occasion was how she had met Alex. A lover and humility, both gained in one day. She laughed softly at the memory and took another draw on her cigarette.

"Another drink?" the waiter asked.

"Double espresso," she said. "Some warm milk on the side?"

"Sure." He gathered up her empty cup and replaced her ashtray, and she breathed in his scent. *He lives on a lemon farm*, she thought. *Works here in the day just to get away. Someone else tied to their family.* She glanced up and the waiter offered her a cautious smile. *Not sure of himself, but he should be. Nice face. Strong shoulders and arms. He's probably breaking someone's heart and doesn't even know it.* The waiter went to fetch her drink, and she returned her attention to the pedestrians passing by her table.

She'd spotted Alex working on his laptop in a café on the other side of town. His white shirt had been open almost to his waist, sweat dribbled down his temple, and he'd been nervously biting his lip as he typed. She'd smiled, because something about his total involvement with what he'd been doing had been alluring. And so she'd begun her game. *Student, British, maybe Irish. Given the opportunity to study here by parents who can ill afford it, but he's messing things up, and soon . . .* He'd looked up and smiled, and Franca had been frowning even as she glanced away, her heart jumping and a flush warming her cheeks. *What the hell . . . ?* It was never like her to react like that.

The waiter brought her drink and disturbed her from her reverie. He breezed off between the tables, approaching a group of four fat men and women in stark white shorts and colorful tops. She guessed at their nationality, their relationships to each other, and when the fattest one started talking to the waiter in slow, ponderous English, as if to make him understand better, Franca laughed out loud. One of the women looked over, and Franca held her gaze until she looked away again.

She took a sip of her espresso and thought back to that first meeting with Alex. She'd been so, so wrong. He was American, for a start, and he was an engineer, not a student. He had been poring over his laptop, composing an email to break up with his girlfriend from several thousand miles away. Most of the nerves had been because of his fear at her family's reaction to the split; he worked for her father. All this she had learnt over several more coffees, and perhaps it was his inscrutability that led her to seek much, much more of him later, in his hotel room. After a passion-filled twenty-four hours—and after missing two important lectures and one assignment deadline—Alex began to talk about staying.

The next email had been to his ex-girlfriend's father, severing his employment.

Franca sighed. They were already talking about love. After breaking away from her family, she was so cautious about intimacy that when it presented itself to her like this, she knew it must be real.

A bus came along the road, edging around parked cars and scattering scooters before it like fish before a shark. Franca stubbed out her cigarette and glanced at her watch. Almost two P.M. This was probably the one, though whether Carlotta had even made it on, she was not sure. She'd tried her cousin's phone several times but it had been turned off. She really must be worried about something.

Franca left the café and stood at the curb, watching the bus disgorge it passengers on the opposite side. Just as she thought Carlotta must have missed the bus, she saw her cousin peering cautiously around the vehicle's rear.

"Carlotta! Over here!" Franca waved, and she saw Carlotta wince and look around. Damn, she really was wound up tight.

Carlotta walked quickly across the road, head down, eyes raised to look at Franca. A smile spread across her face. When she finally reached her, Carlotta laughed out loud and grabbed Franca into a hug.

"It's so wonderful to see you!" she said. "Oh Franca, you have no idea how happy I am."

"To be away?" Franca asked.

Carlotta shrugged, still hugging her cousin, but she said nothing.

"So," Franca asked, "how's the family?" She pulled back and stared into the younger girl's eyes, instantly shocked at how startled she looked. She glanced left and right, searching for searchers, and Franco knew instantly what the girl was going to ask.

"Is there somewhere we can go? Somewhere quiet and . . ."

"Safe?"

Carlotta nodded, then shrugged, but not with apology. She blinked slowly, then let out a sigh that sounded filled with far too many terrible burdens. "Franca, I'm in danger."

"What? How? What sort?"

"I don't know, exactly. But you're the only one I can trust. I've found out some things, and . . ." She reached into her shoulder bag and pulled out a file bulging with notes, clippings and pictures.

Franca glanced at the file, and when she looked up again, the girl was pale and terrified.

"I need help," Carlotta Esposito said. "In six days, on my eighteenth birthday, I think something will come to kill me."

Franca took her cousin back to her apartment. This had not been the sort of reunion she had expected. Carlotta had hinted that she was worried about something, yes, but Franca had expected some vague family matters, or perhaps the girl had gone and got herself pregnant. Nothing like this.

Nothing about death.

Carlotta seemed to relax once they were inside, and she looked around the apartment while Franca prepared them some food.

Cooking pasta, stirring the simple tomato and basil sauce, she watched her cousin, waiting for the girl to start talking rather than prompting her.

Carlotta ran her hands across the shelves and shelves of books on archaeology, history and ancient Mediterranean civilizations, and she barely paused when she passed a full set of *Calvin and Hobbes* paperbacks. She strolled slowly around the cramped room, looking at framed pictures of Franca and her friends at various digs, gently touching some old pottery stacked unceremoniously in an open storage cabinet, and she seemed not to notice the empty wine bottle and two red-stained glasses on the coffee table in front of the huge sofa. She was looking, but not seeing; touching, but not feeling.

"Hey," Franca said. Carlotta glanced around. "Sit down. Chill. Do you need a drink?"

"Maybe just orange juice, if you have some?"

"Wine?"

"I've got to go back."

"Today?"

Carlotta nodded.

Franca went to say more, then turned and delved into the refrigerator for some juice. When she looked through the serving hatch into the living room again, her cousin had slumped onto the sofa, head resting back with her eyes closed. *She's comfortable with me*, Franca thought. *That's good*. But still she was unsettled by her cousin's surprise pronouncement. *I think something will come to kill me*.

She dished up their food, broke some crusty bread and dropped it into a big bowl, then carried everything through on a tray. Sitting beside the girl, she half expected to finds her asleep. But Carlotta was only staring at the ceiling.

"Here," Franca said. "Call it a birthday meal from me."

"Mmm."

The two cousins sat and ate in silence for a while, but Franca soon noticed that Carlotta did not seem very hungry. Still, she finished her own meal, sipping at the glass of wine she'd brought in for herself. Then she sat back and waited for the girl to begin.

"Company?" Carlotta asked, nodding at the empties.

"Alex," Franca said. "An American. Extremely sexy, intelligent and easy to wind around my little finger." She cringed at the lie, but the other girl laughed without apparent humor.

"Trust my cousin." She sat back as well, less than half her food eaten. "A boyfriend. I so wish for that, one day."

"There's no one?"

Carlotta shrugged. "Some admirers. A few kisses. And one boy, earlier this year . . ." She stared into space, then shook her head. "Adamo scared him away."

"Not grand enough for the Esposito family, eh?"

"Who is?"

"Huh." Franca drained her glass and wished she'd brought the bottle in with her. "So . . ." she began, looking at her cousin. She wished that Carlotta would hurry and elaborate on her fears, but at the same time she suddenly didn't want to know. She felt an instant of fear and panic so intense that her heart fluttered, and her eyes went wide. She gasped and coughed. *What was that?* she thought.

Carlotta seemed not to have noticed. "The family's cursed, Franca," she said. "And it has been for centuries."

Franca laughed. It was reaction to Carlotta, but more so, it was her way of combating the sudden trepidation. She couldn't help herself, even though she saw how it annoyed Carlotta. She had to hold her hand over her mouth to press in any further nervous giggles. "Cursed? You sound like the Elders, Carlotta. Damn, you need to get away from them like I did."

"You don't believe in curses?"

"Of course not."

"You've never seen anything, never dug anything up, that makes you believe?"

Franca shook her head, feeling a tension leaving her shoulders that she was not even aware had been there. *So this is all*, she thought. Something had happened to Carlotta, she had seen something that made her believe in the unbelievable. All it would take—

"You remember Maria?"

Franca's smile faded a little, stolen away by the memory of their aunt. "Of course I remember. I'm older than you."

"You were seven, I was four," Carlotta said. "La Casa Fredda was preparing for Maria's eighteenth, but three days before her birthday she vanished."

"Ran away," Franca said. "Fled that family just as I have, and—"

"And just as dozens of others have down the centuries? All on or around their eighteenth birthdays?"

Franca stared at her cousin, blinking slowly. *She believes every word she's saying*, she thought. She drained the final drops of her wine, staring up at the ceiling through the bottom of the glass, and she heard Carlotta emptying the folder across the sofa.

"They were killed, and I have proof," the younger girl said. "Some from old family records, and some I stole from the Elders' library. Some, from Adamo's room itself." She spread the papers around, then paused, staring down at her own hand, tapping the pictures beneath them as though playing a piano. "I still move. I still live. But now it's my turn to disappear."

"Wait," Franca said, and she returned to her kitchen for the rest of the bottle of wine. She had a feeling she was going to need it.

CHAPTER 2

Naples

Another café, another wait, but this time she was not allowed to smoke.

Franca watched the world go by, playing her usual game and wondering where people were going to or coming from. The tourists were obvious and did not interest her, but there were some people who had the look of escape or pursuit in their eyes. She was surprised that she had never noticed them before. It was a look that Carlotta had only recently made her familiar with, and she was haunted by just how many there were.

Is the world really so bad that this many people have to be running from something? she mused. She waved to the waiter and ordered another coffee. She had always loved airports, enjoying the feel that this was a place where old existences were ended and new lives embarked upon. Now, with Carlotta's story at the forefront of her mind, she knew that some things were not so easy to flee.

Sometimes, we carry the bad stuff with us.

She still had grave doubts about what she had done. When she'd told Alex about Carlotta's amazing, disturbing story, he had immediately tried to persuade her to place the call. *I only ever saw him from a distance,* he'd said. *The first company I worked for called him in when they found an old lab, deep in the Brazilian rainforest. Turns out it was an old Nazi place, set up after the war but long since gone to ruin, and he has a thing about Nazis. But this . . . this is* just *the sort of thing the B.P.R.D. is set up for!*

She'd doubted him, and she still doubted Carlotta's strange, disquieting story. But she'd made that one call just to keep Alex happy, and from that . . .

To this.

She sighed, and thanked the waiter when he brought her a fresh coffee. Lifting the cup to her lips, she saw a commotion across the concourse.

"Hellboy," a voice said from somewhere far away, and another took up the name. They were muted, quiet voices, not shouts or shrieks of excitement. And then Franca saw him, and the cup paused halfway.

Damn, he was one big son-of-a-bitch.

He strode through the curious crowd, coat flapping about him even in this heat, kit bag slung over his shoulder, and an empty holster hanging from his belt. A *big* empty holster. In his left hand he carried a lockable metal gun box, and in his right hand—

But no, she realized. That *was* his right hand. And on his head . . .

She'd heard about these things on his head. Some said they were horns. A chill went through her, and she drained her coffee before standing.

Hellboy paused by the café and looked around. His eyes locked on hers almost immediately, and he smiled. Franca smiled back, and a rush of relief swept through her. He might be big, red, and have the stumps of horns growing from his high forehead, but his face looked so damn *human*.

"Hellboy," she said, walking through the tables and approaching him with her right hand automatically extended. He gripped her hand—his own right hand was cold, and heavy, and it felt like he could crush hers to jelly with a squeeze—and shook.

"So they say," he said. "And you're . . . ?"

"Franca Esposito."

"Right." He smiled again and nodded, looking her up and down with frank curiosity.

"Er . . . do you want a coffee?" she asked. "Something stronger?"

"Yeah, but not here. I hate airports. Full of people running away from things."

Franca laughed. "I was thinking just the same thing."

"You were?" Hellboy asked. He seemed both surprised and interested, and Franca could not detect an ounce of sarcasm in his voice.

"We should go," she said, unsure whether to be unnerved or charmed. "My car's outside, and if it's all right with you, we'll go straight to Amalfi."

"Sounds good to me," he said. "You can fill me in on the way."

"The B.P.R.D. didn't give you all the information?"

"Only the basics," Hellboy said. "But I've come straight from Iceland. They called me there just after I'd finished another job. Told me about this one, and damn, I've been cold for long enough. Italy sounded good. Amalfi is a place I've never visited."

"And you're concerned about the possible family curse, of course," Franca said, unnerved by his apparent casual approach.

"Of course I am," he said quietly. "The surroundings are just a bonus."

"I'm sorry," Franca said. "It's . . . thrown me, that's all. To be confronted with the amount of evidence Carlotta presented is . . . well, I've never really believed in such foolish things." She glanced sidelong at Hellboy, biting her tongue.

"Don't worry," he said without looking at her. "I'm flesh and blood." He paused inside the main exit from the arrivals lounge, shifted the kit back from his right shoulder to his left, and his face suddenly turned grim. "So who's this joker?"

Franca followed his gaze and gasped. Entering through the sliding doors, flanked on both sides by young, fit, hard-looking men dressed all in black, came the oldest man she had ever seen.

And she had not seen him for years.

"Oh, my God," she whispered. "Adamo Esposito."

"Family Patriarch," Hellboy said. "That much I do remember. Well, I guess this is as good a place as any to start."

Franca could say no more. Adamo looked up from his feet and directly into her eyes. He gasped as he came to a stop, but none of the men offered a helping hand. He'd brush them off, she knew. Adamo was proud.

He grinned at her. And in the space of a few seconds, Franca remembered every terrible thing that Carlotta had claimed about this little old man.

Crap, Hellboy thought. *I could have done with a shower, at least.* He sized up the welcome committee, and they weren't very big. Even after settling the agitated spirits of a glacial graveyard in Iceland, flying several thousand miles sat next to a seven-year-old kid obsessed with sharing every move he made on his Nintendo DS with the big red guy next to him, and having not slept for about forty hours, he figured he could take these goons without raising his heartbeat.

The old guy, however . . .

Hellboy had learned long ago that it was the old guys you had to watch.

"So she sent for a demon to haunt our family," Adamo rasped.

"I'm no demon," Hellboy growled.

"Surely that's not for you to say?" the old man said, his English heavily accented yet precise. "Isn't it for the people around you to decide?"

Hellboy stared at the man, refusing to rise to the bait.

Adamo laughed, like dry dead leaves on concrete. The smile left his face just as quickly, and he straightened, staring up into Hellboy's face. "I see a big, red, ugly man before me, and so I see a demon."

"I'm not that big."

Adamo switched his gaze to Franca, and that let Hellboy stare at the six goons. Oh, they looked heavy enough, with their tanned faces, slick black hair, obviously fit bodies, an occasional scar, and bulges beneath their jackets. But they were hire-a-mob—Hellboy could sense that with a sniff. Guys like this paid too much attention to looking hard to actually be hard. And he took great pleasure in staring every one of them down.

It took about ten seconds, in all.

"Dear Franca," Adamo said. "It's been a long time. How are your studies? Still digging up the past to learn about the present?"

"Adamo, I'm well, thank you. And you look younger every day." Hellboy could sense the tension in the young woman's voice. They were still speaking in English, and that could only have been for his benefit.

Adamo waved a hand, dismissing her compliment, and his smile looked genuine for the first time. "You've grown into a fine young woman," he said. "So sad you felt you had to leave. Your parents still miss you very much."

"I still talk to them," she said. "But I was . . . stifled. It's just the way I'm made."

Adamo shrugged and nodded his head from side to side, weighing things up. "It's a pity, though, that you were so willing to listen to such a disturbed young girl. Don't you understand how much damage entertaining such nonsense can do? Carlotta is . . . challenged. The whole family is having difficult times with her. Like much of the youth of today, she was drinking too much too young, and there were *men*." He sighed, crouching down again as the weight of his years hung heavy. "You've been gone for four years, Franca. Some family business is no longer *your* business."

"Forgive me, Adamo, but she came to me for help."

"And you called this?" He waved a hand at Hellboy.

"Take a look in the mirror, granddad," Hellboy muttered.

"I only wanted—"

"Help? Yes, I'm sure. Admirable, in a young woman such as you. But you've merely helped Carlotta strengthen her delusions." He shook his head and reached out a hand. One of the goons held his arm, steadying Adamo, and Hellboy saw the show in every movement. *Strong as an ox*, he thought.

"There is no family curse," Adamo said, looking at Hellboy. "We are a large family, and there are unfortunate tales in our past. But that's just what they are: unfortunate. Curses? Pah! You believe in such things?"

Hellboy raised an eyebrow.

Adamo laughed, that grating sound again. "Yes. Of course you do. But no such superstitious drivel hangs around the Esposito family. We look after our own here, and we won't welcome the likes of you."

"I appreciate your feelings," Hellboy said. "Really. But you're not the one who called us in. And from my experience, the more someone doth protest too much, the more likelihood there's something rotten in the state of Denmark."

Adamo chuckled, shaking his head. "And so you never give normality a chance, is that it?"

Hellboy blinked slowly. "Your English is very good."

"I'm old," Adamo said. He tapped his head. "But this still feels young. My body fails me, so I fill my time with learning."

"And research?"

"Oh, yes. I know an awful lot about you, *Hell*boy."

"Huh." Hellboy scratched his chin with one finger, swinging his big right hand by his side. "You'd be surprised how *little* you know."

Adamo came closer. He was shrivelled with age, but as he looked up into Hellboy's face there was no sense at all that he was a small man. His presence was palpable, and Hellboy could not help respecting him. For an old guy, he was full of vitality.

"Listen to me," he said, so softly that no one else but he and Hellboy could hear over the hubbub of the airport. "The Espositos have been in Amalfi for a thousand years. We're one of the city's oldest families. My ancestors were one of the greatest shipping families in the Mediterranean, and we have royalty to our name. But such a large, tenacious family attracts other names as well. There are madmen, and wrongdoers. There are murderers. These times are strange, a difficult challenge to someone such as me, trying my best to keep the family name. Our youngsters . . ." He shrugged, glanced across at Franca. "They have no respect."

Hellboy nodded, scratching his chin again. "Hmm."

"If you come to Amalfi and start digging around, it will be our ruin. Because you *will* find things, Hellboy. You will find that my great-great-grandfather enjoyed the company of young men. You will discover that there was a lady bearing our name several centuries ago who plied the world's oldest trade through the harbors and ports of the Amalfi coast. And there is Guiseppe Esposito of the seventeenth century, a murderer and defiler of little girls."

"Nice of you to want to keep such a family name alive." Hellboy looked down into the old man's eyes, and for a beat he felt ashamed at the barbed comment.

"A few among many hundreds," Adamo said, stepping back and raising his voice once again. "You bring attention with you, Hellboy. We don't want it. There is no curse. Please, honor me and respect my family by leaving."

Hellboy was aware of other passengers parting around their little group like river water around a rock. They were unmoving, but soon the time would come to split. The question was, should he fight against the tide, or go with the flow?

"Of course," he said, and he felt Franca's eyes burning into him. "Last thing the B.P.R.D. wants to do is upset an old man."

"I've already arranged for you to leave on the next flight," Adamo said, nodding his thanks.

"No need. I'll buy my own ticket." Hellboy glared at the goons again, amused to see their confidence return now that they thought he was going. By tomorrow, they'd have made themselves believe they'd had a hand in scaring him off. And by next week, they'd be telling their kids bedtime stories about how they'd fought Hellboy, and won. So it went.

"But—" Franca said.

"And you, my dear Franca," Adamo said, stepping forward to kiss the woman. "Don't leave it so long before your next visit. La Casa Fredda misses you deeply."

"Of course," Franca said, angry and confused.

When the old man turned to leave, his thugs casting warning glances back over their shoulders, Hellboy hefted his bag and walked back to the café. He was already sitting down when the doors closed behind the men, and the waiter left a menu with him, though Hellboy already knew what he wanted. Italy meant pizza.

Franca stood before him and cursed briefly, vehemently in Italian. "What the hell was that?" she said. "You come all this way then turn tail at the first sign of—"

"Lady," Hellboy said, "*no one* tells me to leave." He perused the menu, looked up at Franca, and grinned. *And there*, he thought, *is one tough woman.*

He'd rather take on Adamo's goons any day.

They waited at the café for an hour, eating excellent pizza and drinking slightly less excellent coffee, and Hellboy only asked a few small details about Franca's cousin. He knew it would be better to hear the tale from the girl's own mouth, so that the story would not be so distorted in the telling. Already there had been a confrontation, and tension, and Franca's take on things could have shifted without her realizing. And besides, Hellboy liked her company. It was a while since he'd spent time with a good looking woman who couldn't read minds, set fires, or talk to ghosts—or want him dead.

"So how much of a 'family' is the family?" he asked between mouthfuls of his third pizza. He'd been subjected to too much airline food lately, and he regarded this as cleansing his system.

"Nothing like that," Franca replied, smiling.

"Those goons?"

"Adamo always hires security when he leaves Amalfi. As he said, it's an old family, and it has lots of money. He's always been afraid that the Espositos would be targeted by kidnappers or the like."

"But none of the people who went missing were kidnapped?"

Franca shrugged. "Who's to say?"

"Hmm." Hellboy finished his coffee and sat back, stretching his arms over his head. His shoulders ached, his arms were sore from the workout they'd had in Iceland, and he was hoping this would be a quick, quiet one. He'd have liked a few days back at HQ before coming out again, catching up with Liz, seeing how that thing in the Kenyan lake had panned out for Abe. But hopefully this one would be done in a day or two. Get in, find out what was really going on, get out again.

No fireworks, no fights. No tentacles.

He could hope.

"I guess he'll know we're coming," he said.

"I'm not so sure. Adamo likes to give the impression he has a long reach, but Amalfi is his whole world. I've got away from the family, and I only live here, in Naples. Not a million miles away."

"Why get away?"

"I felt smothered."

"You weren't afraid of anything?"

Franca frowned. "What, like Carlotta? No, not at all. At least, I *wasn't*."

"But now?" Hellboy asked.

"Now . . ." She trailed off, pushing crumbs around her plate with her fingertip. "Well, Carlotta showed me some stuff that's pretty hard to deny, or forget." She shook her head, frowning.

"If it's okay, I'd rather hear it from her. I just wanted to know where you stand."

"It's thanks to my boyfriend that you're here, actually," Franca said. "He met you a while ago in Brazil."

Hellboy frowned, mentally rifling through memories of cases and monsters, wraith and dark places. "Ah," he said a beat later.

"Brazil." He frowned, trying to slam the drawer that particular case file had popped up from. *Damn Nazis!*

"His name's Alex Westerfield."

"Alex," he said, nodding. "Young guy. Cocky."

"Well . . ." she said uncertainly.

"Oh, hey, didn't mean to—"

"No!" she said, laughing and holding up one hand. "No, it's okay. He was, once. His father's influence, I think."

"But no more?"

"I don't like cocky men," she said, and Hellboy grinned. He liked strong women who looked him in the eye.

"We should go," he said, glancing at his watch. They'd waited over an hour. If Adamo and his goons were still watching to see if he really had left . . . well, let them. He was full of pizza. And he really needed a shower.

Chapter 3

Amalfi

Franca had not been back to Amalfi since leaving four years before, afraid that if she did return she would be caught and consumed back into the family, like a fly trapped forever in amber. All her hopes, all her ambitions and aspirations hung on a thread so long and so thin that it could easily be broken, and that realization came hard. She had promised herself that the time would come when she *would* go back, because she loved her family, and she missed her parents. But she'd given herself time to adjust, that time had gone on, and there was a selfish comfort in being away that had succeeded in overlying the duty she felt. *They can come and see* me, she thought. *They can call* me. But few of them ever had. Carlotta was one, and her mother, but most of the others seemed to have shunned her, as though by fleeing Amalfi she had left their world forever.

She had never believed that it would feel like coming home.

They had left the airport apparently without being spotted by anyone Adamo had left behind. She'd been aware of Hellboy glancing around as they'd walked to her car, and he'd sunk into the seat, groaning and resting his head back. He seemed to take comfort in being in the enclosed space of the vehicle, and she guessed it must be a challenge being out in the open when you were so . . . distinctive. She'd seen recognition on many people's faces, and fear on some. By the time she'd driven past the airport perimeter, Hellboy had been snoring lightly beside her. She didn't have the heart to wake him up.

Sitting with a stranger sleeping in her car, she made the journey alone. The reason for her return felt good and honest, but its consequences were difficult to comprehend. La Casa Fredda loomed large in her imagination, and thinking of that place made her both excited and unsettled.

She'd cast Alex aside with a phone call. He had tried to convince her not to go, of course. He knew some of her past, and the concern in his voice had given her butterflies in her stomach. *It's family*, she had told him. Perhaps that was unfair.

It was only as they approached Amalfi that Hellboy came awake.

"Sorry," he said. "I haven't been very good company."

"No worries."

"Where are we?"

"Almost there." *Almost home*, she'd come close to saying. And everything she saw sparked memories.

They followed the coastal road into Amalfi, hugging the cliffs, and she was as aware as ever of the sheer drop to their right. The sea looked stunning this late in the afternoon, with the sun sinking towards the horizon and casting its light across the surface like liquid fire. Familiar landmarks appeared along the road, guiding her in, and she found that she wore a melancholy smile. She had grown up here, and much as she had disassociated herself with her past, a happy childhood like her own left echoes.

"Wow," Hellboy said as they rounded the final bend. The road dipped steeply down towards Amalfi's harbor and small beach, and much of the city was laid out to view. The sun was catching it just right. White buildings clung to the hillside in defiance of gravity, their orange roofs faded with dust from a long, hot summer. The beach was speckled with parasols, the parking lot at the front was a riot of cars and buses, and the lemon groves on the hillsides above were a deep, luscious green.

"It's said that Hercules founded this city," Franca said. "He buried his wife Amalfi here. I once went out with a boy who swore he'd found the grave."

"I'd like to meet him," Hellboy said, chuckling.

"You've seen a lot of strange things," Franca said, a question that came out as a statement.

"A few, here and there."

"You'll like Amalfi." She suddenly felt fiercely protective of her birthplace. Hellboy was here because of her, partly, and because of her troubled younger cousin, and she'd do her utmost to make sure he left here with good memories. "Just through here, and we're close."

They passed through the tunnel onto the Via Matteo Camera, sweeping down to the seafront, and instantly they were swallowed up in the traffic. Horns blared, and drivers hung out of their windows, gesticulating wildly. A bus had bumped a big Mercedes, and the two drivers were standing beside the bonded vehicles staring at the dents. One of them said something, the other shrugged, and they continued to stare. They seemed impervious to the chaos their fender bender had caused.

"I've heard a lot about Italian driving," Hellboy said.

"Hey! Remember who you're talking to." Franca tried mock-stern, but it didn't work. The big red guy looked genuinely cowed. "So what's with the hand?" she asked.

His eyebrows rose in surprise. "Pretty forthright, aren't you?"

Franca shrugged, then leaned on her horn for a couple of seconds, adding to the cacophony.

Hellboy shifted his big right hand, flexing his fingers, turning it this way and that in his lap. Franca glanced down. It didn't appear at all cumbersome or unwieldy.

"You tell me," he said at last.

"You were born with it?"

"I've always had it, yeah."

Franca nodded, and while the car was stationary and Hellboy's attention was taken by two young kids squabbling in the street, she looked him over. His face was strong, his jaw square and determined, and his strange eyes were both intelligent and hard. She saw the end of his tail, curled under him and laid along the edge of his seat. He'd already slipped a huge pistol back into its holster—she'd love to know how he wrangled a licence to carry *that* in Italy—and his belt seemed heavy with pouches and pockets.

And, of course, he was red.

"You haven't asked how we're getting into the house without being seen," she said.

"I assumed you had a plan."

"There's a side door that's usually kept locked. Old servants' entrance, when the family still employed them. I'll call Carlotta when we're close, and she'll make sure that door's unlocked."

"If I'm seen," he said quietly, "I'm sure your Adamo will hear about it soon enough."

"That's why I want to keep you in the car. I'm hoping anyone who sees you will just think you're a sunburned tourist."

She was aware of Hellboy turning to stare at her, and she kept her eyes forward, trying but failing to hold in a smile. Even then, she could not tell whether he was amused or offended.

The traffic jam resolved itself eventually, and Franca steered the car around the wounded Mercedes. She had walked these pavements a thousands times, browsed these shops, drunk in these cafes and eaten in these restaurants. She'd had her first kiss down on the beach, and once a rich Frenchman had taken her to his room in the Hotel Luna, where they had sat on the balcony after making love and looked down on the harbor as daylight faded and street lamps made a fairytale of Amalfi.

"So many memories of this place," she said quietly, and Hellboy was silent, giving her room to welcome them in.

• • •

Amalfi dripped with history. While Franca weaved the car through streets that looked too narrow to negotiate on foot, let alone drive along, Hellboy soaked it all in. The buildings exuded age, and when they passed the cathedral on their right, its impressive steps rising thirty feet to the main doors, he could imagine that the city was built on ghosts. He sensed depths to this place: new foundations built on old; and old, on ancient. The city had been here for more than a millennium, and anywhere that old had a thousand buried secrets and long-forgotten hollows filled with age. He closed his eyes and could smell Amalfi's stories on the air. Some were good, some were bad. A few stung his senses, and he opened his eyes to allow in color and bustle once again. Sometimes, he thought that everywhere he went he could find work.

"It's a beautiful place," he said.

"It has its moments."

"You don't sound so sure."

"You're seeing it for the first time. I grew up here, remember. It's all memories for me. Don't you remember where you were born?"

"Not exactly. But I remember where I grew up. Military base in New Mexico."

"Oh. Sounds interesting."

"It had its moments."

The street wound steadily upward from the sea, into the hills and towards the dramatic cliffs inland. Franca took a left between two buildings that almost seemed to lean in to touch each other, then right, and Hellboy noticed an instant change in atmosphere. Gone were the pizza restaurants and seafood places, the cafes and the souvenir shops, and doorways became blank wooden shutters in shadowy recesses, several of them apparently guarded by old women dressed entirely in black. Washing was strung on lines between buildings to dry, and even that seemed leached of color. It was like driving back in time a hundred years.

"Don't the tourists come back this far?" he asked.

"Some do. The more adventurous ones, those who like to take a path and see where it leads. But most are happy staying where they feel they belong." She eased the car around an incredibly tight corner, the wing mirror passing through a wound worn in the cornerstone over time. In the narrow street beyond, she stopped. "Almost there."

Franca took out her mobile phone and dialed a number.

"On foot from here?" Hellboy asked.

"I'll park around the corner, then yes, on foot. Sorry the car's so small."

"No problem," he said, thinking that perhaps his knees had seized up at last.

After several seconds Franca disconnected. "Hope she heard that," she muttered. She pointed from the window. "Past that overhanging roof, you can just see one end of La Casa Fredda."

"Up there on the hillside?"

"That's it. Surrounded by lemon groves. The views from up there are astonishing."

"You miss the place," Hellboy said.

Franca did not reply, and that was answer enough.

She drove another thirty yards and then parked the car tight against a wall. She had to crawl across the seats and climb out Hellboy's door, and they stood together looking up at the Esposito family home.

"It's a steep climb," she said. "Narrow paths, worn steps, and then the door will hopefully be open."

"You're sure about this?" Hellboy asked. The woman was nervous; there was a quaver in her voice, and he could see beads of sweat on her nose and upper lip.

"Sure. I promised Carlotta. And I need her to tell you what she told me."

"Then lead the way."

Hellboy followed the woman up a narrow set of steps, then onto a path that curved into shadow behind and between buildings, more steps, and eventually past a garden that spilled luscious branches heavy with sweet-smelling blooms he could not identify. They crossed a wider path, Franca glancing both ways first, then started up an even narrower set of steps. These twisted and turned, and in several places the steps had crumbled away. They had to stride up three or four risers at a time, and once when Franca slipped Hellboy automatically reached out to hold her up. She grasped onto his heavy right hand, running her fingers across its surface and glancing back at him, wide-eyed.

After fifteen minutes of climbing, they faced a high boundary wall topped with heavy orange tiles. There was a doorway set into the ancient stonework, almost completely hidden away by the bougainvillea that tumbled over the head of the wall. Franca shouldered her way through the hanging plants and tried the heavy iron handle.

"Shit!" she hissed.

"She hasn't opened it?"

"It's a side door to the house Carlotta is leaving open for us. This is just a garden gate, I don't remember it ever being locked. I don't think it even had a lock *on* it."

"Let me try," Hellboy said. He pushed through the plants and rested his hand on the old oak, close to the handle. He shoved gently and heard the grate of metal on metal.

"We could go around and—"

He shoved harder, and something snapped. "No need." He eased the gate open, pleased that the plants on the other side seemed to be even thicker. They'd hopefully camouflage their entry.

"Let me go first," Franca said. Her voice had dropped, and Hellboy perceived a nervous tension in her shoulders and legs as she squeezed past him and through the gate. "It's okay," she whispered without turning around, and for a moment he thought she was talking to someone inside.

He followed her through into La Casa Fredda's garden. It was a wild, lush place, given over mainly to a dozen species of rose, some quite small and contained, others having grown into huge bushes with stems as thick as his wrist. It reminded Hellboy of the fairy tale of the sleeping princess, and how even as a kid he'd always thought that some sleeping things were best left alone. Many times over the years, he'd come to recognize the truth in that idea.

Franca darted across the garden to the wall of the house, and Hellboy followed in her wake. Nobody shouted out, no alarms were raised, and no guard dogs came slavering and growling after them. That was the one thing he'd been worried about, because dogs usually reacted to him in two ways: unsettled, or savage.

"Yes!" Franca hissed. "Carlotta's an angel." She pushed the door open and beckoned Hellboy in behind her.

"Terrified is what she is," he replied. "The old man knows she let us in here, I'm guessing she'll be punished."

"Maybe," Franca said, clicking the door shut without elaborating. She turned around, breathing in deeply and sighing as she exhaled again. "Home. It always smells the same."

"Smells of garlic to me," Hellboy said.

"Yeah. Come on, this way."

They were inside. Hellboy was excited and alert. Officially, he supposed, he was on a job, though so far he'd encountered nothing more dangerous than Italian drivers. That didn't mean he could get slack. The girl Franca had brought him here to meet was obviously serious about this curse thing, and he had to keep his eyes and ears open.

He rested his hand on the gun holster's flap and popped the clip. He'd keep that open, too.

"More narrow stairs," he said, and he had to turn sideways as they ascended, taking care not to let his right hand knock or scrape against the wall. The staircase was lit by a couple of small windows higher up, but they were dirty, and the air was gloomy and thick.

"Like I said, servants' entrance. Small room up here they used to use for storage, then we're into the first of the house's main corridors."

"So how many people live here?"

Franca paused at the head of the staircase and pressed her ear to the door. "Lots," she said. "If you follow me, and keep quiet, I'm hoping Carlotta is the only one we'll meet."

Hellboy grinned. A hard taskmaster. Yeah, he liked strong women a lot.

They worked their way up through the house, Hellboy staying alert to sounds or other signs of threat to their covert entry. He wondered at a house so large that had no alarms or other signs of defense, but Adamo had been very old, and he knew that sometimes older people trusted technology least.

The place was filled with old stuff, too. He was no expert, but Hellboy figured there was a fortune in antiques and collectibles here, including one long cabinet in a first floor corridor containing a whole range of chipped, reconstructed earthenware. He wondered whether Franca had been responsible for some of this before leaving, or whether her choice of career had been prompted by being raised here. But the time to ask her that would be later.

Following her deeper into her childhood home, he realized that she was taking a big risk in coming here. This was a place that she'd done her best to distance herself from, an outmoded idea of family that this modern, sassy woman had eschewed in favor of a career and independence. Coming back, effectively breaking in and bringing an intruder with her, could be regarded as foolhardy in the extreme. It could also, he acknowledged, be one more way for her to flick her family the bird.

At the end of the first floor corridor, they came to a large hallway, floor lined with ancient marble, a set of main doors at one end, and a large skylight giving the space a bright, airy feel. There was a wide staircase leading up to a landing, balustrades intricately carved as spiral serpents. At each side of the hallway stood three heavy timber doors, and beyond the staircase, at the end of the narrow space on either side, Hellboy could see steel shutters. They were bolted shut and padlocked, and their appearance seemed incongruous against the rest of the well-appointed space.

He nudged Franca and pointed them out.

"Basements," she whispered. "Wine cellar, storage. There's a way into some old caves down there, too, though it's difficult to crawl through."

Hellboy nodded grimly. *Old caves. There you go.*

"We need to go up," Franca whispered, and the front doors opened.

Hellboy grabbed her and backed up the way they'd come, leaving the doors at the end of the corridor open and hunkering down behind the display cabinet. The corridor here was poorly lit, and he hoped that whoever appeared in the bright hallway would not be able to see too far along.

"Oh," Franca said, and she buried her face in her hands.

"What is it?" Hellboy asked. She only shook her head.

And then he heard the old man's voice, and the voices of others. All old. So these must be the family Elders the old guy had mentioned at the airport.

Adamo came into view in the hallway, pausing at the bottom of the staircase and turning to the others. Several men and women milled around him, chatting and laughing, but Hellboy's Italian wasn't good enough for him to understand more than one word in five. *Wine*, he heard, and *delight*, and *garden*. And someone—an old crone with more skin hanging from her neck than covering her face—growled something about *shame* and *party*.

Adamo laughed at that, and the others seemed to fall into a respectful silence.

Franca looked up slowly, and when she saw her old family members she slumped back against Hellboy, seeming to seek comfort against his heavy body. He put his left arm across her chest and hugged her softly.

"I've let them down," she whispered.

"No," he said, but he didn't know what else to say.

The Esposito Elders parted company, some of them climbing the stairs, others disappearing into a doorway out of view. When the hall was silent again, Hellboy stood, pulling Franca up after him.

"Let's get to Carlotta's room," he said. "I'm relying on you, you know that. Leave me to my own devices, I'm liable to—" He shrugged, and his right hand struck the display cabinet, setting an ancient vase swaying dangerously close to the edge of its shelf. Hellboy's reaction was lightning fast; he stilled the vase, and released his held breath. *Crap!* he thought. *Didn't even do that on purpose.*

"Come on," Franca said.

As if seeing the Elders had emboldened her, she seemed to move faster through the house; more confident, or perhaps less cautious. They climbed the staircase, crept along the landing, then went up a second, much narrower staircase to the third floor. There was a short, carpeted corridor here, with high stained glass windows at both ends bathing the hall with a spectacular splash of colored light.

Franca pointed along the corridor at the last door on the right.

Hellboy nodded, then pointed at the woman. *You should go in first.*

Franca stepped to the door, knocked quietly, and entered.

Hellboy heard a squeal from inside, then someone rushing across the room.

Damn! He leapt at the door, shoving it wide with one knee so that he had both hands ready to fight . . . and he felt such a fool.

The two women stood hugging each other, and over Franca's shoulder Hellboy stared into the bright, teary, terrified eyes of Carlotta Esposito.

"Tell me you can help," Carlotta said. "Tell me you know what's happening, and can make it go away." She was trying her hardest not to cry, she really was, but the pressures building within her these past few months were immense. Here was Franca, her cousin, long past eighteen and the time of danger, and escaped from the grip of the family home. And here was Hellboy, the strangest man Carlotta had ever seen. She'd read about him in magazines, seen him on TV, but in the flesh he was . . . intimidating. Franca said that he'd come to help, that he knew about such things as curses, and worked for an organization committed to protecting normal people against abnormal things.

"Can you?" she whispered. "Can you help?"

"I can only do my best," Hellboy said. "First, you have to tell me everything you've told your cousin, and show me what you have."

"Of course," Carlotta said. She slipped from her bed and reached beneath, lifting the basket containing old clothes she rarely wore anymore and pulling out the file. She'd gathered it all together after showing it to Franca, making sure every single scrap of evidence she'd accumulated over the past few months was still there. *Here it is*, she thought. *The proof that I might die in two days' time*. She took a couple of steps towards Hellboy and held it out.

"Want to talk me through it?" he asked. "You Espositos seem to speak English better than me. And I'm not the best at stuff like this."

Carlotta nodded, amazed at the man's red skin, his eyes, his huge, weird fist. And those things on his head . . .

"Shall we sit on the bed?" he asked, looking around her large room.

She nodded and sat, and when Hellboy sat beside her the bedsprings creaked ominously. She glanced across at Franca, but her cousin seemed lost in contemplation, her head back and eyes half closed. *I asked her back here*, Carlotta thought, and a pang of guilt bit through her. But she hadn't forced her cousin to help her.

"First, I don't want you to think I'm crazy," she said.

"Hey, I've seen crazy," Hellboy said, "and so far you seem pretty sane to me."

"Some of this is quite . . . tenuous, really. And a lot of it is guesswork on my part. But the facts of what I've got in here speak for themselves, and everything else in between . . . well, even if it doesn't add up quite the way I've supposed, there's still something terrible going on."

"A curse on your family," he said.

"I think so, yes."

"Caused by what?"

"What do you mean?" Carlotta asked, instantly defensive. *Already he doubts me!*

But Hellboy held out his hands and shook his head. "Hey, I'm only asking. Sometimes if I know the source of a curse, I might be able to read it better, or understand when the time comes to tackle it."

"You think you can do something about this?"

"That's what he's trying to find out, Carlotta," Franca said.

Carlotta nodded, and a flush of gratitude almost overwhelmed her. She gasped, tried to speak, but tears stole her voice. She felt like such a fool.

"Hey," Hellboy said, and he touched the back of her shoulder. So gentle for such a giant. "Take your time."

"I can't," Carlota said. "I don't *have* any time." And she took a deep breath, and began.

CHAPTER 4

Amalfi

She opened the file and wondered where to start.

"Here," she said. "Antonia Esposito, lost at sea in 1546." She looked at the facsimile of an old, faded painting, trying to see herself in this girl's eyes. But she could not. Antonia looked peaceful and happy.

"Long time ago," Hellboy said, taking the print.

"She was lost three weeks after her eighteenth birthday, so the old accounts say." Carlotta read from another copied page, this one from the old book she'd found in the basements. She'd tell Hellboy about that soon. Everything at once might be too much, and she wanted—*needed*—him to believe.

"Okay," he said, handing the picture back and obviously expecting more.

"Amalfi has always been a great seafaring port," she said. "I assume you know a little about the place?"

"Ah . . . can't say I had much time to research, no," he said, glancing away as if embarrassed.

"It was once a great power," Carlotta continued. "A long, long time ago, at least. But five hundred years ago, when Antonia was lost, much of that former glory was gone. It was a fishing port then, though war galleons were often known to dock here. A cosmopolitan place, there would be a dozen languages spoken in the town squares, and the women of the area gave birth to babies of many hues. But the Espositos were a very powerful family back then, perhaps even more so than now. And they would *never* have allowed such a young daughter to go to sea."

"So you're saying it's a cover-up?" Hellboy asked.

"Of course."

"How can you be sure?" His eyes bore into her with a stark intelligence.

"Well . . ." Carlotta took the sheet from him and folded it away. "I can't. Not for certain."

"Show him what else you have," Franca said. She was still sitting in the chair, head resting back and eyes closed.

Carlotta sorted through some of the file contents, looking for a particular piece of paper. She was aware of the loaded silence in the room, waiting for her theories to fill it. Now her ideas should start to seem ridiculous, presented to someone else, their tenuous threads and links stretched and snapped by a second opinion. But she found the account she was looking for, and she felt more certain that ever.

"In 1743, Emilia Esposito was kidnapped, raped and murdered by sea bandits who were raiding all the coastlines of south-western Italy at the time. She was taken on her eighteenth birthday as she swam in the sea at the foot of the old Saracen watchtower. She'd gone swimming on her own, against her family's express orders, and her body was never found."

Hellboy nodded, expecting more. But Carlotta had no more to give him . . . and therein lay the proof.

"So, the bandits were caught and punished?" he asked.

"No one was ever held accountable."

"So how do they know she was kidnapped, raped and murdered?"

Carlotta shrugged. She watched the big man's eyes glaze as he looked into some middle distance, one finger scratching the bristly tuft that grew on his chin.

"Could have drowned," he said. "Could have run away with a lover, been eaten by a shark, or been kidnapped by slave traders."

"Or she could have been taken by sea bandits, raped and murdered," Carlotta said, holding out the paper to him. Hellboy shook his head and nodded at the file. More.

Carlotta started pulling papers out at random. There were copies from the book—which she would tell him more about soon, when his doubt needed one final push to be expunged forever—some old newspaper clippings, printouts from the Internet, and a couple of official forms she'd requested from the registrar of births, marriages and deaths. They each told a story of someone else, another unfortunate member of the Esposito family victim of a freakish accident or something terrible. They all happened on or close to the victims' eighteenth birthdays.

And they were all women.

After another few minutes, and four more accounts, Hellboy held up his hand.

"Okay, let's think about this," he said. "Old friend of mine said you have to interrogate things from every angle to urge the truth to show. When I was young, I'd interrogate with my fists, but I'm a little older now. Maybe even a little wiser. So, this occurs to me: you've given me accounts from a five hundred year period, and in that time, there must have been plenty of male Espositos subject to strange accidents and disappearances as well."

Carlotta smiled weakly. "Of course. And I've thought about that, too. But the only ones mentioned in the book are the girls. All missing. No bodies found, Hellboy. *Ever.* And all so close to their eighteenth birthdays. Interrogate that."

"Book?" he asked. "What book?"

Carlotta glanced at Franca. Her older cousin was watching her now, eyes glittering with concern and something that might have been anger.

"I found it in the basements," Carlotta said. "I went . . . exploring. It was deep down, in a room that looked like it had been used hundreds of years ago. There was an old table, a chair with three legs, some rotten tapestries on the walls. I thought maybe a monk had hidden down there long ago, or someone else trying to escape something. I was *fascinated*. I rooted around a little, trying not to disturb too much, but then I found the book. It wasn't as dusty as everything else. And the last entry was 1945."

Hellboy raised his eyebrows. "Huh. A good year."

"It's like a register," Carlotta said. "A family account of Esposito girls gone missing. Sometimes there's ten years between disappearances, sometimes fifty. And it's long overdue to happen again."

"So what in particular makes you think it'll be you?"

Carlotta glanced at Franca, a flush of guilt making her feel sick. "Only that Franca escaped it."

Franca snorted. "That's no reason—"

"I can't help it," Carlotta said. "It started before I even went and found the book, Franca! I felt watched, all the time, whatever I was doing. I'd walk around the city and feel eyes on me at every moment."

"You're a pretty girl," Hellboy said.

"It wasn't *like* that. I *know* what that feels like. This was . . . predatory. I'd come home, sit in my room reading, bathe, and it always felt as if I was the center of someone's attention. Even at dinner, or out with friends when there were so many other people around, I felt singled out. And then I found the book, and it all began to come together."

"Or you put it together," Hellboy said. But he sounded distracted, and Carlotta could see the concentration on his face as he pored over some of the other copies from the file. "You managed to steal the book?"

"Only for a morning. I copied as much as I could."

"And it's back there now? Down in the basements?"

"Yes. Hellboy, I don't want to end up a new entry on one of its blank pages."

"You won't," he said, and he sounded very firm.

"You'll help me? Protect me?"

"I'll stay until I find out for sure." And though that answer still entertained doubt, Carlotta felt a surge of relief.

"Thank you," she said, and the tears she had been holding back began to flow. She shuddered, desperate not to appear weak or scared, but unable to prevent either. Hellboy put his arm awkwardly around her shoulders, but then Franca came across and sat on her other side, and Carlotta leaned into her. "Thanks for coming," she said. "You came back here because of me, and I can't thank you enough for that."

"It's not a problem," Franca said, and Carlotta could sense that her cousin was not lying. "I've sort of enjoyed coming back here."

"Those basements," Hellboy said. He'd been quiet, and Carlotta thought it was in deference to her teary outburst. But maybe not. She glanced up, and he was still frowning, looking down at his feet—

Hooves, she thought, *he has hooves*!

—and concentrating.

"Who has access to them?"

"Only the staff, I assume," Franca said. "I've been down there once or twice. I think most Esposito kids have, just to explore. It's dusty and dirty, though, and most children aren't much interested in wine cellars."

Hellboy looked up at them both, and Carlotta saw how dangerous he could be. It wasn't his red skin, or his build, or that heavy right hand he rested in his lap. The danger was entirely in his eyes.

"The book's been down there for a long time," he said. "Girls been disappearing for a long time. Damn it, I don't like the sound of this at all. I need to speak to the old guy."

"Adamo?" Carlotta asked.

"Yeah, him. This time without his goons around."

"You don't think he can have anything to do with this?" Franca asked.

"Someone in your family does."

"The book doesn't prove anything. It's a family account, and—"

"Then why keep it hidden away?" Hellboy asked. He stood and paced the room, his hooves making a strange sound on the floorboards. "How well hidden *is* it down there?"

"Anyone can see it, if they go down far enough."

"Maybe . . ." Carlotta said, and she felt Franca tense. "Maybe Adamo and the Elders *do* know what's happening, and they're ashamed. Or scared."

"If they know, then someone's told them."

"Who?"

Hellboy stood by the window and looked out, his expression grim. "That's what I have to find out."

Basements, he thought. *Why is it always basements, or caves, or old temples buried for thousands of years? Why can't the bad guys ever live in nice condos, or airy apartments with all-round glazing and views of the sea?* The moment he'd seen those metal doors down behind the big main staircase, something had tingled inside. Not a warning, not another sense, but just . . . recognition. He'd gone through doors like that before, and more often than not he hadn't liked what was on the other side.

And it hadn't liked him.

The view from the window was stunning; the city of Amalfi clung to the hillsides below La Casa Fredda, all the way down to the deep blue sea. The chaotic arrangement of orange-tiled roofs surrounded the dominant cathedral, and in the streets and alleys in between, people moved like colored ants. Speed boats and sailing craft cut white lines in the water, and further out, a small cruise ship drifted close by so people could get some nice pictures of the coastline. It all looked so peaceful. He took in a deep breath and smelled the scent of roses. And hidden somewhere behind that smell, a weaker hint of lilies.

In the garden below him, he sensed movement.

"Oh," he said, looking down. "So *there* are the dogs."

"They're out?" Carlotta asked, panicked. She stood from the bed and looked around, as if searching for something long-lost.

Franca sighed and came to stand beside Hellboy. "Inevitable, really," she said. "They know we're here."

"Makes what comes next a little easier, I guess," he said.

"Adamo?"

"Just a chat. Maybe he'll offer me some coffee."

"You don't know Adamo," she said.

"Time to get acquainted. Will you lead the way?"

Franca stepped away from Hellboy and stood beside her worried cousin again. They hugged, chatted in Italian, and Carlotta looked at Hellboy across Franca's shoulder for the second time. This time she looked a little less scared. But just a little.

"Hey," he said. "I'll speak to the old man. Offer my help. I'd be happy to stay here for a while, at least until your birthday. Anyone tries something on you, they have to come through me, first."

Carlotta managed a smile. "And that wouldn't be easy, right?"

"Many have tried."

"Well, you can suggest it to him," Franca said without turning around. "But I think I'll know exactly what he'll say."

"Then I'll do my best to persuade him," Hellboy said. "Besides, I wouldn't mind a look around those basements. Who knows? Maybe that's where Hercules buried Amalfi."

Franca turned and offered him a weak, worried smile.

Hellboy sighed. He wasn't sure what he'd find when he spoke to Adamo, but one thing already seemed certain: this was family business.

Maybe he was too relaxed, and he ignored the senses that had saved him many times before. Perhaps he was tired from Iceland and the flight down here, and the details Franca and her scared cousin had told him were still circling in his mind, threatening to coalesce into something sinister. Whatever the reason Hellboy had let down his guard, he did not acknowledge the feeling that something was wrong. The temperature rose around him, and he put it down to some strange atmospherics Amalfi might experience now and then: a breeze from the sea, a breath from the hills. A soft hiss increased in volume somewhere beyond the room, and perhaps it was the ocean, or the sound of an aircraft floating low above the attractive, rugged coastline.

"It's so hot," Franca said, concerned, and as Hellboy reached for the door, he glanced back over his shoulder at the two women.

The metal door handle scorched his hand.

"Back!" he managed to shout, and then the heavy wooden door burst inward.

Hellboy closed his eyes and brought his hands up as fire and splintered wood erupted around him. He staggered back, trying to keep his footing, but he tripped on a rug and fell, left hand going for his gun.

Explosion? he thought, but he'd heard only the impact of something heavy on the door.

Carlotta was screaming, and Franca was shouting something in rapid-fire Italian that Hellboy could not understand.

He rolled and stood, bringing the gun up to bear on the ragged door opening. Wood was burning, and smoke rose from the old carpets. Fire filled the doorway, roaring so loud that it hurt his ears, shifting this way and that as a breeze blew through—

But there *was* no breeze.

And as fiery fingers curved around the doorframe and pulled the thing through, Hellboy realized that that Carlotta's fears were well-founded.

There was nothing to shoot at—bullets couldn't hurt flames—but he fired anyway, and the roar of the gun provoked the reaction he'd been hoping for. The fire-thing came through the door and paused, its touch igniting the doorframe, raising itself to its full seven-foot height and turning its strange head in Hellboy's direction.

"What *is* that?" Franca said, her voice misleadingly calm.

Seen some things in my time, Hellboy thought, shifting the gun so that it aimed at the fire-thing's head. It was vaguely humanoid in shape—two arms, two legs, a torso—but its head was elongated, with white-hot burning stars where its eyes should have been. Inside its mouth, behind fire teeth and the flickering, wavering flame that was its tongue, there was a black hole leading down, down into whatever passed for its insides. Such blackness, such void, should surely not exist within a fire of this intensity. It had a wide chest, and long shifting flames on its fire-hands in place of claws; oranges and yellows glimmered across its body like fur in a breeze. *Seen some things, but nothing like this.*

He'd fought werewolves in the Balkans, and this thing . . . it looked like a werewolf made of flames.

As it howled, Hellboy pulled the trigger again. He saw a glimmer of fire parting on the creature's head, but the blaze closed again instantaneously. He holstered the gun.

"Okay," he said, lifting his hands. "Let's do this the old-fashioned way." He took a couple of steps sideways so that he was between the fire wolf and the women, and waited for it to come.

It surged forward on its hind legs, the air around it a shimmering heat-haze. It howled again, the sound of a conflagration sucking air through a small opening, and the howl finished in a low, liquid chuckle.

"Laughing at me?" Hellboy asked.

"Hellboy!" Franca said. "You can't fight *that*!"

"Watch me," he muttered, the words meant for both the woman, and the beast. And he made the first move.

The fire wolf seemed surprised when he came at it. It even flowed back a little, leaving a scorched black area on the carpet, and then Hellboy swung his left fist around. He'd been expecting some sort of impact, but there was none, and the lack of resistance sent him off balance. As he stumbled forward and fell, he saw the monster thrash at the air for a moment, flames flashing out from where his fist had swept through it like blood and flesh spurting from a wound. But even as Hellboy hit the floor he looked up and saw the thing reforming, the fire wolf taking shape once more. And it lowered its head to look into his eyes.

The pain of the burns kicked in then, rippling across the skin of his lower arm. As he gritted his teeth, something flew over his head and erupted in flames in the guts of the fire wolf.

"Another!" Franca shouted. Hellboy glanced up and saw Carlotta handing her a pillow from the bed. Franca launched this second pillow, and it too combusted the moment it hit the thing.

But it gave Hellboy precious seconds, and he took them, rolling away from the flames and back towards the two women.

"Nice moves," he said as he stood.

"Baseball," Franca muttered. She never took her eyes from the creature in Carlotta's ruined doorway. "Hellboy . . ."

"Leave it to me," he said. "This is my thing."

He went forward again, desperately trying to hide his confusion. *How do I punch something that's all fire? How can I grab hold of it before it takes Carlotta?* The fire wolf gave that gruesome howl again, then it leaped at Hellboy.

This time he went for a hold, not a punch. He felt the flames envelope him, smelled burning hair, heard the fire sizzling in his ears, and he tasted soot and acrid steam. And grabbing with his right fist he felt . . . something. It wasn't solid, but it was more tactile than fire, something *inside*.

Then the thing shrugged him off and he fell to one side, striking the wall beside the ruined doorway, chunks of plaster bursting out around him and scratching at his eyes.

From behind, someone screamed.

Only my right hand can feel its insides, Hellboy thought. He spun around and launched himself again, his vision a blur but good enough to see what he was aiming for. He dragged up a big rug as he went, swinging it around his head and towards the fire wolf like a toreador. The heavy weave dropped across the thing's head and it fell, already scorching through the material but still forced down for a precious few seconds.

"Take her and get out!" Hellboy said, pointing at Carlotta, talking to Franca.

"Where?"

"Hide. Somewhere close to water."

Franca grabbed Carlotta's hand—the younger cousin was staring wide-eyed at the thrashing fire thing, sweat dripping from her brow and staining her blouse—and pulled her towards the door.

The fire wolf reached out a blazing hand and closed its flames around Franca's ankle.

She screamed, pulling back, but Hellboy could smell scorched skin, and then burnt flesh. She kept hold of Carlotta's hand as she fell, trying to pull the girl behind her.

Hellboy threw himself on the burning rug, hoping to trap the fire beneath and maybe even extinguish it. But it was a vain hope, and within seconds he knew that he could not win like this.

Franca was leaning back against the wall, sweating, pale, her eyes dipping shut.

"Franca!" Hellboy shouted. Then he turned his attention to the girl . . . but she was petrified, frozen in fear, and he did not even see her blink.

He punched at the rug, spluttering on burning shreds of material. His coat smoldered, and he could feel the skin of his chest and stomach blistering. The pain he could take, because he knew he'd heal and get over it.

Losing, he could *not* accept.

"Son of a bitch!" he hissed, rolling across the remains of the rug and kicking out with his hooves.

The fire wolf rose on all fours and reformed, glancing at him almost dismissively before leaping at Carlotta.

Hellboy had a flash of what could happen in the next few seconds: if he was too slow, the intruder would grasp Carlotta to its bosom; her hair would smolder first, then her clothes would ignite, and finally her skin and flesh would start to melt. And he would have lost before he even knew what he was fighting. Another Esposito tragedy, reading to be marked down in that old book in the basement . . . except that this one had witnesses.

And that was why after Carlotta, the thing would turn its fires upon Franca and him.

That all occurred to him in a blink, and a heartbeat later he was launching himself across the room at Carlotta. He landed and flicked out his hand, knocking her from her feet just as the fire wolf scorched through the air where she had been standing. It washed against the window like a wave striking a beach, spreading, rippling then retreating back into its old shape.

Carlotta landed, Hellboy heaved himself over her, and the thing came one more time. But this time, he'd seen something that might just help.

He smashed the table legs, then swung his hand back as the vase fell from the table. He caught it just right; the vase shattered against his knuckles, sending six beautiful roses and several pints of water showering into the fire wolf's face.

If that hadn't worked, Hellboy would have been at a loss. But whatever supernatural bastard this thing might be, it also seemed to obey some earthly laws as well. And fire did not like water.

It howled and hissed, steamed and spat, and then flung itself at the window. The already weakened glass cracked and shattered under the heat, and the creature fell out, tumbling three floors to the ground below.

Hellboy stood quickly and went to the window, burns stinging across his body, skin stretched. He grabbed the window frame, knocking out more glass, and leaned out, looking down at where the fire wolf had fallen. He was just in time to see it blazing across the garden, leaving a trail of burnt foliage in its wake. The living plants gave out thick gray smoke as they died.

"You okay?" he asked Carlotta. The girl had crawled across to Franca and she lay shivering on the floor, hugged up against her cousin. Franca seemed to have fallen unconscious from the pain. He knew he should stay, but . . .

"Two minutes," he said, then he jumped from the window.

He landed hard, grunting as air was knocked from his body. He started running, following the path of scorched and dead plants the thing had left across the garden and around the corner of the house. No sign of the dogs, for which he was glad. In seconds he reached the boundary wall. The resplendent bougainvillea was dried and stick-like where the creature had flamed right over the top, and Hellboy jumped, scrabbling up and swinging over the wall. He landed in the alley close to the garden gate by which they had entered, and looking down the narrow path and steps he could see the air shimmering from the heat of the fleeing fire wolf. He ran, pumping his arms, hissing in pain as his coat rubbed against the burnt parts of his skin.

At a junction of the path he looked left and right, heard a startled scream some distance to the left, and went that way. Soon there was another junction at the corner of three buildings, and here there was no sign of which way the thing had gone. Washing overhung two of the twisting, shaded alleys, none of it burnt, so he took the third, turning corners, descending steps towards the city's main thoroughfare and the harbor. He passed a little old lady sitting on the steps outside an open wooden door.

"You seen a fire demon come this way?" he asked. The woman looked up at him with milky cataract eyes, hands raised to show she did not understand. Hellboy didn't have time to try his shaky Italian.

He ran on some more, reaching a small square with a fountain at its center. There were five routes leading out from here, and none of them offered up any immediate clues. He might be lucky once or twice, but he needed much more than that right now. Besides, he figured the flower vase had probably worn out his luck for the day.

A small group of tourists entered the square, one of them squealed, and then cameras flashed at him. A fat man asked for his autograph.

Hellboy cursed and began retracing his steps. He smelled singed things in the air, and he wondered whether the scent came from him.

He climbed the garden wall again, and this time, the dogs were waiting for him, having apparently forgotten their obvious fear of the burning thing. They came close as soon as he landed, alternately growling and whining, uncertain at this strange man who had invaded their domain.

They crouched down, ready to leap.

• • •

How can I ever escape that? Carlotta thought. She looked down at her burnt cousin, the painful mess of her ankle, the sweat on her beautiful face, and it was all her fault. *I led it here . . . it came for me . . . it will come for me again, and next time . . . .*

Carlotta stood and backed away from Franca, as if distance would lessen her guilt. But it did nothing to assuage the responsibility she felt, unreasonable though that may be. She struggled to see sense through her tears, searched for light at the end of her fears, but there was neither sense nor light to be found. Only darkness, lit by the jumping orange flames of the thing that had come for her.

She could hear shouting elsewhere in the house. Her loved ones, and those who loved her, coming to see what the commotion was.

When it comes back, they will be here as well. She remembered the thing's flaming claws closing around Franca's ankle, and imagined them twisting the heads of small children, burning the gray hair of her older relatives, and pricking burning fingers into her mother's eyes.

Carlotta gasped, shivering even in the heat. Hopelessness had made her ice cold. She went and stood at the smashed window, and even sunlight could not ease the chill.

Then she heard people in the room behind her, frightened and concerned, voices she knew saying things she did not understand, because everything came to this:

It wanted her.

Looking down, the ground did not seem so far away.

Hellboy heard a scream. The dogs glanced back towards the house.

"Beat it," Hellboy growled, and both dogs slunk away. *Carlotta!* Damn it, he should have never left her alone. He ran back across the garden, skidded around the corner of the house and looked up at the shattered window. He saw a pale, old face there, staring straight down, eyes wide with shock. And then the scream came again, and Hellboy stopped when he saw the shape before him.

Carlotta was splayed on the ground, a pool of blood spreading across the cobbles beneath her broken head. Beyond her stood a middle-aged woman Hellboy had never seen, squeezing her face so tightly that her features distorted and made the third scream sound very far away.

He went to Carlotta and knelt by her side, aware of the shouts and calls coming from inside the house, and sensing also the other people rushing to gather around. But he only had eyes for the girl. He'd seen enough dead people to know that she was one too, but still he went through the motions, blinking quickly when tears blurred his vision.

I should never have left her alone!

He touched her neck and felt no pulse. He moved his finger close to her half-open eye, and she did not flinch. In the blood beneath her head, there was other matter; that poor young girl's brain, so filled with fear as she approached adulthood, and he . . .

"I let her fall," he whispered. He touched her cheek and said he was sorry, hoping that somewhere she might hear.

The middle-aged woman shouted something in Italian, and it was a harsh word that Hellboy knew well.

"No," a weak voice said, and Hellboy looked up at Carlotta's window. Franca stood there now, looking weak and in pain, staring down at her dead cousin. "Not murder," she said. "She fell. I saw. I saw and . . ." Hellboy saw her eyes flutter and he stood, ready to catch her should she fall as well. But Franca disappeared back into the room, and he heard a soothing voice trying to whisper her pain away.

He moved back a few steps as more family gathered around the body, some of them speaking rapidly into mobile phones while others fussed about her, trying to find life where he already knew there was none.

Someone shouted. The people parted and Adamo hobbled through, sweating, panting as his old man's legs carried him forward. He glanced at Hellboy, but only once. When he saw the dead young girl his eyes turned fluid and he fell to his knees.

When the first wail came, Hellboy turned away.

Chapter 5

Amalfi

When she opened her eyes he was there, sitting at her bedside and looking as if he was snoozing. She watched for a while, and listened. The room was completely silent, and in the house beyond she could hear nothing; no voices, no chatter of excited children, no deeper drone of the Elders in conference.

She turned her head slightly and looked at the window. It had been swathed in polyethylene, a rough new frame nailed into the old to hold it in place. Sniffing, she could still smell burning. She thought perhaps that smell would never leave her.

They didn't put me in another room, she thought. But then she knew why. Injured though she might be, she could also be partially to blame for Carlotta's death. None of them knew what had happened, none of them had seen . . .

When she closed her eyes she no longer saw darkness, but light, and the flicker of flames across her consciousness.

I've seen that thing before...

She opened her eyes again, and he was looking at her. He smiled.

"How do you feel?"

Franca tried to speak but her mouth was dry. Hellboy leaned forward, handing her a glass of water. She sipped and swallowed, blinking over the glass at him. He only watched her. *He must be so full of questions*, she thought, and silently thanked him for holding back.

"Sore," she said. "Leg hurts. But you?" She sat up, wincing but waving away his concern. "You were fighting it, tangled with it. You must be burnt?"

"A little," he said, looking at his left hand and patting his stomach softly. "I heal easy."

Franca lifted the single thin sheet and looked down at her foot.

"Some old doctor came," Hellboy said. "He was about a hundred and fifty. Patched you up, left some painkillers and some cream to rub in."

"Family doctor. He's been on retainer to the Espositos for decades." *We're edging around the subject*, she thought, and when she glanced at Hellboy again she knew he was aware of it as well. He looked away, searching the room for something unseen.

"They let you stay?" she asked.

"Police want to talk to me. They're in with Adamo and the others right now. Selecting the lining for my coffin, I guess."

"She jumped, Hellboy. I barely saw . . . I could hardly see. But she stood at the window, and when people came in there was shouting, some screaming, talk of fires and explosions. I tried to sit up but the pain held me down, made me feel faint. I reached out for Carlotta, but she didn't even turn around. Didn't seem to hear. And then she jumped." France felt a single tear streak down her cheek, cool and lonely.

"I'm going to find it," he said. "Gotta speak to a friend of mine, see if she has any ideas. But I'm not leaving, Franca. Whatever the old man says, I'm going to stay until that bastard is sorted out. Carlotta's will be the last name in that book, you hear me?"

"I hear you," she said. But she felt weak and tired, and as sleep beckoned she was more than happy to welcome it in.

I'm sure I've seen that thing before, she thought. *I just have to remember where.*

The Carlotta that accompanied her down into sleep was a younger, more carefree girl, whom Franca had played with as a child in the large gardens, walked with through the sweet Amalfi streets, and talked to about their future while sitting beneath the protective spread of the largest rose bush. A girl who still knew how to laugh.

"Hey, Liz."

"Hellboy! Damn, it's good to hear your voice."

"You too." He smiled into his cellphone, waiting for her to speak. Liz Sherman represented somewhere he felt at home, somewhere he belonged, and she was one of his closest friends. The fact that she was a member of the Bureau for Paranormal Research and Defense and able to start fires with her mind made her all the more special.

"So I hear they shipped you straight off to Italy!" she said. "I was hoping we could catch up after your Iceland jaunt. I'm sitting here at H.Q., twiddling my thumbs, and—"

"Don't twiddle too much, you'll burn the place down."

"Screw you."

"Ha! Liz. It's *good* to hear your voice." He was sitting in La Casa Fredda's garden, watching the sun sinking into the sea and looking out for any flame-lit regions of the city. He sighed, breathing in the stench of burning flesh. He really should take a shower soon.

"What is it, H.B.?"

"You know me so well."

"Got a bad one?"

"Yeah, it is. I thought it was nothing at first. Young girl approaching eighteen, scared of a supposed family curse, sees shades where there are none, conspiracies in family whispers. I didn't take her too seriously, really, and now she'd dead."

"Oh, no." Liz's voice changed little, but Hellboy knew she could empathize. She bore more than enough guilt for both of them, and though she was growing to handle it, the ghosts of her childhood would always be with her. "What happened?"

"Some sort of fire monster came for her. I fought it off, it ran, I chased. When I came back, she'd killed herself."

"After you saved her?" A note of hardness there, but Hellboy had not even considered feeling angry at Carlotta.

"She was terrified, Liz. All her months of paranoia were confirmed to her. She saw the thing injure the cousin she loved, and she must have been certain it'd be back for her."

"Monster made of fire . . ." she said, trailing off.

"Yeah. You remember the Sahara?"

"Fire dogs."

"Well, this thing . . . It wasn't the same. Nowhere near. But I was just thinking . . ."

"Just thinking that since it's made of fire, I could help."

"Nah. I know you won't have a clue. Just wanted to hear your voice."

"Screw you again."

Hellboy laughed, and it felt good. Speaking with Liz, he was thousands of miles away back in Connecticut, not huddled down in this dusky garden waiting to talk to the police. She had a way of making his pains less heavy.

"How did you chase it away?"

"Threw water over it."

"Hmm. Figures. What did it look like?"

"Well . . . this may sound crazy, but—"

"H.B., I've known you a long time. Crazy doesn't even begin to perturb me any more."

"Yeah. Well, if the thing hadn't been made of flames, I'd have said it looked like a wolf."

"A wolf, like, hooowwwlll!"

"A wolf on two legs."

"Werewolf."

Hellboy shrugged. "Teeth, claws, fur, all made of fire. White-hot eyes. But the throat, that was the freaky part. When it howled, its throat was pitch black."

"Dark as the void," Liz said, in a mock-1950s horror-movie voice.

"Actually, yeah."

"Creepy," Liz said, no longer mocking. "Kate's been researching something to do with werewolves. Black Sun prophecy, she calls it."

"Yeah, she's mentioned that to me. But this is very different, Liz. This thing was made of *fire*."

"Water scared it away, though," she said.

"Seemed to. Looked like it hurt it, actually."

"Then change that big cannon of yours for a water pistol."

Hellboy chuckled, not quite dismissing the idea out of hand. "I'm gonna sniff around," he said. "Whatever's happening, there're people in this family aware of it. I'll get to the bottom of it."

"You know where I am if you need anything," Liz said.

"Yeah, you're on panic-dial on my cell."

"You need me out there, H.B.?"

He thought about that, and the idea of having Liz here with him was comforting. Yet there was still that uncertainty about her abilities, which she was as ready to acknowledge as anyone, and a fear that the power she held could never be completely under control. Confront her with something like this, and that power might well take over.

"Nah, not right now," he said. "If I do, I'll push that panic button."

"I think I'm going to Seattle," she said, and he sensed the disappointment she was trying to hide.

"Oh?"

"Haunted sailing yacht. Tom says it smells like an insurance scam, but I'll go check it out."

"Great seafood in Seattle."

"Don't get fat on pasta."

"Your concern is noted," Hellboy said, and he wanted to say more, tell her what a friend she was to him. Seeing that poor young girl take her own life had left him feeling maudlin.

But he never needed to tell Liz those things, and that's what made the two of them together so special.

"Take it easy, H.B," she said

"You know me."

He heard her mocking laughter as she broke the connection.

Hellboy sat there for a while, watching the city below lighting up as tourists headed out for their evening meals. Mopeds buzzed along the streets like fireflies, and out at sea, expensive yachts bobbed at their moorings.

"Hellboy," someone said.

He stood and turned quickly, hand resting on his holster. Adamo stood a few paces behind him, hands crossed on a walking stick that had not been with him before. He looked like a shrunken man.

"Mr. Esposito. I'm sorry for your loss."

Adamo nodded, glancing past Hellboy at the view he must have seen a million times. He sighed, seemed about to say something, but then turned and walked back towards the door. "The police will see you now," he said.

"After that, can you and I—"

"In the morning, if you will. I can't talk to you now. I can barely look at you."

Hellboy felt a flush of anger, but then the atmosphere of the house gave him pause. This old, beautiful place was stilled by grief tonight. He could give the old man a night to cry his pain away, at least.

"In the morning, then," he said in acknowledgement. "But if it's all right with you, and pretty much also if it isn't all right, I'll patrol the grounds tonight."

Adamo waved a hand above his shoulder, a dismissive gesture.

Hellboy took it as a yes. He had grave doubts about whether he'd be able to sleep. And as night fell, the taint of fire left the garden, and the scent of roses on the air was fine.

The pain should have kept her awake, but the doctor had given her ointment for the burns and painkillers to fend off the discomfort. So she slept, insisting that she stay in Carlotta's ruined room—

her parents had come to see her at last, and they had made the offer to move her elsewhere—and as she drifted away she heard the familiar sounds of Amalfi coming through the polyethylene windows. Dropping into sleep, she was a girl once more, and La Casa Fredda was her home and always would be. That young girl could never imagine living anywhere else. With her family around her, everything felt safe.

In her dreams she walked the darkened corridors of the house while everyone slept. She seemed to know where each creaking floorboard was positioned, because even she could not hear her footfalls. There was a tension to the air, as if it was thicker than usual. She had to push through. It pressed against her, caressing her skin and compacting her ears.

Downstairs, she turned around the staircase and approached the metal door leading down into the basement. She expected it to be locked, as always, but the door hung open, and through the crack she saw the dancing flicker of flames.

She was afraid but fascinated, and she thought, *I have seen you before.*

Opening the door, she saw a small room, much smaller than the tunnels and basements she had expected to find. It contained nothing but a table, and upon the table sat a book, open to the last page. Above the book, blazing like the hottest fire, bright as the sun, floated the familiar fire demon.

She went to step back, but her legs took her forward instead.

The fire demon eased back from the book, displaying what it had been writing with one burning claw, letters and words scored in carbon on the slightly scorched paper. As she viewed the book, the room around her shook, and the only sound to be heard in her dream was a subtle, distant roar.

She knew what she would see, and she prepared herself for that sadness once again.

But it was not Carlotta's name marked on that final page.

It was her own.

• • •

The cool night air soothed his burns. The doctor had offered to take a look at his wounds, but Hellboy had declined; he figured paranoia was now a healthy option. He'd heal soon enough, and for now they gave him some physical sign of the fire wolf. As he walked, he dwelled upon just what that thing could be.

If everything that Carlotta had claimed was right—and the Esposito family was under some strange, ancient curse—then it could surely not have been a fire wolf responsible for every disappearance. It would have been seen down through the centuries, and noted somewhere in family history or whispers. So, that meant that the threat had changed, or who- or what-ever was taking the girls had altered its tactics. A demon or a wraith, the creature had certainly been real enough, both affecting this world and being affected by it.

If and when he met it again, at least he would know that water worked against it.

He passed around the garden, one of the guard dogs walking several steps behind him. The Doberman had taken an interest in him, and though it had yet to come close enough to be stroked, Hellboy quite liked its company.

"So did you see it, dog?" he asked, pausing and turning around. "Did you smell it?" The dog stopped and cocked its head. "Carlotta and Franca saw it. Stands to reason others in the family must have as well." He'd spoken with some of the others that evening—Franca's parents, Carlotta's older brother, a few others who spoke good English—but grief was a heavy weight upon every Esposito, and few of them had welcomed his questions. Rumor had already spread that his arrival here had initiated the events, and Hellboy had an unsettling suspicion that could have been the case. The fire wolf had come for Franca when there were others around to witness it, but perhaps only because it knew of Hellboy's presence. If Franca had not called the B.P.R.D.—if she'd put her cousin's fears down to teenaged delusions—the creature, or something connected with it, would have come unseen.

Carlotta would still be dead, but not of her own will.

"Damn it!" he snapped, startling the Doberman into the bushes. His frustration and grief at what she had done could not transpose into anger, much as he felt it should. He'd fought the thing and saved her life, but still she had done *that*.

Terrified that the thing might return, perhaps.

Or certain that it *would*.

Hellboy walked the gardens that whole night, and saw no sign of the fire wolf. By the time dawn peered over the hilltops, a much more benevolent fire, the Doberman was walking by his side, sniffing at his big right hand and letting him pet its head.

And Hellboy had questions for Adamo.

When she opened her eyes there was fire at the window. She tried to scream, but her throat and mouth were so dry that she could utter no sound, so she thrashed her hands and knocked a glass from the bedside table before she realized she was seeing the sunrise.

Franca's heart fluttered in her chest, and she sat up in bed against the instruction of her pain. *Lie still*, it said, *or you will hurt even more*. But at least the pain told her that she was alive. Every time she blinked she saw Carlotta lying dead below this very window, blood spreading beneath her pretty head. And between each blink was only the sunlight, a mocking heat. Neither gave her any respite.

Even her dreams had been bad, though right now all that she remembered was her name in a book.

Her mother had been with her on and off through the night, but now she was gone. Franca had vague memories of the woman sitting upright beside her bed, and exuding from her had been a confusion of concern and blame. *It wasn't me*, Franca had wanted to say, and perhaps in her sleep she had spoken those words. But now her mother was gone, and her absence from the bedside of her wounded daughter spoke volumes.

She swung her legs over the side of the bed, stepping gingerly onto the floor. The burn around her ankle and lower leg stung, but it was not as bad as she had expected.

I've seen that thing before, she thought absently, sending the idea away in the hope that she would chance upon the truth via a casual approach.

She walked to the shattered door and moved aside the curtain that had been hung in its place. The police had urged against remaining in the room, cautioning that officers would wish to examine the window and door. But the Espositos were an old, respected family. And Franca had no doubt that money had changed hands. A suicide was an embarrassment, but nowhere near as scandalous as a murder.

She left the room and the stink of burned carpet behind. *How did they explain that?* she wondered. But that was something for later. Now, she had to find Hellboy and speak to him about what had happened.

I've seen that thing, she would tell him. Perhaps his questions would prompt her to remember where.

He met Franca in the downstairs hallway. She was limping slightly, and she looked tired and drawn, but he was glad to see her up and on her feet.

"Hey," he said, "how're you feeling?"

"I'm fine. You?"

Hellboy shrugged his shoulders, cricked his neck. "Bit sore this morning." There was plenty he wanted to say about Carlotta, but right now did not seem the time.

"Shall we breakfast?" Franca asked. "Some of the younger family members seemed pleased to see me, at least."

"You go ahead," Hellboy said. "I'm going to visit Adamo, if I can find him."

"He'll likely be in his rooms on the third floor. He always breakfasts alone. At least, he did when I lived here."

"You did a brave thing, you know," he said. Franca looked away, but he touched her chin and turned her to face him again. "Coming back. That took guts, and I know Carlotta appreciated it."

Her eyes watered at the sound of her dead cousin's name. "Did we do this?" she asked.

"What?"

"By coming here, did we cause this?"

"You're smarter than that, Franca," he said.

She blinked quickly for a couple of seconds, banishing her tears for a better time. "Then that thing knew we were here," she said, "and it came early."

"That's what I figure. That's one of the things I'll be talking about with the old man."

Franca actually managed a smile. It was dazzling, and it touched Hellboy's heart. "Best of luck," she said. She nodded at a door across the hall from them. "I'll be in there. Breakfast room. If they haven't tarred and feathered me by the time you come back."

"You'll be fine," he said. "Go. Eat. I'll see you later."

"Hellboy . . ." she said, her smile wiped by an instant frown.

He waited for a few seconds, giving her time.

"Never mind." Franca shook her head, but the frown was still there. "Later."

"You sure?" he asked.

Franca nodded. "Bad dreams."

"That happens."

She surprised him by giving him a brief, strong hug. Then she headed for the breakfast room door, glancing back with a soft smile. He watched her through the door and heard a few welcome greetings from some of those inside. From others, he sensed silence.

He started up the staircase, and by the time he reached the third floor—and the house took on the air of an old, deserted place—he knew he should have pressed Franca to say what she had been thinking. But there was always later.

Two of the Elders were standing on the third floor landing, talking in hushed tones. One of them, a man, offered him a curt nod.

The woman simply stared at him, the piercing eyes in her wrinkled face wet and full of malice.

"I did my best to save Carlotta," he said, but neither Elder responded. Maybe they couldn't speak English. "Adamo?" he asked, pointing along the corridor one way, and then the other.

Again, the woman only stared at him, perhaps manufacturing a dozen suitable tortures for this red-skinned man in her old woman's mind. The man pointed to the corridor behind them, and as Hellboy moved on, he maintained eye contact until they were behind him.

A door opened and he paused, waiting to see if Adamo emerged. But it was another of the Elders, a woman so withered and twisted that she reminded Hellboy of an ancient tree.

"Hellboy," the woman said in heavily accented English, "the man who is not."

"I am what I am," he said, immediately on the defensive. She smiled, showing crooked teeth and a constantly shifting tongue, like a snake in its hole.

"Come here to help, and brought something with him."

"Lady, that thing was here before me, believe me."

"The fire demon?" she said, shrugging. "Maybe. But you brought something else, Hellboy. Death. I smell it on you." She pecked her head forward in a mine of sniffing. "I see it on you, in every red crease."

"I'm here to see Adamo," he said. "I'm truly sorry for your loss, lady. Carlotta was a brave girl."

"Carlotta," the woman said, and something seemed to fade from her eyes. She looked past Hellboy into a distance he could not view. "A great loss, yes. To all of us." Her eyes snapped back to Hellboy. "Be gone."

"Not yet, lady." *No one tells me to be gone*, he thought, bristling with awkward anger. These people were grieving, he had to remember that, but he had something to do here. A hundred questions had been asked, and now was the time to start answering them.

He walked on, aware of the woman's gaze burning into the back of his neck. When he reached the next door he glanced back, but she was gone, along with the other two Elders. Down for breakfast, he supposed. He only hoped they were kinder to Franca than they were to him.

Hellboy knocked at the door, and a heartbeat later it opened. Adamo stood there in the doorway, chewing thoughtfully on a croissant. There was a flake of it on his top lip. He stared at Hellboy, but some of the anger from the previous night seemed to have gone. Indeed, he seemed almost friendly as he waved the big man into his room.

Weird.

"Join me for breakfast?" Adamo said. "My great-great-grandson, bless him, always brings me too much. An old man doesn't burn as much energy as his younger descendants, alas, much as I like to think of myself as still . . . athletic."

"You're as old as you feel," Hellboy said.

Adamo actually chuckled. "Then this morning, I must be the oldest man on Earth." He ushered Hellboy over to a table placed inside a tall, wide window. Shutters had been drawn back and the windows were open, allowing in a pleasing breeze that carried the scent of the garden with it. Beneath that, the unmistakeable smell of the sea. Hellboy sat, looking out at the stunning view afforded down across Amalfi.

"Coffee?" Adamo asked.

"Please." He watched the old man pour, then heaped three teaspoons of sugar into the cup.

"You ruin a good coffee."

"I'm a creature of habit," Hellboy said. He stirred and sipped, and Adamo was right, it *was* good coffee.

"Today, ours is a sad house," Adamo said. "I feel the weight of grief, even up here, and I dread descending those stairs this morning. It's a very . . . private time for us, in our loss. Do you understand?"

"Of course. And I appreciate how difficult this is. I've lost people close to me, and—"

"But have you ever lost family, Hellboy?" The old man stared right at him, the question loaded.

"My father was murdered," he said.

Adamo nodded, then reached down for his coffee.

"As I was saying, I'm sorry. But I can't simply leave."

Adamo glanced up at him again, his welcoming manner evaporating like spit on a hot sidewalk.

"You know some of what's been happening here, Adamo," Hellboy said. "Carlotta found that old book down in the basements. She showed me pages from it, and—"

"She found a history of this family's grief and sadness," Adamo said. "It surprises you that I keep the book hidden away? It shouldn't. It's not exactly bedtime reading."

"Who else knows about it?"

"The family Elders," Adamo said, sighing. "Supposedly no one else, but I'm aware that some of the children go into the basements on occasion, against strict instruction. It's a challenge for some, an adventure for others. And if they find the book, well, so be it. But it remains hidden away. It's full of sad times, and it has no place in a happy family home."

"So you keep it buried."

"I keep it out of the way."

Hellboy picked up a croissant and bit into it, scooping honey from a stone jar on the table and smearing it inside. It tasted good, and he had barely realized how hungry he was.

"But you or those before you continue to fill in the book," he said. "You record the cursed deaths this family endures—"

"There is no curse!" Adamo said, almost spitting the words.

"Then what the hell was that thing that came here for Carlotta?" Hellboy asked leaning across the table. It became a ridiculous staring game, and he could not help but be impressed by the old guy's resilience. Most people would have looked away from him long ago. He smiled and glanced down at the table, seeing if there were any pastries left.

"That, I cannot answer," Adamo said. "And I did not see it. No one saw it, other than you and Franca."

"And Carlotta."

"Ahh, sweet Carlotta. Dead, now. Unable to tell what she saw, or why she fell."

"She jumped, because she was terrified of—"

"A fire demon?"

"Something like that."

"Ha!" Adamo spat. "Preposterous. But then, a man like you would see demons everywhere."

"What do you mean?"

"I made that clear before, Hellboy."

"Well, officially, I'm as human as you."

"And unofficially?"

"I'm just a guy doing a job."

Adamo laughed, a bitter, hacking old man's laugh.

"This isn't about me," Hellboy said. "It's about Carlotta, and why she jumped from—"

"Jumped or was pushed. Either way, she fell." Adamo was shifting from mockery to anger now, less able to hide it behind civilities and platitudes.

"I want to look at the book," Hellboy said. "I want to go into the basements."

"Impossible. You're not family." Adamo finished his coffee and clunked his cup down, going to stand and finish this audience as quickly as it had begun.

Hellboy poured himself some more coffee. "I'm not finished," he said.

Adamo glared at him, half out of his chair. Then he sat back down with a groan, leaned back, and closed his eyes. A tear leaked from the corner of his left eye, and Hellboy looked away.

"Whatever visited La Casa Fredda yesterday, the Elders believe that your arrival brought it," Adamo said. "I believe the same. The

Elders believe, therefore, that you are responsible for Carlotta's death."

"And you?" Hellboy asked, taking a measured bite from his croissant.

"Angry as I am, I do not think that," Adamo said. "Carlotta saw lies in every word, conspiracies in every wrinkle of history. A troubled girl, and yet not as passive in her fears as I believed. Finding the book was the worst thing for her, because it gave so much scope for those insecurities to take root. And they did, expanding and growing into terrors, fears and certainties. And in the end, the certainty that she was cursed is what killed her."

"There's truth in what she was claiming," Hellboy said. "And I intend to find it."

"As you wish. But I cannot in good conscience allow you to remain here any longer."

"You're not afraid of that fire wolf?"

Adamo shrugged. "I'm an old, old man. I've seen many things to scare me, but at my age, something I cannot see holds little fear for me."

"If it returns, you'll know it."

"If it was Carlotta's curse, as you seem to believe, then it will not return, will it?"

Hellboy stood, wiping crumbs from his coat. "The curse is your family's, Adamo. Carlotta was simply its next victim."

"Take Franca with you," Adamo said quietly. "She's not been welcome here for years."

"Such sentiment," Hellboy said, bitterness giving his voice bite. But the old man remained unmoved.

"Goodbye, Hellboy."

"Arrivederci, Adamo Esposito." Hellboy left the room, closing the door behind him and barely able to restrain his instinct to rip it from its hinges and crunch it over his knee. He took a few deeps breaths as he walked along the deserted corridor, and as he started back downstairs, he tried to formulate a plan. But he was never very good at this covert, scheming stuff.

Damn, he thought, *maybe I should have asked Liz to come after all.*

The breakfast room was bustling. He hadn't realized just how many people lived in this huge old house, but as he entered and faces turned this way, he looked around and did a quick count. He saw several Elders spotted around, including the three cheery souls he'd encountered up on the third floor. There were maybe a dozen younger men and women, ranging in age from early twenties to their fifties or sixties. He did not see Franca's parents among them. And he counted fifteen kids, at least. They were seated around several large tables arrayed around the room, flitting to and from a breakfast bar set up along one wall. This contained fresh fruits, cereals, croissants, and a mouth-watering array of fresh pastries.

Franca was sitting at one of the tables, and she offered him a brief smile.

Conversation had faded as he entered. Some people, mainly the kids, stared at him. Some of the adults turned away, but some of the younger ones seemed keen to catch his eye, and as he looked around, he received several friendly nods and smiles. *Love me or loathe me, I'm here*, he thought, and he allowed himself a small, grim smile in return.

"Here," Franca said, touching the table beside her.

"I've eaten," Hellboy said. "Can we talk?"

As Franca stood, a teenager ran into the room from a door in the far corner. He was speaking Italian at a hundred miles per hour, and the only word Hellboy managed to catch was *Vesuvius*.

Most of the room stood in unison, streaming towards the door and piling through.

"TV room," Franca said, frowning at Hellboy, distracted. He nodded and watched her go with the others, knowing that he should see for himself what was happening. But something kept him back. *Take advantage*, a voice whispered in his head, and maybe that was Abe Sapien's calm, controlled influence over him.

The Elders around the room seemed in shock. They stared at one-another, then quickly became conscious that Hellboy was still standing in the doorway. Most of them stood and headed for the TV room, but the man and woman he'd first met on the third floor pushed past him into the hallway, not even sparing him a glance.

They're distracted, Abe's voice said, *and isn't there somewhere you need to be?*

He backed into the hallway and watched the two Elders climb the stairs. For old people, they were very sprightly. *Olive oil and fish*, he thought. Liz always talked about the good Mediterranean diet. He walked gently across the marble floor until he stood before the great staircase, listening to doors opening and closing upstairs, and the muted grumble of many voices from two rooms away.

Then he walked quickly around the staircase and approached the metal door. Bolted and padlocked. But that should prove no problem.

He was crossing a line now, and he knew it. But it was a line he had not drawn himself, so it might as well not be there at all.

Clutching the first of the padlocks in his right hand, he began to twist.

CHAPTER 6

Amalfi

"Vesuvius is erupting!" Mario had shouted. He was another of Franca's cousins, and he'd grown up a lot since she'd left. "It's all over the news, and they're talking of evacuation!"

Franca followed the others into the TV lounge, remembering spending long cool evenings in here watching history programmes and period-piece movies. Even as a girl she'd been fascinated with the past.

Where the hell have I seen that damned fire wolf before? she thought, jostled by her family as they all craned to see the big TV in the far corner of the room. But her thoughts trailed off when she saw the TV picture.

The great, shattered hillside of Vesuvius took up the bottom half of the screen, and the camera was focused on a trail of smoke standing vertically from the hidden crater. It rose for perhaps a thousand feet before being caught by a breeze and dispersed into the air. The smoke was almost pure white, and it looked calm and peaceful. But what that wisp might herald imbued it with a more sinister meaning.

Some of the kids ran around the room, jumping on and across furniture in an impromptu game of tag, and Franca's aunt gave a terse, loud shout to quiet them. Franca was impressed with how quickly the children obeyed, dropping onto a sofa and watching to see what had gotten the adults so agitated.

She glanced behind her for Hellboy, but he had not yet appeared.

"Turn it up," someone called. Her Uncle Alfonso, who had not once made eye contact with her since her return. Even her dead father's brother could not accept the fact that she had her own life to lead.

Someone found the remote control and raised the volume, and the bustle in the room immediately settled as the reporter's voice came through.

" . . . evacuation procedure that has been put in place for such an eventuality. The first tremors were felt several weeks ago, and a team from Naples University and the Disaster Emergency Committee have been monitoring the volcano closely ever since. There are frequent rumblings, they say, but this recent tremor—and the fact that the volcano is now venting gas—is a significant step towards eruption. I repeat: there is no apparent immediate threat of Vesuvius erupting, but please be aware of regular updates on TV and radio, and if you live within the boundaries of the Vesuvius Evacuation Plan, please review and be familiar with your procedures."

The live feed vanished, replaced by some clever CGI of Pompeii almost two thousand years ago.

"The most famous eruption of Mount Vesuvius destroyed the towns of Herculaneum and Pompeii in AD 79, burying much of Pompeii and preserving it for . . ." The words trailed off for Franca, her senses withdrew, and she closed her eyes and saw what she had been reaching for.

Yes, I have *seen it before!*

What that meant, she could not guess. But the idea that there was a connection between the two—the thing that had burned her yesterday, and the fresco on that excavated wall in Pompeii—sent a chill into her heart.

She opened her eyes again. Some of the others were already drifting away, and she noticed that there were no Elders among them. Perhaps they were avoiding her.

"Is the volcano going to erupt, Franca?" Mario asked.

"Of course not," she said, distracted by the familiar images of Pompeii being played across the screen.

"I hope it does!" one of the children yelled. "Exciting! Boom!"

"Hellboy," she muttered. "We really need to talk." She turned around and moved quickly through the breakfast room. Sunlight glanced from the window and into her eyes, and she squinted, heart stuttering and then racing at the thought of fire against her skin.

Out in the hallway she paused, watching Uncle Alfonso and her aunt—his wife, married into the family almost twenty years ago—climbing the staircase. He turned around and then away again, as if she was not even there, and she was assaulted by an overwhelming memory: she and Carlotta playing on this very marble floor, dolls scattered around the base of the stairs, and Alfonso accidentally stepping on one as he came downstairs. Franca had cried, and her uncle had scooped her into his arms and hugged her, whispering that he was sorry. Carlotta had handed over one of her own dolls as replacement, and they had played on into the evening, performing an imaginary funeral for the dead doll. Such innocent love.

She watched her aunt and uncle disappear out of sight along the second floor corridor, then she went for the big front doors, thinking that Hellboy might have gone outside. Touching the handles, she paused.

I've eaten, he had said. *Can we talk?* He must have eaten with Adamo, but they had not been together for very long. If the conversation was that short, it must have been because Adamo was trying to send them away again. And though she had only known Hellboy for a day, she knew he would not take kindly to such advice.

Perhaps it had prompted him to move things on in his own way.

She turned and walked back to the staircase, glancing up before edging into the narrow space by its side. Ahead of her, a broken padlock hung on the metal door to the basement, and it had been pushed almost shut.

He's in there, she thought. She had to find him, and soon. She had something to tell him. And together, they had to go to Pompeii.

A nervous thrill sang through her as she pushed the door open. It had been a long time since she'd been in here, and the last time she'd been a little girl. Entering again as an adult, she wondered what she might find.

It was quite a hole. Hellboy was used to these underground places, and he liked to think he'd become familiar with the signs that were portents of trouble. He kept his eyes and ears open.

The basement smelled old, dry, and musty, not used to the flow of air. There was a light switch just inside the metal door, and when he flicked it, bare bulbs turned on in the first room. He sensed the emptiness of more rooms beyond, and hoped that the light circuit was all on one loop.

The first room was smallish, and given over mainly to storage. On the left was a metal shelving rack stacked with cardboard boxes. He could see clothes spilling from a couple, and another was home to a selection of unwanted cuddly toys and teddy bears. He found that a little sad. Plenty of kids upstairs, but he supposed they mostly wanted their own toys, not ones handed down from generations past.

The other wall housed banks of electrical distribution boards and fuse boxes, spaghetti heaps of wires leading here and there and tied haphazardly with plastic clips. None of it looked very safe, but the power in the house seemed to work well enough.

He moved on into the next room, ducking through the low doorway. He had to descend several steps through the thick basement wall, and he guessed he was down amongst the house's ancient foundations now, carved into the rock of the Amalfi hillsides many centuries ago. He paused impressed, when he saw the next room, and wondering whether this had always been a wine cellar.

The racks lined one long wall, floor to ceiling. They were half full, containing perhaps a thousand bottles or more. He was certainly no expert, but he'd wager that some of these bottles were worth quite a bit. A stack of empties piled along the facing wall was testament to the fact that these wines were here to be enjoyed, not to accumulate value, and he found that reassuring. Adamo and the other Elders might be weird and a bit up their own asses, but they liked a tipple. *Olive oil, fish, and red wine*, Liz would have said. *These people will live until they're two hundred.*

There was a closed door at the far end of the room. It was unlocked, and when Hellboy opened it he caught a faint whiff of dampness. He paused and sniffed again, but the scent was gone, swallowed in the aroma of dust and age that pervaded this next room. More storage, it looked like, and some of the furniture had been down here so long that it was mouldering into one unsightly mass. Perhaps some of this might have been valuable as antiques, were it cared for, but when it was brought down here it was probably at a time when it was commonplace. A dumping ground for three-legged chairs, a graveyard for cracked tables and broken beds, it was a sad place that spoke of the passage of time.

Another door at the end, this one locked, and Hellboy did not hesitate to give it a shove. Wood splintered, and the door fell open. Beyond was a short tunnel carved into rock, and at its end a small room, its ceiling rough stone. One bare bulb hung from a wire pinned to the ceiling. At the room's center was a table and another three-legged chair, leaning against the table so that it did not tumble. And on two walls hung rotten tapestries.

Hellboy went to the table, but he could already see that it was empty. Its surface was covered with a thick layer of dust, at its center a clear rectangle, and from there towards its edge, an obvious drag mark. He ran his finger across the clear area and examined it; dust, but only a little. Carlotta said she'd taken the book for a morning to get those copies and then returned it, but since then someone had spirited it away. Adamo? The Elders? He suspected one or the other, or maybe both.

Pity. But that wasn't the only reason he'd come down here.

Hellboy could feel the weight of the land around him, the millions of tons of rock and history exerting gravity on every molecule of his body. That weight both pulled and crushed, playing on his mind as well as his flesh, and he closed his eyes in an effort to sense what lay around him. When he looked again, he saw one of the tapestries deform before his eyes. It was a very slight effect, as though the air between him and the wall had suffered a rapid temperature change, and it made him dizzy for a couple of seconds. He couldn't focus on the tapestry—its distance from him was uncertain and unknown—and he had to blink and clear his vision before looking again.

"There we are," he said. His voice was surprisingly loud in the subterranean room.

Carlotta had said that perhaps a monk had once used this room, and she may have been right. But in truth, it could have been a bolt hole for anyone. And a bolt hole always needed more than one way in and out.

Hellboy lifted the tapestry he'd seen move and looked into the dark space beyond. A breath of air wafted out against him, the land sighing because he had found its secret, and he closed his eyes and breathed in deeply. He could smell nothing threatening through there, but little manmade either; no rotting furniture, no boxed possessions given to the darkness.

He dropped the tapestry again and rummaged around in his belt pockets. It took a few tries to find what he wanted: a little flashlight, the size of a pen but very powerful. Last time he used this, it had illuminated the face of a monster.

He hoped the batteries still worked.

Tapestry tucked aside, he shone the flashlight into the hole beyond. It was hacked through the rock, barely wide enough to fit him, and the thought of crawling through there made him shiver. The light revealed a slow bend in the tunnel, no end, and he tried not to entertain the thought that it would end in a blank wall. He knew that could not be the case; air wafted against his face, and he could feel the openness beyond. But the idea persisted, something to do with everyone's fear of being buried alive: he would crawl in, negotiate a couple of gentle bends, then be faced with trying to crawl backwards all the way out again. And if his belt caught on a rocky protrusion? If he heard something entering the narrow tunnel behind him, saw its fiery light filling the void, felt its furnace breath on his hooves . . . ?

"Idiot," he muttered. "Don't be such a wimp." He bit the flashlight between his teeth, made sure it was angled ahead, and eased his shoulders and head into the hole.

The going was slow, but once he started crawling, those fears began to evaporate. This wasn't like him. The things he'd seen, the things he'd fought off and defeated, the counts of almost-certain death he'd survived, and a hole in the ground worried him?

The tunnel curved to the left and dropped slightly, the slope gentle but noticeable. The stone ceiling brushed his head while his goatee touched the floor. He had to kick with his hooves to advance, and a panicky feeling started to descend again, the knowledge that if it *did* end suddenly, the chances of him backing up such a narrow, curved tunnel were minimal.

"Quit it!" he said. His voice was muffled, without echo, and he paused and stared ahead. The walls of the crawl hole disappeared, and the light spread in a diffuse haze. "At last." He shuffled forward, and when the floor disappeared from below him, and the walls from either side, he paused to take a look around. He looked down first of all, eager to ensure that if he fell he could climb up again. The floor of this buried chasm was barely two feet below the lip of the tunnel, so Hellboy eased himself out and broke his fall with outstretched hands. They encountered cool, dry rock, speckled here and there with the damp grittiness of something else.

Then he looked up and around, and a million eyes were watching.

He gasped, the light dropping from his mouth and bouncing from his knee. It struck the rock and spun, flicking its glare around the huge cavern and reflecting in the eyes that stared at him from ceiling and walls. There was a sense of constant, rippling movement in the cavern, and for a beat Hellboy thought that he had entered the belly of a beast, upsetting its rest and causing a quiver to lap through its gargantuan body. But then the light came to rest by his feet, and in the sphere of its influence, he saw the flutter of bats disturbed by his presence.

Hellboy drew a few deep breaths before bending to pick up the light, feeling ridiculous.

He took a good, slow look around. The cavern was huge, and there were thousands of bats. If there were bats that meant there had to be another way in and out, and that lessened his anxiety. But where did that anxiety come from in the first place?

He started walking, sinking ankle-deep in bat guano. The stench was terrible, a rich ammonia stink that stung his nostrils and burnt his throat and lungs. This couldn't be healthy.

The flashlight picked out several dark openings around the cave. Without exploring further, there was no way of telling where any of them went, but in the middle of the cavern, another breath of air wafted past Hellboy. He closed his eyes and breathed it in, trying to filter out the stink. Water, definitely. He waited for a while and another subtle breath cooled his skin, then another, coming in rhythmic gasps.

Something breathing, he thought, but it did not concern him too much. He knew the smell of the sea well enough. One of these tunnels must lead all the way down through the cliffs to the ocean.

If the fire wolf had entered La Casa Fredda this way, there would surely be signs of its entry. Hellboy could see no scorched, blackened bats; no trail of cauterized bat crap; and the carved tunnel he'd crawled through had not been coated with soot. The tapestry was old and fragile, so dried out by being hung over the crawlspace opening for many centuries that he thought it would probably ignite if he coughed on it. He'd come down here seeking secrets, but all he'd found were forgotten histories. Centuries ago, this had been an escape route from the old Esposito house, and it bore remembering. But right now, there were more important things he could be doing.

Like finding out what that kid had been shouting about Vesuvius.

Franca would be looking for him, no doubt, and he had to figure what to do now. He had to leave the house for a while, that was sure. No good could come of him going against Adamo's wishes. But that didn't mean they had to leave Amalfi.

Sighing, Hellboy faced the dark hole in the cave wall again. Tingling inside his head, too high to really hear, the bats' calls seemed to see him on his way.

He wiped the flashlight, popped it in his mouth, and started crawling.

"You scared the hell out of me!" Franca was cowering against the far wall as Hellboy pushed the tapestry aside, and he grinned at her as he climbed from the hole and stood. He stretched, hearing his joints protesting at the way they were being treated.

"Sorry," he said. "But if you go snooping around subterranean rooms, you've gotta expect to see some weird things."

"I guessed you'd come down here," she said. "The broken padlock's a dead giveaway."

"Yeah, well, I figure Adamo can afford a new one."

"So he told you to leave?"

"Yep. And to take you with me." He brushed himself down, not liking the feel of grit on his skin. "Said you weren't welcome."

"I've known that for years." She looked around, saw the dust trails on the table, and her eyes grew wide. "The book?"

"It's gone." Hellboy shrugged. "Guess the old man really didn't want me snooping."

Franca's shoulders sagged, and she looked around the little room her cousin had described.

"So," Hellboy said, "I figure we leave the house, go down into Amalfi—"

"Hellboy, we have somewhere else to go." Franca suddenly seemed motivated again, her eyes wide and scared, but excited as well.

"Where?"

"Can't you trust me?" she asked.

"Can't you tell me?"

She pressed her lips together and frowned. "Not straight away. Just in case I dreamed it. I have . . . nightmares. More frequent since Carlotta first contacted me, told me about all this. And if *this* was a nightmare as well, I'll feel stupid dragging you all the way there to—"

"All the way where?"

"Pompeii."

Hellboy nodded, and cogs clicked into place in his mind. "Vesuvius."

"There've been rumblings," Franca said, but she didn't seemed as surprised at his perception as he'd have hoped. "Smoke coming from the crater. But it's not that."

"So what's in Pompeii?"

"If I'm right—if it wasn't a dream—there's something there you need to see."

Hellboy brushed more dirt and dust from his skin and coat, then slipped the flashlight back into a belt pocket. "Why not?" he said. "I'm all done here."

"So what's down there?" she asked.

"A cave. Bats. Bat crap." He shrugged, and as Franca turned and he followed her back through the basement rooms, he couldn't shake the feeling that he'd missed something vital.

Chapter 7

Amalfi/Pompeii

"He sent someone to follow us," Franca said. "Five cars back."

"What are you, some kind of secret agent?"

"No. Just angry. Something killed my cousin. I don't care that she stepped from the window herself."

Hellboy took a final drag on his cigarette and flicked it from the window. He'd quit the habit, but this thing was vexing him, and Franca's pack had been open on the dashboard. Half an hour and three cigarettes later the sea was behind them, and they were heading across the root of the peninsula towards Pompeii.

"Besides, they're the same men who met us at the airport. And they're making themselves very visible."

Hellboy leaned forward slightly and looked in the wing mirror. The car—it was big and black, of course—weaved across the road, crossing the central line when there was nothing coming the other way. They were keeping back, but Franca was right: they weren't keeping their presence a secret.

He needed to ask Franca what was in Pompeii that she suddenly found so important, but he also respected her wishes. If she had doubts, it was best she lay them to rest herself before revealing them to him. She was very obviously scared. There was grief mixed in with that, too, and Hellboy knew only too well that together they made a poor combination. So he scratched absently at the burns already healing on his stomach and chest, and sat back to watch the scenery drift by.

There were quite a few police cars and army trucks on the road today, and Franca had said it was part of the big evacuation plan. Vesuvius was grumbling, and though the experts said there was no definitive indication that there would be an eruption, the initial stages of the plan were being readied. He could barely imagine the chaos that would ensue were the volcano to blow. Though there was a plan in place to get everyone to safety, he knew people: some would not want to leave. The old ones, the determined, those who had lived in their homes their whole lives, they'd want to stay behind and challenge the might of Vesuvius.

As for the Espositos, Hellboy didn't know. They were outside the evacuation circle and well away from the lava zone, but a big eruption would fill the air with poisonous gases, ash, and fireballs, maybe even as far as Amalfi.

Volcanoes and the fire wolf. Any connection? The link had seemed obvious to begin with, but for now he put it to one side. *For later attention*, he marked it in his mind. He'd wait to see what came once they reached Amalfi.

Passing Castellammare di Stabia, their followers seemed to back off. They took an exit from the main road, and Franca seemed to settle in her seat, driving more confidently.

"More than halfway to Naples," she said. "They must assume we're making for the airport. They'll park somewhere, have a big meal, then get back to Amalfi for evening. Might even tell Adamo that they saw us onto a 'plane.'"

"Clumsy of them," Hellboy said, doubtful.

"Thugs for hire," Franca said. "They're not Espositos. Just some local characters he uses sometimes."

"So why doesn't Adamo use people from the family as his heavies?"

"We're not like that, Hellboy," Franca said, and it was the first time he'd heard her speak positively of her family in general. It surprised him, but also shamed him a little. He was painting people with a brush of his own choice, where in reality there were different shades and textures to everyone.

"I don't mean to jump to conclusions," he said. "But I saw the reaction you got back at the house."

"Not from everyone. My father might be dead, and my mother . . . distant. But I do still have family. Going back there was . . . well, you called it brave. But it wasn't brave. It was painful."

"And you knew it would be. For me, that's the definition of bravery."

"Being hurt?" she asked bitterly

"No. Facing pain for someone else."

Franca gave a derisive snort, but then lit a cigarette and drove in silence for a couple of miles. Finally, as she turned off the main road and followed signs headed for Pompeii, she asked, "Do you think you can help us?"

"I don't know," he said, and the honesty hurt him. *So we're both brave today*, he thought. *Brave little soldiers*. The heat of that fire wolf's bite haunted him, and he knew for sure that he would feel such a bite again. "Show me what's in Pompeii. Maybe then I'll have a better idea."

An hour later Franca stopped the car in a big, dusty parking lot to the west of Pompeii. Usually, she told him, this place would still be buzzing with tourists at this time of day, but the reason why the whole area was deserted was patently obvious.

In the distance, the shattered peak of Vesuvius breathed fumes at the evening sky. The setting sun caught the rising column of smoke and cast it blood-red. And here and there, in the clouds forming high above, lightning cut stark blue lines in the deepening dusk.

Beautiful, terrible, Vesuvius's grumbles reached Hellboy through his cloven hooves.

With every mile they had drawn closer to Pompeii, so Franca's fear had grown.

She slammed the car door behind her and heard Hellboy do the same, but she only had eyes for Vesuvius, that constant scar on the world that stood sentry above Pompeii and silhouetted a reminder of what it had done against every dusk, every dawn. Its fury two thousand years before had blasted a cubic mile of mountain into the atmosphere, pulverizing it before dropping it again in showers of rock, dust, and ash. It had destroyed itself to bring destruction to everyone and everything around it. And now, it was breathing again.

She had not been to Pompeii since she had attended an archaeological dig here over a year ago. That first time had unsettled her, but perhaps the fear was now in her blood. She'd been here for its history, not its present, and she had seen and felt how these thousands of people had died: suffocating, burning, crushing, breathing in poisonous gases. Mothers had held their children as they gasped their last, fathers had hugged their wives, and Vesuvius had rocked the ground with its monstrous laughter. Most people blamed the citizens of Pompeii for not heeding the warnings, but Franca knew them as living, breathing people, not those horrific plaster casts of human suffering that tourists so delighted in photographing.

She blamed the volcano.

"Heard a lot about this place," Hellboy said. "Always wanted to visit."

"It's a graveyard," Franca said, and she felt Hellboy taking in a cautious breath behind her. "Come on. What I need to show you is this way."

Her skin crawled as she walked, goose bumps rising along her arms and down her sides, reacting to a coolness that was not there. She was not used to this place being swamped with such silence. When she had been here before there had always been tourists; the scraping of their tired feet, their mumbled appreciation of times gone by, their curious comments as they stood outside the dig and peered through empty windows or over worn walls. Now her footsteps echoed from stonework, and the only other sound was the impact of Hellboy's strange feet.

He sounded . . . more at home. She could not exactly pin down the feeling, but there was something about the way he walked, and his silence sounded contented. *He comes from places like this*, Franca thought, surprised at the idea, but flowing with it. *Old places, graveyards, where the dead whisper and the living never feel at home until it's their time to depart as well. He's welcome here, and he welcomes it.* She glanced back at Hellboy, and he smiled softly.

"Interesting place," he said quietly.

"It's trapped in time," she said. "I'll tell you about it." And as she started to talk, her nervousness bowed down beneath the words. Perhaps it was just the sound of her voice, or the act of concentrating that drove away the feeling of dread. Or maybe it was knowing Pompeii that made it easier to be here.

"The streets are all like this," she began. "Sunken in the middle for wagons and cattle, raised on the edges for pedestrians. If you look closely in places, you can even see where the wagon wheels have worn ruts in the rock." She paused at a junction of two roads, looked around the place herself, then smiled. Yes, she knew this Pompeii well. Sharing it with Hellboy would distract her attention from the volcano, its breath, its distant mutterings . . .

"Over here," she said, jogging along the narrow street to her left. Some of the buildings along here still retained their roofs, and there were a few interesting places to show him on their way to where she was headed. "Look." She pointed at the bottom of a wall.

"Hmm," Hellboy said. "Pipes."

"Two thousand year old lead plumbing, actually."

"You're kidding me."

"Not at all. Water can still flow through it, too. Though you'd end up with lead poisoning, of course."

"Well," he said.

"Want to se the brothel?"

"Is it open?" he asked, smiling.

"This way," Franca said. She led them along the street, then left through the ruin of an old family home. She pointed out some frescoes on the wall, their colors still vivid and extravagant, and it reminded her of where they were going. She tried to shut that out. *Just for a few minutes*, she thought. *That's all I ask, a few minutes of normality.*

She had the sudden, painful certainty that once they reached the half-buried building with the mosaic, normality would be a thing of the past.

After passing several buildings along the next street she paused outside an innocuous structure, the doorway open to the elements. Hellboy stood before her and stared at the darkened doorway. He seemed distracted.

"What is it?" Franca asked.

"Old place," he said. "It has echoes."

"I know," she said. He glanced sharply at her, and she walked inside, not sure that she could explain even if he asked.

It's like I've been here before, she thought. *Before that time I was at the dig. Long ago*. She wondered if Hellboy felt the same.

She crowded into the small reception area with him and looked around.

"Priapus," she said, pointing to the waist-high column in the corner.

"Impressive." He pointed up at the colored pictures above each alcove, the detail still obvious, the colors darkening in the dusk but still patently fresh. "What's this, Roman porn?"

"It's a menu," Franca said. "Lots of people who visited here were sailors, so the prostitutes wouldn't be able to speak their language. They'd peruse the menu and choose. Each alcove, a different speciality."

"Wow," Hellboy said. "Imagine that." He looked around at the images above each alcove, pausing once or twice.

"This was a whole city dug out of the ashes," Franca said. "It's really quite remarkable, and unprecedented. Pompeii was forgotten for almost two thousand years, and it's been frozen in time."

"And the people who died, their bodies were mummified by the ash, right?"

"That's what most people think. Actually, their flesh and organs rotted away, leaving hollows in the hardened ash. When a hollow is discovered, plaster is poured in. When it sets, the ash is carefully moved away, and voila! The sculpture of a real person's agonized death. Bones, and all."

"Hmm," Hellboy said. He took one more look at the menus for sex and pleasure, glanced into an alcove, then stepped outside. Franca followed, not sure whether the big man had been embarrassed or uninterested. For her, his enigma deepened.

He was standing in the street outside, turning his head left and right with his eyes closed. The sun was settling into the western horizon, and its dying glare gave his skin a scarlet hue. He seemed not to notice her presence for a while, as if he were seeing or listening to something else entirely, and Franca felt far removed from this strange man's world.

"Hellboy," she said, "what is it?"

"All old places have old ghosts," he said. "Here, I can hear one calling to me."

Franca felt a chill pass down through her body. Her back and neck prickled, her stomach grew cool, and she had never heard anyone say anything quite so terrifying.

"Come on," he said quietly. "This way."

"You're supposed to be following me," Franca said.

"I'd hazard a guess we're both aiming for the same place." Hellboy walked along the street, coat flapping about him as a gentle evening breeze came in from the direction of the sea.

Franca hurried to catch up. She suddenly had a fear of being left behind, alone, here in Pompeii as the sun went down and the volcano announced its presence. There appeared to be no one else here, but the ancient city might still be inhabited, with people who chose to hide themselves away, or ghosts that waited for the silence before showing themselves. Franca wanted to meet neither.

Hellboy stepped over the root of a tumbled wall and she followed. They were in the old bakery, with grain grinders and kilns, and she wanted to tell him all about it. But she could see that his mind was now elsewhere. He walked steadily, but without any sign of being stopped. He reminded her of a dog following a scent, but this dog had its head tilted to one side, listening to something she could not hear.

She tried. She opened herself up to this place, but she was too scared. Pompeii was bad enough, but at her back now rose the shadow of the mountain, and in its base she sensed doom gathering in molten, gaseous fury.

"Close," Hellboy said after a few minutes. "Just along here."

"Yes," Franca said, because they were on the right street, and he was pointing towards the building where she had dug. He seemed to realize what he had done, because he stepped back slightly and waved her forward.

"You brought me here," he said. "So show me what we came to see."

"Then what?"

"Then I'll have a better idea of what to ask this ghost."

Something whispered then, like a breeze blowing through the broken doors and walls of the dead city, but Franca knew she heard its voice only in her head.

She let out a strangled cry and turned to run.

"Hey," Hellboy said, sweeping Franca against his chest. She was panting, breathing hard, and he didn't want her to run out on him now. There was more here than ruins, and this was not a place to be fleeing blind with panic on your heels. "Take it easy, Franca. It's just an old dead thing."

"I heard . . . I heard . . ." She sobbed against his chest, drawing the comfort he offered, but still terrified.

He knew this was her first time, and that the next few minutes would change the way she viewed the world forever. She had already seen the fire wolf—an impossible thing—and he'd been impressed with her resilience after it had wounded her. But soon she would hear a voice.

"This will help us," he said.

"It can't help Carlotta."

"No, but you wanted answers." He stroked her hair, listening, ready to hear what the old thing had to say. But first he had to find it.

"I don't know if I can do this," Franca said.

"Show me what you came to show me. It's important."

See, the thing whispered in his mind, *heed*.

"It's in there," the girl said. "Through the door, then right, on the wall. An old mosaic, and I think . . . I'm sure . . ."

See! the phantom hissed. *Heed!*

"You can wait!" Hellboy said, and Franca jumped in his arms. "Hey, not you." She looked up at him as if he were mad, and who was he to contradict? "Lead the way."

Franca grabbed his left hand and held on tight. That meant he couldn't reach for his gun, but he felt no danger here. He'd met things like this before, old dead relics who still had something to say. Mostly they hated being woken and questioned, but this one seemed to have been awake already. Waiting to speak.

In his book, that didn't bode well.

Franca was shaking, and she was cold, and when she stepped through into the ruined building's interior and turned to look at the wall, her shock was palpable.

"I was right," she said.

Hellboy stood beside her and followed her gaze. Really, he should not have been surprised. But the jolt that the image drove through him was real enough.

Its implication, terrible.

He'd seen mosaics like this before, but there was a simplicity to this one that gave it resonance. It showed a version of Vesuvius that no one alive had ever seen: a mountain with a true volcanic peak, not yet destroyed by the tremendous cataclysm that would bury Pompeii.

Out of that peak's smoky mouth rose a shape that Hellboy knew. The fire wolf, imagined here in random shapes of red and orange, its fur created from varying shards of yellow. Its eyes were signified by plain white pebbles, and its mouth was a hole in the wall.

"I knew it," Franca said. "That's what we saw, isn't it?"

"Yeah, that's it."

"What does it mean?"

He sighed and scanned the wall for more, but there was nothing else. From the frieze's rough edges, he guessed this had been a rush job.

"I guess it means we're in trouble."

"So now you're going to—"

"Somewhere close by," he said. He looked around the half-excavated room, and that voice began niggling inside his skull once again.

Here, here, *turn and see, dig down, can't you* see *me,* can't *you?*

"Damn it, lady, you're already getting on my nerves." Hellboy knelt in the corner of the room, tapped the ancient ash grown hard as rock, and pounded down with his big right fist. He heard Franca gasp at the impact, and he glanced back once to give her a reassuring smile. She was standing there, looking at him, back at the mosaic, at him again. He wasn't sure which she found most terrifying.

I don't have time to talk her through this, he thought. *Maybe later, when I know what this old buried thing knows, but not now.* He scraped and bashed, crushing rock, breaking the solidified ash through fault lines laid two millennia before. *She'll just have to watch and learn.*

He pulled out several chunks of rock, going deeper and scooping out handfuls of dust and sand. All the while that old, reedy voice rustled in his mind, but he tried to cast it aside. Franca seemed not to hear, or, if she did, then she was handling it very well. She'd sensed that first breezy gasp of the dead thing, and then no more. Perhaps hearing it now had something to do with who and what he was.

Hellboy, the voice said. Time had bled it of character; age diminished it. It was impersonal writing in his mind. With these old, mad things it was what they said, not the way they spoke.

"How d'you know my name?" he said.

It's in the air, in the rock, it said. *This place has been expecting you.*

"Yeah, right." He dug deeper, and after another couple of minutes his hand brushed against something twiglike at the bottom of the hole.

Ah, you've found me. It's a long time since I've been touched like that.

"Shut up and brace yourself," Hellboy muttered. He pulled more stone from the ground, then clasped the thing he'd found and tugged. It moved strangely, lifting from the hole in jerky jumps, its stick arms and legs catching on rocks, hair tangled in a mess of rock and ash. For a beat Hellboy thought he could actually smell the disaster; the heat of fire, and the stench of gas like rotting eggs. He dropped it to the ground.

"Oh, God!" Franca said. She stepped back against the wall, unconsciously blocking the fire wolf frieze from view, and stared down at what Hellboy had found. "It's still there," she said. "Mummified. But how?"

"Some people aren't so keen to die," he said, "and some hang around if they have something to say."

So much to say, the thing said. *But so much of it I've forgotten. It took you a long time, Hellboy!*

"I asked you how you know my name," he growled.

You know the likes of me, it said. *You question me, but do not step away. Your heart beats true, your mind is unclouded, and I'm no surprise to you. But the likes of me are never quite alone, down there, in the shadows, in the place where the light fades away and the dark starts to bear weight.*

"Save me," Hellboy said, yawning.

And of those myriad spirits that bless me with company, there are some that whisper your name.

"Right. I'm guessing they're not people I've made a good impression on," he said.

The voice laughed, a terrible, high keening sound that seemed to pierce his ears. Franca winced and drew away, her eyes going wide.

He went to Franca then, holding her wrists and pulling her hands from her ears. "I think maybe you need to hear this," he said. "If you're ready, that is."

"Ready?" She stared at the mess of bones, dried flesh and skin that he'd pulled up out of Pompeii's history, disbelief evident in her eyes, belief obvious in her voice. "If it's about my family, being ready doesn't count. I have a duty."

"Brave," Hellboy said.

"I didn't say I wanted it to hurt." She frowned. "How can I listen? You're talking at it like you hear voices, but all I hear is . . ."

"Whispers in the breeze?" he asked.

"Yes. Whispers." She blinked, and Hellboy saw that she sensed true meaning behind those sounds.

"It's the language of the subconscious," he said. "Not real words, just understanding and perception. You'll just need a little help to hear it." He started rooting through the pouches on his belt. There was stuff in here he hadn't seen for years, and things he'd forgotten about; charms and talismans, potions and herbs. And here and there, a weapon.

"I know it's here somewhere," he muttered.

"What are you looking for?"

"Something . . . Ah, this might be it." He pulled out a twisted lock of hair, holding it between two fingers. "Yeah. Huh. An old woman in Ireland gave me this, long time ago. Her husband had died, and every night he came to the room, demanding his conjugal rights. I ran him off. Then I asked if he'd left anything personal to him. Turns out she snipped this off before his funeral." He handed it to Franca.

"I don't want it."

"It'll help you hear the dead."

She shuddered, folding her arms tight across her chest. "Yet more reason not to have it."

He held it, turning his fingers slightly so that the dusky sunlight brought out the hair's auburn tinge. He hadn't seen the lock for more than twenty years. Weird. He wondered what else he'd find, should he go rooting around in those pouches. But sometimes it was best not knowing.

"You know, you should be impressed by my memory," he said. "It's not usually that good. And if this old thing tells me something today, I might forget it by tomorrow. That's why I think you should be able to listen."

Franca reached out.

"Careful, though," Hellboy said. "If you hear other voices, don't pay them any attention. And tell me."

"Oh God," Franca said, and she fisted her hand around the hair.

She closed her eyes, and it was like being in a cave with a hundred people bearing secrets they were desperate to share. Some shouted, but their voices were very far away. Most whispered, and she heard them well.

One of them sounded afraid.

You're the one I have to tell, that scared voice said, *because there's something about you, a heat, or perhaps a coldness so cold it feels like heat, and I know you're the right one, you're the one who can help, can stop it before—*

"It?" Hellboy said out loud, and Franca knew she was hearing the correct voice.

I'm listening to a ghost, she thought, staring in amazement at the thing Hellboy had hauled up out of the ground. Its face was hidden beneath the tangled branches of its bent arms and splayed fingers, looking down at the ground beneath it as if eager to feel its rocky embrace again. She could see its skull in places where the scalp had withered and split, the skin on its back was sunk between ribs and across the ridges of its spine, and its legs were pulled up in a fetal position. There was nothing about it that was alive. Yet she heard its voice, and when she closed her eyes she felt a third presence there in that ruin with Hellboy and herself.

The fire demon, the voice said. *I came here to send it down, but I failed. Too strong, it was! Too weak, was I!*

Hellboy knelt beside the dried corpse and rested his hand on the back of its head. It was almost gentle.

"I can put you to rest," he said. "But first, I need to know—"

Need to know, Hellboy? You trust me to tell you, even though—

"You just *said* I was the one you wanted to speak to!"

A long time down here, though, ages buried, waiting, and the scheming *a woman like me can do, the* deceptions *I can plan.*

"Did you make the mosaic on the wall?" Franca asked. The ruin fell silent. Hellboy looked up at her, surprised, and the scratchy voice in her mind seemed to hold its breath. Her heart fluttered like a trapped butterfly in her chest, taking her breath away.

Ahh, the voice said.

"Did you?" Franca asked again, emboldened by the silence.

I did. A warning to those who would come after the volcano. I expected weeks, maybe months. Not centuries.

"But we're here now," Franca said, and when Hellboy nodded at her, it fortified her against the weirdness of the situation.

So long, the voice whispered, and it chilled Franca's insides. *So long, and still I remember. I was summoned here by those who knew, who had seen the demon escape the mouth of Vesuvius. I was to put it down and send it back. But it was far stronger, and far stranger than I could have imagined. How do you fight fire? How to you hold down something you cannot touch? The monster swept over and through me, fleeing Pompeii and leaving the city to its doom. Vesuvius screamed, many died, and I knew then the best I could do was to warn.*

"That was so long ago," Franca said, trying to ally what the ghostly voice said with what she knew. "And yet we saw the fire wolf yesterday."

Fire wolf? The spirit recoiled in terror then, a piercing, painful shimmer of utter fear that sent a pulse through the ruin, distorting the evening air like a heat haze and bringing Franca out in such intense goosebumps that she winced at the pain across her skin. *Fire wolf*, it muttered. *An apt name.*

"What do you know of it?" Hellboy asked.

It rose from the volcano and fled across the land. The volcano was angered. After that, I know nothing, buried as I was.

"Perhaps it went back," Hellboy said. "Just comes out now and then."

It will never return of its own accord, the spirit said. *In my brief moments conversing with the demon—the fire wolf—the one thing I learned was its utter terror of where it had been, and its endless determination to escape. The only direction I strove to push it was towards Vesuvius, and that was the only way it would not go.*

"Then where has it been all this time?" Franca asked. "And why did it come for Carlotta?"

Peace, the spirit said, *rest, oblivion, I crave these things.*

"You've waited so long to tell someone this, a couple more minutes won't hurt," Hellboy said.

Foul beast! Cruel teaser, harsh master, cold demon!

"Hey, lady, that's the second time I've been called—"

"Why was the volcano so angry at its escape?" Franca asked.

Because this is more than a volcano, fool. It's a resting place of something . . . beyond words. Now honor me! Give me darkness, give me rest! Take me from this world of pain and filth.

"Better stand back," Hellboy said, picking up the dried corpse.

"But there's so much more to ask!" Franca said, grasping the lock of hair in her hand. It was strange, hearing the voice inside her head much like her own thoughts, while hers and Hellboy's voices actually stirred the dust of this place. The spirit was little more than an echo of an echo, yet she was still so strong.

Ask away, girl, the voice said, suddenly quiet and calm once again.

"Oh no you don't." Hellboy dropped the corpse back into the hole he'd pulled it from, then held out his open right hand to Franca.

"What would happen if the fire wolf—"

"No!" Hellboy said. "Hand it back, Franca."

She's only asking, Hellboy, the voice whispered, soothing and soft. *Only giving me her questions, lending me her words.*

Franca swayed with a sudden bout of nausea, feeling her stomach clench and her throat constrict.

"Franca!"

She stepped forward and held out her hand, but she could not release the hair. Her fist remained tight.

Such a sweet girl, such a young girl, so full of heat and blood and . . . lust for you, Hellboy. Lust, for you.

Franca blinked and tried letting go. She felt Hellboy's big fingers prying her own apart, delving into her fist for the lock.

Give me a moment of your time, sweet young girl, the voice said, *just a moment to sing you a song of the ages, a poem of the time I've spent waiting—*

And then Franca heard no more. The voice shed itself to the breeze, echoing between ruins as it had for these past two millennia, haunting the night but touching no one. She leaned against a wall, feeling the mosaic image of the fire wolf scrape against her shoulder as she slid down.

Hellboy dropped the hair back into a belt pouch, then bent over the hole. He looked as if he was still listening.

I can help, the old ghost whispered. *I know things you don't. Take me with you.*

"Don't you *want* to be at rest?" Hellboy muttered.

Waiting for so long, a little while longer won't hurt. Not if it means finishing what I began so long ago. And you need me, Hellboy . . . do you know how to stop the fire wolf? How it hides? Its link with Vesuvius?

"You're playing with me."

The ghost remained silent, but there was restrained laughter in his mind.

And damn it, the old thing was right. He knew nothing about the fire wolf, and she had been down there for two thousand years with nothing to do but think about how it had defeated her.

"Fine," he said. "But just so we're clear, you'll be with me, and me alone. You start screwing around and you go back in the dirt."

He looked down into the hole, contemplating the awkwardness of lugging around her dusty, withered remains. After a second, he reached down and closed his fist around her right index finger.

"This'll do," he said, then snapped the bone. As it cracked he heard a cackle, and bringing the bone back up out of the dark, he knew he had her. The finger would let the spirit stay with him, but she'd be tethered to her grave no matter how far from it he traveled.

"Be good," he said, but he knew ghosts. They were tricky, and he'd have to be very careful indeed. So he wound the finger bone in a leather thong and dropped it around his neck, tying the knot in a very particular way—a way he had learned from a dying witch doctor in Africa, who had tied his own spilled guts to take with him the demons he had expelled from his three wives—and thereby binding her spirit to silence. He knew it would piss off the ghost, but without that . . . well, she'd been waiting for a long time. She'd have a lot to say. And when he needed to speak to her, the knot would be undone.

Lust for you, Hellboy, the lost spirit had said. Franca closed her eyes, seeking to question its truth. She felt no lust for this big, strange American. Curiosity, perhaps. A measure of fear, certainly, and maybe even a slowly growing affection. But lust?

She looked again, and Hellboy stood from his task, tying something onto a leather thong around his neck.

"What's that?" she asked.

The breeze died down, fading away to silence with a whisper of dust across the ancient ground. It was the dust of a dead city, comprised of bones and ideas of those long-gone. The sense of peace was exquisite.

"Nothing," Hellboy said, still facing away from her.

"What was she trying to do?" Franca asked. "It felt . . . dangerous."

He looked at her then, and for a while she thought he would not answer. The silence between them felt heavy. Finally Hellboy sighed, brushing down his coat and resealing the pouches on his belt.

"Don't worry about it," he said. "She was nuts."

That was no answer to her question, but right then Franca wanted to know no more. What she craved more than anything was to leave the ruin of that dead city. Beyond that she could not see.

The unreality of what was happening seemed remote right now, and she was accepting much that she would have questioned just a day ago. There was something in the human mind that defended against such instances, she believed, allowing the person to function when in reality they should be a quivering, crying mess. It was the same with grief. When her father had died when she was fifteen, she'd been consumed with a fear that she would never be able to move on past his death. But something inside had stepped up to guide her through those terrible days and weeks. At first she'd put it down to instinct: thousands of years ago, humans would have had to deal with such grief while still being alert for dangers, hunting food, and ensuring that their families were safe. But she had come to believe that it was something even deeper than instinct, a spiritual function in the human soul that took death, no matter how close its victim, for what it was: the most natural consequence of life.

She felt the same protective filter around her now. She had just been talking with a ghost, and she could accept that, and deal with its resultant information.

"Hey, you okay?" Hellboy asked.

"Yeah." Franca nodded, hugging herself and looking around the ruin. She saw the mosaic of the fire wolf and looked quickly away, hoping that would be the last time she would ever have to set eyes upon it.

"We really need to get back to Amalfi," he said. His voice sounded uncertain, as though weighed by something heavy he could not express.

"Amalfi," she said. "You know we won't be welcome."

"Were we ever?" Still that hesitancy.

"You think Adamo knows something about the fire wolf."

"Yeah," he sighed, and relief lightened his voice. "I think he knows a lot about it, and the disappearances."

"If what that woman said is true, and Vesuvius erupted because it was angry . . . why hasn't it done so again?"

"Because its anger is being sated."

Realization hit quickly. "Human sacrifice," Franca gasped, barely believing such words could pass her lips. *Like an old Hollywood movie.*

But here in Pompeii, with the dust of ages stirred in the air around her, such a phrase did not sound so ridiculous.

"That book from the basement is like a . . ." Hellboy shrugged.

"An order book."

"Yeah. Or a score sheet."

"Can we go?" Franca said. True darkness was falling now, and shadows were stretching out from where they hid beneath walls and under the parts of the old city yet to be excavated. The thought of what might be down there, feeding these shadows . . .

"It's okay here now," Hellboy said, gesturing her to him. And hand in hand with someone she had twice heard called demon, she guided them both out of Pompeii and back towards her car.

She carried with her an increasing fear of Hellboy and his world, and a burgeoning fascination. And, perhaps . . . perhaps the old ghost had been right.

CHAPTER 8

Pompeii

Leaving Pompeii, their path was illuminated by lightning. Hellboy turned back in the passenger seat and looked through the rear window at Vesuvius. Just before arriving at the car, they'd felt the ground vibrating beneath their feet, dust and grit had danced, and then a booming explosion had rolled down the mountain slopes towards them. Now, the mountain had a snaking head of lightning and staggered splits in the sky above the smoking crater, ripping through the clear evening air and the billowing mass of steam and smoke alike. It lit the expanding and rising cloud from the inside, giving it shape and texture and the appearance of great, ponderous movement. It looked like a monstrous tentacle slowly birthing from beneath the ground, and Hellboy could not help but feel chilled by the notion. He hated tentacles.

"That's one pissed-off volcano," he said.

Franca drove. Her hands were tight on the wheel, knuckles a pearly white. She stared grim faced through the windscreen, concentrating on where they were going, not where they'd been. She was terrified.

"Hey, don't worry," he said. "It's just bluff and bluster right now. All bark, no bite."

"First time I came to Pompeii, over a year ago, I was scared," she said, still not taking her eyes off the road. She was driving faster than she should, but she seemed a more than competent driver. "It was like walking into a place where I'd been before but having no memory of it. Does that make sense? Things seemed . . . familiar, but it was my first time there. Really disturbing."

"Fate has a way of messing with us," Hellboy said.

"This time, it was worse. I can't wait to leave. And the volcano . . ." She looked in the rear view mirror and shivered. "That just scares the crap out of me."

"Where'd you learn English?"

"School. And TV. I like American cop shows."

Hellboy sat back in his seat and watched her drive. Being so intent on the road, she did not seem to notice him sizing her up. He knew she was strong, and intelligent, but now he noticed for the first time just how attractive she was. He'd seen it before, but not really acknowledged it.

Can't do this, he thought. *Can't get mixed up with her, especially as she's one of Adamo's. An Esposito*. He felt uncomfortable at that. He'd only known Franca for a couple of days, and already he felt a level of trust and respect growing between them. But he had to be sensible.

He had to be *cautious*.

"I remember the voice of my father when he was angry," she said. "And Vesuvius sounds worse."

"Let's just keep driving, then. We'll be away from it soon."

"Really?" Franca asked, and she looked at him for the first time since leaving Pompeii. Doubting or desperate, her question went unanswered.

When they hit the main road, traffic was much heavier than was normal this time of evening. With the sky darkening, the roads were alight with rows of traffic, flowing like the rivers of lava they were keen to escape. Franca turned on the car radio and listened to the news, translating for Hellboy. While a major eruption was still not expected—the gas and steam were the results of minor ventings, so the experts said—a limited evacuation of those areas susceptible to pyroclastic flow had been put into action. The greater evacuation, if it was ordered, would take up to seven days, with almost a million people being transported to other parts of the country. There was a sense of excitement in the announcer's voice. This was still an adventure, not a disaster.

While Franca drove, Hellboy thought. The fire wolf obviously had Adamo Esposito in its thrall. He'd dealt with parasitic scumbags like Adamo before, keen to serve because they thought doing so would gain them some unseen, unknowable benefits—immortal life, endless power, other stuff. Occasionally they were coerced, or even threatened into working for some stronger master such as the fire wolf, but Adamo did not seem to be the frightened type. The more he thought about it now, the more Hellboy recognized a smug complicity in the memory of Adamo's eyes, and a confident swagger to his pronouncements. Here was an old man, apparently preparing a member of his own close family for sacrifice to something horrible, and he could still wear a smile.

That pissed off Hellboy. He closed his eyes, and imagined smacking that smile right off the old bastard's wrinkled face.

Take a deep breath, a voice said, and Professor Bruttenholm spoke to him from the past. *Leaping to conclusions is easy, but holding back when you get angry is more difficult.* He had tried teaching Hellboy to be more analytical, encouraging study and research in place of action. But it was moving, searching, fighting that made Hellboy feel alive. There were plenty of others back at B.P.R.D. headquarters who were paid to pore through books and come up with their theories. He was out in the field. And sometimes the field got hot.

That worked best for him. He never liked taking too much time to sit and ponder things.

When he had a chance, he'd unbind the spirit and confer, but right now he was sure he knew what had to be done. The fire wolf had been out for two millennia, and every now and then it made a sacrifice to Vesuvius to keep it happy. Hellboy had no idea how that worked, and he glanced again in the wing mirror, going cold at the sight of that billowing, almost living cloud. Lightning still thrashed above the volcano. It did not look like a nice place to be.

But that was where he had to go. Confront Adamo, find out where the fire wolf laid low, then take it to the volcano and throw it back in.

Piece of cake.

"Hellboy?" Franca's voice stirred him from a doze, and it took Hellboy a few moments to come around, dregs of fiery dreams melting away as he opened his eyes. When he'd nodded off they'd been nose-to-tail in a traffic jam, the oppressive heat aggravated by exhaust fumes, but now they drifted quickly along an unlit road. There were a couple of lights in the distance—lit windows on a hillside, he thought—but there seemed to be no other cars around.

And then he saw the solid bridge ahead, and the soft glow emanating from beneath.

He snapped awake quickly, sitting up in his seat and reaching for his gun.

"You know this road?"

"Yes."

"And that?"

Franca stopped the car a hundred yards short of the bridge. "Never seen it before."

"No new buildings down in the ravine? No mad modern artist's come along and lit the bridge up?"

Franca shrugged, and he just caught it in the darkness.

"Well, maybe—"

The glow beneath the bridge moved. It expanded and brightened, and then it started to flicker as it turned from an even light to a textured, billowing fire. It was like seeing the wound in the land forded by the bridge filling with lava. And then it flowed over the parapet and onto the bridge, and the fire wolf sped along the road towards them.

How it knew which route they had taken, where they were, *who* they were . . . these were all questions that sprung up in Hellboy's mind and cast themselves aside for later. The priority right now was to survive.

Though silenced, he felt a wave of fear emanating from the demon-hunter's spirit.

"Jesus Christ!" Franca whined.

"What's below the bridge?"

"A river."

He clasped her arm, hard, because he knew she needed nudging from her shock. They had maybe three seconds. They needed action. "Franca, *drive*!"

In the darkness, the fire wolf seemed much larger than before. It loped along the road, its long legs stretching in fluid motion, and it carried with it a wide field of illumination. Bushes and trees on the scrubby hillside beside the road danced with their own shadows. As the thing closed on their vehicle and opened its mouth, its maw was darker than the night.

Franca was moving again by the time the thing hit them.

The fire wolf flowed right over the car. Metal sang and pinged as it expanded rapidly, and the windscreen glass cracked under immense heat. Hellboy squinted against the bright firelight, then fired his gun once through the roof when he thought the thing was on top. It had no discernable effect.

The vehicle bounced once from the roadside barrier, then it was on the bridge.

"Stop here!" Hellboy said, turning in his seat. The fiery demon was squatting in the road behind them. As it spun around, black slicks of melted tarmac flicked from its fingers.

"Shouldn't we drive?" Franca asked.

Hellboy strained against the window and looked over the bridge parapet. The narrow valley was not deep, and he could see the shimmer of a river flowing along its base.

"We're near water here," he said.

"Oh God, you don't mean we have to—"

"I get burnt, I'll get over it," he said, glancing quickly down at Franca's clothing, up at her hair.

"Here it comes!" she shouted.

The fire wolf struck the rear of the car. This time it was a heavier impact, driving them squealing along the road for several yards. It drove forward, gnashing at the broken glass and shaking its head, a thousand diamond-shaped glass shards ricocheting around the car's interior.

"Damn it!" Hellboy roared. He looked the thing in the face . . . and realized what it was trying to do. "Franca, out!"

"But—"

"*Out!*" He reached past her and pulled the catch on her door, snapping it off in his hand as the door fell open. Then he shoved her hard, falling across her on the road in case the gas tank went up before they could get away.

The fire wolf made a terrible, sickening noise; a laugh, with the amplified rumble of flames echoing from the bridge parapet and vibrating in Hellboy's chest.

He reached for Franca as she went to stand and swung her forward. She scraped across the road, crying out as the grit burned into her hands and knees. Then she fell into a roll, and as she saw Hellboy coming after her, she kept rolling.

The car exploded. Hellboy was certain that beneath the roar of erupting gasoline and the screech of pained metal, he heard an ecstatic sigh, pleasure in heat. He fell forward and shielded Franca with his body. Something hard glanced from his back, slashing across his shoulder and spinning over the edge of the bridge. Heat blossomed behind him and threw his shadow forward, across Franca and past her, merging with the darkness beyond.

"Stay close to me," he shouted in her ear. "You can't let it get you on your own!"

Franca looked up at him, her eyes wide and filled with reflected fire. She nodded, then her eyes went wider as she saw past his shoulder.

Hellboy pistoned himself up from the ground and turned, bringing his big right hand around in a circle and using its weight to give the punch force. The fire wolf was already upon him, and his fist passed through its head, the flames slicking out around his hand and almost seeming to stick to it, pulling tendrils out and streaming them through the air. Hellboy felt resistance again as his fist moved through the monster's furious head. It roared, flame and sound emerging from the hollow dark pit of its mouth, and Hellboy squeezed his eyes closed as its rage parted around his own head. When he looked again, the fire wolf had fallen to the side. It stood on the ground beside him, legs staggered, head lowered, the road beneath it melting and flowing from the intense heat.

"Well, you ain't so—" he started, but then the fire wolf struck out with one of its thick, shimmering back legs. It struck him across the throat, a heavy, hot blow that sent him staggering back. He tripped over Franca and landed across her, frantically reaching for her even as he struck, desperate not to leave her exposed to the thing's attention.

It's after her, he thought. *It wants her, not me, I'm just in the way.*

His hand found Franca's and he pulled, using the force to help him stand and drag her away from the fire wolf at the same time.

It stood to its full height again now, but it shook its head as though dazed. *There* is *something harder than fire in there*, Hellboy thought. *I felt it when I punched.*

He stepped forward and struck out with his left hand, and it was like punching air. The fire wolf snapped at his forearm with its flaming teeth, and he actually felt them penetrating, slipping hotly through skin and flesh and closing around his tough bones.

Which was just what he wanted. Hellboy punched again with his right hand, his fingers splayed out and ready to grab as soon as they felt something more solid. A risky experiment, but it seemed to work; while the fire wolf concentrated on trying to rip his left arm off at the elbow, Hellboy's right hand closed around something deep inside.

It felt like thick porridge, sludge, tapioca, and he was careful not to grip too hard. Then he pulled.

The fire wolf screeched in surprise, and what could have been pain. A sheet of fire sliced skyward from its mouth, forming a rainbow of flames as it twisted its head left to right in an attempt to shake his hold. In doing so, it lifted Hellboy from his feet. His right closed through whatever he was holding, and the momentum sent him flying.

"Crap!" he shouted, then hit the road and slid hard into the bridge parapet. The impact knocked the breath from him, but still he stood, staggering forward again, blood flowing down his left arm even though some of the wounds had been cauterized, and he had only one thing on his mind: Franca.

The fire wolf was crouching, ready to jump.

Franca scrabbled backward on her behind, pushing with her feet, desperately trying to back away from the demon.

"Oh, no you don't," Hellboy said, and he jumped at the same time as the fire wolf.

They met in mid-air, directly above the screaming Franca. Vicious and deadly though the fire demon was, Hellboy was heavier. They struck the ground beyond Franca and rolled into the opposite parapet.

They were tangled together, Hellboy's legs wrapped around the thing's waist, right hand grabbing inside the flames of the thing's body, his fingers tangling again in whatever semi-solid stuff went to make up its insides.

Wish I could talk to that old ghost right now, he thought. But he'd taken his attention from its head for a split second, and that was a mistake. He just managed to twist his own head to one side as the thing bit down.

He shouted as fire-teeth sank into his neck and shoulder.

And then Franca was there, pulling at his arm, shouting in incomprehensible rage as she tried to tug Hellboy away from the fire wolf's grasp. He punched the thing ineffectually with his left hand, pulled with his right, and for an instant when it let go with its teeth he felt relieved. But then he saw where it was looking. Its white-hot eyes were fixed on Franca, and liquid fire dripped from its bottomless mouth.

The decision he made next was pure instinct. He grabbed Franca with his left and stood, pushing at the fire demon-with his right. And keeping himself between the two, he leaned against the parapet . . . and tipped over.

The fall was a strangely calm, almost beautiful moment. The breeze ruffled the thing's flame-fur and whispered past Franca's ears, but other than that all was silence. They fell within an expanse of light from the fire wolf, and the river below them was illuminated as they approached, and then struck.

She had time to draw in a huge breath before water enveloped them, and the current pulled her under.

The coldness took her breath away and she sucked in water. She'd landed against Hellboy and he'd broken her fall somewhat, but then he let go of her, and Franca found herself drifting free. She opened her eyes but what she saw confused her more: the water appeared to be on fire all around, and she had no idea which way to swim. So she let the current carry her for a few seconds, kicking hard and breaking surface at last. She coughed and spluttered, then gasped in lungs full of air, relieved that it was cool.

"Son of a—!" she heard behind her, and she managed to turn while she was drifting and look back towards the bridge. Hellboy had surfaced as well, and around him the river bubbled and steamed, spat and surged. It was lit from beneath, and Hellboy was a shadow against the light. He brought his big hand down again and again on the surface of the river, and in the splashed water Franca saw sickly rainbows.

He looked across at her and nodded at the bank.

Franca started paddling backwards, going with the river's flow and drifting in towards its edge, and she never took her eyes off Hellboy. There was something primal about the fight she was witnessing, as if it had been under way for all eternity. Hellboy punched and the steaming waters splashed, and Franca thought that perhaps his conflict would never end.

But she was wrong. As she felt rocks beneath her back and legs, Hellboy stood taller in the water, lifting his big hand up towards the starry sky. Water hissed and poured from his grip, but there was something else there as well, something gray and limp with weak flame sparking across its surface. *That's fire when it isn't burning*, she thought, the idea preposterous but patently true.

"That's it for you," Hellboy said, and then he went to plunge beneath the surface one more time.

His hand and arm exploded in flames. He shouted in surprise and pain, flipping backwards into the water, but the fire had already parted from him, leaping across the surface of the river and leaving ripples of steam in its wake. It hit the shore thirty yards upriver from Franca, and when it glanced her way she saw its eyes, emphasized even more by the weaker flames surrounding them. The fire wolf left a trail of steam and smoke as it scrabbled at the steep sides of the gorge, pulling itself up the low cliff and standing briefly on its upper lip.

It looked down at the two of them: Hellboy up to his chest in the water; Franca wet and cold on the bank. And in the few seconds before it turned and vanished into the night, its flames grew brighter, and hot with the promise of more pain to come.

Hellboy splashed across to her, and by then she was starting to shiver from the shock and cold. He was grimacing, stretching his left arm out from his body and examining the scorch marks that tattered his coat sleeve and still steamed on his skin. He was soaked through, but the heat of these wounds kept this part of him dry.

The car was still burning up on the bridge, and soon it would attract the attention of the police. *We have to get back up there!* she wanted to shout, but when she opened her mouth to speak, nothing emerged. Her teeth were rattling, her jaw shaking as she tried to form words, and she let Hellboy gather her in his arms and squeeze her tight to his chest. She became aware once again of what an oddity he was: he smelled different from any man she had ever been this close to, and there was a confidence and strength in his arms that belied what he had just been through. He growled something—she could not quite hear the words against the flow of the river and the beat of her heart—and she took immense comfort from the sound of his voice.

"It was looking . . . looking at me," she said. "It wanted *me*."

"And I got in its way."

"Thank you," she said, silently berating herself for not saying that before. *He just saved my life.*

"It didn't get Carlotta, so I figure it wants you in her place."

"But I'm twenty-five."

She felt Hellboy shrug. "Who's to say eighteen is the only age it wants? Maybe somebody else makes those rules."

She knew whom he meant, but the reality of it was painful to consider. There was a safety about family that she had carried with her even after fleeing, a sense that the Espositos were a tight, solid unit, and their influence still touched her though she had removed herself from their immediate sphere. Family was important. So thinking of Adamo in this way . . .

"I've got a lot of questions for that old man," Hellboy said.

"How do we get to Amalfi now?"

"Well . . ." he said, trailing off.

Franca pulled back from him and looked up into his face, seeing the discomfort there, and something else as well. It looked like frustration.

"You beat it, Hellboy," she said. "You saved my life!"

"I only sent it away," he muttered. "And things like that always come back. Believe me, I know."

"Then we need to get to Adamo," she said. "Find out what he knows."

"You're sure you want to be there?" he asked.

Franca laughed, an unconscious, reflexive action. "Right now, I want to be wherever you are!" The big man smiled at that, but as he turned away and she followed, Franca could not help feeling like a burden.

"Back up to the road," he said. "Gotta get rid of that car, then start using our thumbs."

"We're going to hitch a ride to Amalfi?"

"Not we," he said, glancing back at her. "You. Really, would you give *me* a ride in the dead of night?"

They climbed back up to the road, Hellboy going first, and Franca could sense the tension in him. He was ready for action, if any should come his way. Twice now he'd been burnt, and . . . But it would do no good dwelling on things such as that. He was on her side, and that was all that mattered.

Terrified though she was of him. Disturbed by his appearance, his tail, his hooves, those things on his head. Perturbed though she was by the things he spoke of, the histories he alluded to. He was an enigma, but right now, his mystery was starting to feel like her only protection.

Franca thought of Alex, and how far away he felt from all this. She had not spoken with him in two days, and in truth, she did not feel the need. He was so remote from what was happening, what could she really say? If she truly loved him, that love was something that existed in the true, safe world of pavement cafes, evening meals and nights of passion. To speak to him now, she thought, would be like speaking to a child. She knew, and had seen, so much more.

She wondered whether things would ever be the same again.

Franca stood a dozens steps back as Hellboy shoved the still-burning car to the edge of the bridge, leaning against its buckled metal wing as he strained and turned it on its side. The concrete parapet crumbled slightly, and with a roar Hellboy gave the vehicle one final, hard push. It tumbled through the dark, a burning mass mimicking the fire wolf that had fallen with them scant minutes before, and splashed steaming into the river. In seconds, with hissing and the cracks of ruptured metal, the flames had been extinguished.

Hellboy motioned her to him, and together they crossed the bridge and started walking towards Amalfi.

Ten minutes later a car approached. Hellboy slipped from the road and hid amongst rocky shadows, while Franca stood with her hand out and thumb up. The car—a big four-wheel drive—powered past, and then the splash of red brake lights blooded the road.

"A ride," Franca called across to Hellboy.

"Great," he said. "Can't wait 'til they get a load of me."

Chapter 9

Pompeii/Amalfi

What a mess this was turning into.

Hellboy had already tried his phone, but the soaking had ruined it. He wanted to talk with Liz, get her take on things, and maybe ask Kate Corrigan to see if she could pull up some research on what he was dealing with here. She was an expert in European folklore and mysteries, and the fieldwork he'd persuaded her to undertake had made her indispensable. He could think of no precedent other than those fire dogs in Africa, certainly not in the cases he'd dealt with for the B.P.R.D. And those things had been . . . different. They'd sown destruction, but in an aimless, useless manner. This thing had purpose, and if Adamo was as involved as Hellboy suspected, then there was human influence behind these monstrous actions.

That was always when things turned bad. Drooling, roaring, tentacled things he could deal with. It was people who were often revealed as the greatest monsters.

He really needed to speak with the old demon hunter, but right now wasn't the best time. Franca was shivering in the seat next to him, and if he started talking to the bone tied around his neck . . . well, they needed this ride. Last image he wanted to give out was *crazy*.

The little girl leaned forward and looked at him again, giggling behind her hands. Hellboy could not help chuckling, and that got the girl giggling again. Sweet little thing. Franca sat in the middle, and the girl had all but ignored the woman's presence ever since they'd climbed into the vehicle. She only had eyes for Hellboy.

So did her parents. The father kept checking him out in the rearview mirror, offering a tentative half-smile that Hellboy knew so well. It said, *You're that famous one from America*, but it also spoke of its owner's previously-held doubts about whether he really existed. Well, now the guy knew. Hellboy smiled back.

The mother had turned around in the passenger seat, talking to Franca in rapid-fire Italian but spending more time looking at Hellboy. He'd done his best to put them all at ease when he'd climbed in after Franca, but they had their little girl to think of, and he could understand their caution. Good for them. You've got to look after what you love.

He hoped the guy hadn't caught sight of the cannon in his holster as he'd climbed in. He doubted it; darkness hung heavy over these hills, and the roads were unlit.

Hellboy covered his face with his hands, then pulled them quickly away again. "Boo!" The girl squealed in delight, and Hellboy laughed softly.

The mother smiled at him, and he leaned back and closed his eyes.

There was a sense of urgency bearing down upon him, a pressure inside his skull that he could do little to relieve. Amalfi was maybe an hour away, and there was no way he could get there any faster. And all the while, the thought pressed home: *The whole family is in danger.* If the sick contract between Adamo Esposito and the fire wolf had been broken, then what was to prevent the fire wolf from destroying all living evidence of its existence, and then moving on?

Me, Hellboy thought. But he was also aware that if that did happen, he was the one to blame. If it had taken that one girl, everyone would have been safe for another couple, even a few decades. *But I drove the thing away and Carlotta took her own life . . .* He shook his head, frowning, trying to dislodge the guilt that had instilled itself within. He could not blame himself for positive action. There was nothing else he could have done.

"Boo!" a voice said. Hellboy opened his eyes and looked past Franca at the little girl. Who was to say this family wouldn't be next? He smiled and played her game back at her, and only then noticed that Franca was no longer talking to the woman in the front seat. She was muttering into a mobile phone she must have borrowed, and Hellboy realized what a fool he'd been. It should have been the first thing he'd thought of upon entering the Jeep.

Franca snapped the phone shut and handed it back to the woman with a nod of thanks.

"Well?" Hellboy said.

"All's well," she said. "I spoke with my cousin Mario and told him to get those who will leave out of the house. It's night, and Adamo always posts a couple of security guards. And the dogs. But hopefully they'll get out, and they'll meet up in an all-night café I know in town."

"Did you tell him anything else?"

"How could I?" she asked, her eyes wide and innocent. And Hellboy realized her predicament. Suddenly returning to the family, how could she start rumors about fire-demons, and their family patriarch holding some hellish contract with something monstrous?

"So how did you get them to agree?"

"I said it was about what killed Carlotta."

"But she killed herself."

"That's what we know, and what everyone else thinks. But the suspicion worked well."

"Lady, you want a job with the B.P.R.D. when this is all over?" Hellboy asked, but Franca did not reply. She looked between the two adults and out through the windscreen at the road ahead. And he understood that she could not yet even comprehend this being over. She had no idea what was to come next, and she was utterly terrified. *Clinging on by her nails*, he thought, and he clasped her hand.

For a heartbeat she tried to pull away. But then she relaxed, and when he looked again she was resting her head against his shoulder.

The little kid had also nodded off to sleep. Hellboy wondered where these people had come from, where they were going in the middle of the night, but then he heard mention of Vesuvius on the subdued radio, and he understood. Evacuees. The volcano's anger was reaching far.

He closed his eyes again, but could not rest. He touched the bone and sensed the spirit's frustration. *Soon*, he thought. On the canvas of his eyelids there played out nightmare scenarios that he could not entertain: this innocent mother and father dead, their little girl carried back toward Pompeii and Vesuvius beyond, all the potential of her young life snuffed out in a superheated instant.

So Hellboy sat in the back seat and stared at the dark landscape slipping by, watching for the telltale glow of something terrible approaching.

They arrived in Amalfi just as dawn was painting the eastern sky with familiar, dreadful colors. The people dropped them off at the harbor and continued their journey along the coastal road. The little girl knelt in the back seat and waved, and Hellboy waved back, smiling. *Be safe*, he thought.

"This way," Franca said. She headed up into the small city, past the grand steps of the cathedral and the few people out on the streets at this hour: a street sweeper, a fruit seller trundling his cart towards the beach, and several men unloading a truck outside a restaurant. Hellboy's hooves clacked on the stone paving, and a couple of men glanced their way. They stared, and Hellboy stared back. "Mind your business," he said, but even if the men heard they did not appear to understand.

Franca turned left and passed through a narrow, twisting alley. La Casa Fredda was in this direction, high up on the hillside, but she turned north again, following the route of the valley until the alley opened into a small, attractive square. Even in the burgeoning dawn, the flowers here gave off an incredible array of colors and scents, spilling from several huge planters around the square and hanging curtains of growth from window boxes.

"Mario!" Franca called, and Hellboy heard the delight in her voice. She dashed across to where there was a spread of tables and chairs behind the largest planter, hugging the man as he came to meet her. A few lights were on in the building behind the seating area, and Hellboy could see the shadows of people moving out into the dawn. There were maybe eight there, and he recognized most of them from his brief time at La Casa Fredda. A couple of kids ran out too, already lively and alert even this early. They saw Hellboy and stopped, then brought their heads together and muttered behind their hands, giggling. Hellboy smiled and felt a lightness lift his mood. Seemed he was a real kid charmer today.

"Mario, you know Hellboy. He has something to tell you all."

"About Carlotta?" Mario asked. "About why she killed herself?" His English was very good and Hellboy felt an instant of selfish dread: inside, he'd been hoping that Franca would have to translate for him.

"Yes," Hellboy said. "And about Adamo Esposito."

"What about Adamo?" a woman asked. The others were crowded behind Mario now, unsettled and still grieving, and Hellboy hated what he had to say next. But he was quite certain, and he had a duty to these people. Whatever nefarious arrangement had existed between Adamo and the fire wolf from Vesuvius had gone up in smoke, and he could not be certain that the thing would not now kill them all.

"He's brought grief to your family," Hellboy said. "I don't know all the details yet, but he's perpetuating something that—"

"Adamo loves us all," the woman said. Mario made no move to deny that. The others nodded, and Hellboy realized that most of them spoke enough English to follow this. A well-educated family, one of the oldest and proudest in Amalfi, and here he was . . .

"I'm not questioning that," he said. "But it doesn't mean he's incapable of what I'm suggesting."

"So what *is* that, *Hell*boy?" Mario asked. And the way he uttered his name made something clear to Hellboy: Adamo had already spoken to them all. Whatever Hellboy said about the fire wolf—however much Franca backed him up, told them what she had seen, what had happened to them—it was Hellboy who had become this family's demon.

"Right," he said, nodding. He looked at each of them one to the next, and he could see the fear in their eyes. Fear of him. It was only after he had arrived that Carlotta had died, after all. And a few words from their patriarch, the man they loved and who loved them, and seeds of suspicion were planted, guilt was assured. "Right," he said again, nodding. "Franca, I don't think we can gain anything here." She glanced back at him, and he hoped she got the message. *Not here*, he thought, *but maybe up at the house.*

She seemed confused, then her face sagged and she looked down at her feet.

"You bring doom!" one of the women said. "Doom and pain, red man."

"Carlotta dies, and you come here, offend our family, our great-grandfather, and you think . . . ?" The man behind Mario could not even finish, such was his anger.

Oh, crap, Hellboy thought, *they're turning into a mob.*

The kids were still whispering to each other behind their hands, but he could see by their eyes that they were no longer smiling. *Even them.*

"Franca?"

"Listen to him!" Franca said. "You have no idea what we've just been through, what we've seen and heard, and—"

"You left us, Franca," Mario said. And though Hellboy saw some measure of warmth in his eyes, his voice was cold.

"I went to live my life," Franca said. "You know that Mario. You and I talked about it before I went."

If she had expected that to faze Mario at all, she must have been disappointed. "We did," he said, "and I chose to stay with the family. All my heart is behind them."

"And mine!" Franca shouted, the passion in her voice stilling all movement and muttering in the square. "I love the name Esposito as well as any of you, and the fact that I have my own life detracts *nothing* from that! And that's why I'm telling you—"

Mario said something in Italian then, a fast smattering of words that Hellboy could not understand, and they killed whatever Franca had been about to say. She looked at her cousin, her family, and then back to Hellboy.

"We should leave," she said quietly. She turned her back on her family and walked from the square.

"You're making a big mistake," Hellboy said to Mario.

"A threat?" Mario asked. He was strong, and he held Hellboy's gaze. Impressive.

"The truth," Hellboy said. "I came here to help Carlotta, and now it turns out I have to help you all."

"We don't need the sort of help you gave her," a woman behind Mario said, her voice angry through hot tears.

Hellboy sighed and looked down at the little kids. They were staring at him with wide eyes, almost completely motionless, waiting for whatever came next. He gave them a weak smile, turned, and started away.

"I'll still be here," he said, without looking back. "When you need me, I'll still be here." He expected a rebuff, or a final word from the Esposito family's younger generations gathered behind him. But only silence saw him from the square, and the heat of their stares boring into his back.

With Franca ahead of him, Hellboy took a moment to unbind the spirit as he walked.

Damn you damn you damn you!

"Hush," he whispered.

You crush me, you hurt me!

"Lady, I know you don't hurt. You wanted to come, and I'm glad to have you along for the ride, because honestly, I need the help."

Her tone changed instantly. You *want help from* me*, Hellboy?*

He didn't respond. Ghosts, and their damn taunts and word-games . . .

Where is the cursed monster now?

"I don't know. After it went for us on the bridge, it vanished. Thought I'd killed it, pushing it down into the water. It sorta . . . went out for a bit, then—"

It's taken form. Water . . . that hurts, but does not kill.

"So what *will* kill it?"

I never had chance to find out.

"It's sacrificing people to Vesuvius." He passed by an old, old man, who looked up at Hellboy apparently talking to himself. Hellboy waved at him with the finger bone.

Of course. It has no wish to return, and that is why you must take it there. It is what I was trying to do when the thing defeated me, and the volcano . . .

"That won't happen again," Hellboy said.

You seem sure. The voice had taken on a mocking lilt.

Hellboy started winding the cord again as he walked, twisting the two ends into the beginning of the binding knot.

Torturer, defiler! the old ghost shouted in his mind. Then gentle again, it said, *You want the woman, don't you? Of course. But if the fire wolf eludes you, she will be your last hope.*

"Shut it, lady." Hellboy pulled the knot tight and sighed when the presence left his mind. He paused for a moment and looked around, listening for Franca's footsteps and hearing them as she fled her family once again.

She walked aimlessly for a while, wanting only to be away from there. If she could walk for seven days and be out of Italy completely, that would suit her. After a couple of minutes she heard Hellboy's hooves on the stone paving behind her, following at a respectful distance, and she was grateful for the space he was giving her. He would ask her soon, she knew: ask what Mario had said to her in Italian. And hopefully by then she would be able to tell him without sobbing it out.

You bring shame on our name, and we disown you.

Franca had been an only child, and Mario and Carlotta had been as close to siblings as she could have wished for. Now one of them was dead, and the other . . .

She'd known for a long time that she was the black sheep of the family. Choosing to leave Amalfi and pursue her own life had made her such, and however wrong that was—however short-sighted and old fashioned, selfish and unreasonable—she had never shaken the idea that it was her doing something wrong. The guilt ran deep, and though she had enjoyed the years since she had been away with a carefree abandon, some nights she dreamed of the place she would always call home. And some mornings she woke with tears dried on her face, and the dark shadow of shame would haze her day.

Coming back here had crystallized that guilt and shame, but it had also reinforced her certainty that she had done the right thing. Franca was conflicted, and her frustration at not being able to help her family only went to make matters worse.

"Franca," Hellboy said behind her. His voice was deep and mysterious, and she wondered what hidden depths he concealed; what shame and guilt, frustrations and longings. And here he was, doing his best to help.

She stopped and sagged against a wall, holding her face in her hands but fighting back the tears. He was right! She would not let them grind her down, not like this, and not after everything she had seen this night just gone. A minute of weakness now was another minute that she was not helping her family, whether they welcomed that help or not.

"What now?" she asked. Hellboy stopped behind her and put his hand on the back of her neck. It was warm and strong, and meant in the gentlest way.

"Now we play it my way," he said.

Franca turned, anger quickly receding when he saw the big man's face. He understood her anguish, she could see. He could empathize, and she wondered whether unconscious prejudice had made her unable to see that before. *He's human*, she thought, *as much as me, as much as the next person*. And she could only smile, because the truth of that idea was bright in his eyes.

"We should get into the house a different way from last time," she said. "Adamo will have the dogs out, even though he thinks we're gone."

"He's the root of all this, I'm certain of it," Hellboy said. "I absolutely have to speak with him, and I'm done trying to play nice."

"We can't just smash our way in there," Franca said.

Hellboy shrugged and looked over her shoulder, further along the path.

"Hellboy—"

"The dogs I can handle," he said. "Even if they get nasty, I was given something a long time ago by an old woman in Iceland, and if I can find it in here . . ." He patted the pouches around his belt, then looked down at Franca. "But people . . . guards, family, whatever . . . I've had enough of them, Franca. They get in my way, I'll move them gently aside."

She'd seen him fighting that fire wolf, the fury in his eyes, the power in his punches. "Gently?" she asked.

The big red man nodded, but said no more.

Franca turned and led the way. She was determined to be able to enter La Casa Fredda without any trouble, but the closer they drew to her old family home, the more she realized that was unlikely. Adamo was alert now, and Mario and the others had likely called ahead already to warn him that Hellboy and she were back in town.

Gently, gently, she thought, and that was the mantra that kept her going. Hellboy was here to help her family, not hurt them. If and when the trouble began, she would be there by his side.

Amalfi's daytime heartbeat was thrumming by the time they reached the walls of La Casa Fredda. Scooters flitted through the winding streets and along the coastal road, tourist buses were arriving at the harbor, and a lone speedboat was chalking a line across the sea a mile from shore. Birds sang in the lemon groves across the hillsides, and in their shade, local people were moving down towards the heart of the town, to shop or work, or to meet friends for coffee.

Beyond the walls, the house's grounds sounded silent.

Franca had taken a different approach from yesterday, climbing the zig-zag route of a path further inland and then cutting through a small cemetery and closing on the house from the east. This took them near to where one corner of the garden ended in a sheer cliff rising fifty feet, and Franca knew that the wall here was very old. It was even crumbling in places, and family talk had it that it had not been maintained for two centuries.

And below where the dilapidated wall was built into the rock of the cliff, Franca knew of a small crawlspace. It had been used by generations of Esposito teens, the secret way out to meet friends for drinks or childhood sweethearts for love on the hillsides. She had used it herself many times, and she wondered now whether her mindset at the time had been different from everyone else's. The crawlspace was known about by the adults, of course, and most people using it did so with a sort of naïve awareness. When Franca had used it, her secrecy had been deadly serious. At the time it had been her only available route from the family, until she was old enough to make her own adult decision to leave.

Approaching the area of the crawl hole, Franca was struck by a flush of nostalgia. She had kissed her first boy just this side of the wall, after he had walked her home from a dance in one of Amalfi's many hotels. He was a tourist, and had been returning to Britain the very next day, but he had tried nothing more than a kiss. Many times she had wondered whether he held that night in the same dreamy reverence as she.

"Here," she said to Hellboy. "A space beneath the wall."

"And the dogs don't know about this?"

"*Everyone* knows about it. But everyone also treats it as secret. Cute family tradition."

"Huh. Well, there's nothing cute about tonight."

"I know that!" she said quietly. She touched the wall and felt the damp, crumbling plaster turn to dust beneath her fingers. "I'm doing my best, Hellboy. Just hoping this place slips their minds."

"Right," he said, but she could see his doubt. "Well then, I'll go first."

Franca nodded and stepped back slightly, looking at the length of wall to her left. It led downhill towards the house, and she could see the eastern wall of the building from here. Windows were open, and a curtain billowed in the gentle sea breeze. Nothing else moved, and she heard no sign of activity.

Hellboy was pushing himself through the crawlspace. She heard muttered curses and could not help smiling. Then she saw his hooved feet and tail waving below the tattered remains of his long coat, and her smile slipped. She had forgotten to ask whether he'd found whatever he'd been looking for in his belt pouches.

His feet disappeared, and silence descended. She waited for a while, listening; she heard no movement, and no sound of confrontation. A bird landed atop the wall close to her, and she turned slowly to watch it peruse the area. It started singing, and then suddenly it flew away as if startled by a movement.

She turned around first, making sure nobody was stalking close to her from this side. Then, confident that she was alone, she turned back to the wall.

"Hellboy!" she called in a hoarse whisper.

"Wait," she heard, and she hated that he told her no more. *Damn it, I'm not waiting here like a puppy*. She dropped to her stomach and started through the hole herself. For an instant she was sixteen again; she had the memory of a kiss still fresh on her lips, and in her mind's eye the smile of a boy who could not speak her language, and whom she could barely understand. Then she felt the weight of the wall above her, remembered how little it had been maintained, and she was back to the dangerous present once again. Still crawling, she felt a melancholic regret at the loss of innocence. And then a hand clamped across her mouth.

She tried to scream in surprise, and Hellboy pressed harder, mashing her lips against her teeth. With his strange right hand he grabbed her belt and pulled her upright, staring into her eyes. When she calmed, he nodded and let her go.

"Quiet," he whispered. Then he looked down at something on the ground.

It was a dozen feet away, and hidden slightly by some of the lush plant growth in this forgotten corner of the garden, but Franca could still make out the dead dog.

She glanced at Hellboy. He was crouched down a little so that he was no taller than her, tensed, ready for action. His left hand rested on his holster, his right fisted and heavy.

The rear of the house looked peaceful from here, just as it had on warm summer days when she used to live here. Many of the windows and doors were open, balconies bright with the reds and yellows of flower boxes. On the ground floor, the patio area that ran the length of the house was also awash with color, and several large stone tables were surrounded by metal chairs. She could see no one sitting there, and similarly the balconies appeared to be abandoned.

"What killed it?" she whispered.

Hellboy stepped forward and she followed. Even before they reached the dog, the smell was enough to give her a clue. Amazed that she had not smell it before, Franca pressed her hand over her nose and mouth, trying to shut out the rich stench of burnt meat. *It only smells like that when it's freshly cooked*, she thought, and she was disgusted at the brief pang of hunger the smell inspired within her.

The dog was one of the big Dobermans, its right flank and chest burnt black. She leaned forward a little and looked into its dulled eyes, checking for movement. Definitely dead.

"It got here before us," Hellboy said, and as Franca stood she realized the enormity of what might have happened.

It's got here before us . . . and La Casa Fredda is silent.

Shunning her own sense of self preservation, and ignoring Hellboy's startled cry behind her, Franca ran down the slope of the garden towards her family home, dreading what she would find.

CHAPTER 10

Amalfi

He knew that shouting after her would do no good. Caution had fled now that her family was at risk, and the only way to stop her would be to catch up. But Franca was young and fit, and she knew this garden well.

Hellboy pulled his gun and watched the house as he ran, rather than Franca's back. He searched for movement at any of the windows and doors, hoping that if something did appear it would be human. But the house exuded a stillness that he did not like. And Franca was almost there, leaping this way and that as she negotiated her way through a garden she had known since taking her first steps as a toddler.

"Franca!" he called, risking one shout before he lost sight of her through one of the doors. A curtain swished behind her and then settled again, like the house's skin parting to allow her entry. *It won't be so welcoming to me*, he thought, but he did not slow, and did not hesitate. And that was how he ran into Franca immediately inside the doorway.

She went sprawling, gasping as the wind was knocked from her and slipping across the marble floor. Hellboy kept to his feet, just, staggering to one side and slapping his right hand against a wall to regain his balance. And then he saw why she had stopped.

It must have been a sitting room, once. The remains of several casual chairs and a sofa were dotted around, and on the walls there were darkened oil paintings, and a selection of charred masks from around the world. In the corner, sitting on the floor and leaning against a wall, the blackened shell of a burnt human being.

Franca muttered something in Italian, but Hellboy knew the language of humans enough to know that it was an utterance of shock and grief. She knelt up and crawled forward, pausing on a rug that had had much of its surface scorched away, leaving only the bare brown thread of its underside visible.

"Keep away," Hellboy said, and when she turned to look at him her eyes were wide, and a line of dribble stretched from her mouth. It looked as if she did not recognize him. *At least we got some of them away*, he thought, but it was scant comfort. And there was the very real danger that Mario and the others were on their way back here even now.

The fire wolf could still be here.

Hellboy looked away from the corpse—hollowed eyes, cracked scalp, bright grin in its blackened, shrunken face—and tilted his head to one side, listening.

"Hellboy," Franca breathed.

"Shh!" He opened his mouth slightly, listening for anything that could give away what was happening elsewhere in the house. The utter silence promised only that something had already happened.

"Hellboy, that's a child," Franca said, her voice breaking on the last word.

"Yeah," he said. Adrenaline pumped, and his anger was growing with every heartbeat. He did not look at the body again, and he closed his eyes only briefly, waiting for the whisper of a lost spirit but hearing nothing.

"Do you think—" Franca began.

"Only one way to find out." He held out his hand to her, pleased when she took it and allowed him to help her stand. "You ready for this?"

"No," she said, shivering. But there was a strength to her; he'd sensed it before, and he felt it now. She stood by his side and took several deep breaths. "I smell more of this," she said.

Hellboy nodded. He'd already smelled the burning. One dog dead in the garden likely meant that all of them were dead, otherwise the others would either have attacked, or would have been eating the flesh of their dead companion. And one dead Esposito . . .

"We have to find Adamo," he said.

"What about the others?"

"We'll help if we can, but he's the key, Franca. And he can tell us how to solve this. *Stop* it. That's why we have to get to him before the fire wolf does. If it kills him, moves onto another family, we'll lose it. Might take months, or maybe years before it rears its head again."

"But the volcano, what about—?"

From somewhere in the house, a terrible scream rose up. It was shattering, a call of agony that raised Hellboy's hackles and sent a shiver from his scalp to the tip of his tail. It was cut off quickly, and then came a noise like the house gasping a breath.

The curtains at the open door quivered as air moved.

"Fire," Hellboy said. "Come on."

Franca muttered something in Italian as she ran, and Hellboy recognized prayer.

They ran along a short corridor and then emerged into the large entrance hallway. The staircase was to their left, and to the right the dining room door lay open. Hellboy could smell breakfast, and the scent of some other cooked meat. He hurried to the door and flattened himself against the wall, not sure which hand to raise in protection; the gun hand, or the right hand? He decided on both, and as Franca paused behind him he ducked into the room.

The table had been set for breakfast, but it had been scattered and ruined. The tablecloth waved down on one side, and a slick of milk and fruit juice glittered on the marble floor. A wide swathe of blackened, charred food scarred the tabletop, and at the far end, behind a pile of tumbled chairs, lay several bodies. They had been burned so badly that they had merged as one, arms and legs protruding at agonized angles, hair scorched away. The sight of their jumbled, melted bodies reminded Hellboy of something he'd once fought deep below an old church in Moldavia, but this sight was much more sad.

Franca stood beside him and surveyed the ruins of the room. Hellboy guessed it was probably good that the corpses were beyond identifying.

"Upstairs to Adamo?" she asked querulously.

"Yeah, Adamo. If that wasn't him screaming."

Hellboy led them out of the room again and across to the foot of the stairs. *Nothing burning,* he thought. *No curtains have gone up, no furniture . . . just those people.* He juggled the problem for a second or two, then cast it to one side for later consideration. He had more immediate things to worry about right now.

Up on the second floor landing they found another body. It was facing away from them and still smoking slightly, and Hellboy guessed it hadn't been this way for much more than an hour. *Is that bastard thing hunting them all through the house?* he thought. *It must have struck just as Mario and the others left, and is it stalking the survivors even now?* He imagined this huge, still home to contain a dozen people hidden away from the terror visiting itself upon them: wardrobes containing more than clothes; doors shut and barricaded; eyes wide in shadows, hearts thumping in fright.

"Here we are you son of a bitch!" he shouted, rage getting the better of caution.

"Hellboy!" Franca cried.

"Don't worry, I know what I'm—"

"No, look!" She was pointing at the body. And it turned what was left of its head.

Hellboy went to his knees by the burnt woman, looking around to see what might answer his shout. She was keening through her ruined mouth, as if the heat was still inside her and whining for release. Franca shoved him to one side and he almost fell, and all her attention was on the burnt woman.

Hellboy stood again, watching and listening, sniffing the air, waiting for the roar of glare of danger to descend upon them. And he was dreadfully aware of just how exposed Franca would be if and when that happened.

"Hellboy, she's . . ." Franca was leaning over the woman, trying not to touch her burned body. Hellboy wondered if she recognized her, and hoped not.

"What is it?" he asked. The woman was almost dead, he could see that, and he wished that she *would* die. An end to the agony, an end to the fearful pains she must be going through right now. When she turned, he had seen her eyes melted away.

"Ad . . . Ad . . . Adamo," the woman muttered wetly.

"We're going to find him," Franca said, nodding. "We're going to save him, and everyone else." Her voice broke but she did not turn away. Even in his rage, that brought a lump to Hellboy's throat. Franca did not turn away until the woman breathed her last.

She stood, hands pressed against her face as if to hold in the remains of her composure.

"Adamo," Hellboy said. "Let's go."

They ran up the second flight of stairs, Hellboy sniffing the air as they went. The whole house was rich with the scent of cooked meat, and in one room they passed the bed was smoldering. Hellboy ran on, but Franca had paused outside the bedroom door, looking in with mouth agape.

"Franca, we—"

"Mother," she said.

Oh hell. He went back to her and peered into the room again. The bed was burnt, and fire had scorched a terrible trail up the wall and into the curtained window. Cast into that blackened stain was the shape of a person, where they had been pressed against the wall as they were burnt to death.

"No," Franca whined.

"Hey, we—"

She pushed past him and walked several steps along the corridor, before leaning heavily against the wall.

Hellboy took a quick step into the room, looked at the body slumped down beside the bed, and knew that there was nothing to be done.

Franca was facing him as he emerged. He approached her cautiously, ready to hold her if she fell or grab her if she tried to run. She never took her eyes from his, and he could see the grim determination on her face.

"I feel . . . numb," she said, biting back tears. "Numb and empty. Will I feel it all later, do you think, or will it always be like this?"

"There's no wrong way to handle grief."

Franca nodded. "Numb." And she turned and hurried along the corridor.

When they reached Adamo's room Hellboy did not pause: he kicked open the door, barging his way inside and sweeping the room with his gun.

It was empty.

"Hellboy," Franca said, and he was unsettled by the distant look in her eyes: they shifted left and right, but her mind was elsewhere. "The basements. In the war, they used the basements as—"

"A hiding place," he said. "Damn it, I should've thought of that. Come on!"

There were no more screams, and as they reached the large entrance hall again Hellboy darted to the front door. He lifted a heavy curtain aside and looked out through the window, surveying as much of the gardens before the house as he could. There was no sign of Mario and the other, and Hellboy felt torn: leave the house to make sure they did not return? Or go down, deeper, pursuing whoever might have taken shelter down there to lead them out again?

And all this time, where was that damn fire wolf?

He thought briefly of sending Franca from the house to warn Mario, but he could not bear to leave her on her own.

"Down?" she whispered, glancing back at the door behind the staircase.

"Yes," Hellboy said. "Down. You okay?"

"No," Franca said, shaking her head and hugging her arms across her chest. "I'm not."

"Stay with me," he said. He went to her and touched her arms, and she dropped then and wrapped them around his chest. "Hey . . ."

"I can't believe this is happening," Franca said, and Hellboy could smell smoke in her hair. "My family . . . I don't know who's alive and who's dead. Up there, in the corridor . . . I didn't even know who she was . . . She died as I watched, and I *still* don't know . . ."

"Adamo has the answers," Hellboy said softly, still alert for danger. "I can fight that thing again and again, but to stop it, I need to speak to the old man."

Franca nodded against his chest, but she did not let go for a few seconds more. "Fine," she said, wiping tears angrily from her face. She sniffed. "I'm fine. Let's go."

They went.

Someone had come this way recently, and the fire wolf had followed.

As they entered the first small storage room, Hellboy tried to map out the area ahead in his mind. He'd only been down here once, but there were several rooms, and with everything that had happened his memory was a little hazy. First room, storage boxes, with toys leaning over their rims as if killed trying to escape. Last time down here, none of the dolls had blisters across their pale skin, and none of the teddies had melted eyes and shrivelled fur.

"Hellboy, if he came this way . . ."

"If he did and he kept going, he might be hiding down in the caves. Or if not Adamo, there might be others left alive down here."

"But the fire wolf?"

He shrugged and descended the steps into the next room, where the smell of wine was rich and heady. A hundred bottles lay smashed across the floor, and the racking against the long wall on the left was slumped as if something heavy had rested against it. The next room was where the old furniture was piled up, and there were fewer signs of disturbance or fire here.

Passing into the final room, Hellboy remembered the tapestries that had hung on the walls, and that old table at the room's center where the book containing the history of the family's curse had rested. He glanced that way first, not at all surprised to see that the book was still absent. And beyond the table, revealed in the low glare of the dusty bulb, sat Adamo Esposito.

For a second, Hellboy thought the old man was dead. His eyes were wide but dull, and his skin was as dark as a ripe plum's. But wisps of hair lay unburned across his scalp, and though naked, the skin of his stomach and chest seemed untouched.

Adamo gasped, lowered his head and started crying into his hands.

Franca went to him. He had been terrible to her, turning family against her simply because she had left to choose her own path through life, but he was still the man responsible for her being alive. He was responsible for *all* the Espositos, and Hellboy could barely imagine the misery the old man must be going through right now.

"You brought it on yourself," Hellboy said. When Adamo glared at him with a glimmer of bitter humor in his eyes, Hellboy's sympathies flew.

"You know nothing, demon," Adamo said.

Hellboy glanced at the tapestry covering the tunnel that led to the deeper caves. Its center had been completely burned away, and smoke still rose from the ragged edges.

"It let you live?" Franca asked, in English so that Hellboy could follow.

Adamo shrugged, eyes widening with fear again. But behind the fear there still shone that glitter of amusement, and Hellboy knew that the old guy was a good pretender.

"Lots of your family are dead up in the house," Hellboy said. "Whatever you've got going on with that damned thing, you better tell me what it is."

"I'd better? Really?"

"Adamo?" Franca said. Her voice was tinged with confusion, and she stood back from the old man. She had not quite moved close enough to hug him.

"So it's through there," Hellboy said, nodding at the burned tapestry.

Adamo sighed, wiping both hand across his sweating face. Franca still waited by him, but now she looked less inclined to kneel down by his side. She saw no sorrow at his dead family, and no regret at whatever he had done, and that accounted for the look of confusion on her face.

"Adamo," she said, "my mother's dead. If you know what's happening here, Hellboy needs—"

"That tapestry," the old man said, nodding at the wall and completely ignoring his young relative, "is over a thousand years old. It depicts the time when Amalfi drove the Saracens from her lands, after giving them Capri years before as payment for their war efforts. It was a special time for this great city. Amalfi was the most powerful force in the Mediterranean at one time." He sighed almost wistfully.

Hellboy had a bad feeling about this.

"Adamo, the loss of a tapestry—"

The old man looked up at Franca then, as if noticing her presence for the first time. "Girl," he said, but he followed it with nothing else.

"I can help you," Hellboy said, but something was niggling at the back of his mind. He looked from the old man to the tapestry and back again. "Whatever it is between you and that thing, I can break it. Believe me, I've met a lot worse and beaten it in a fight."

Adamo was staring at him, smiling.

"And the fire wolf?" Hellboy said. "Pretty damn dull, if you ask me."

Adamo's smile slipped, just a notch. *And there it is*, Hellboy thought, *the old fool and that thing are more than just passing acquaintances*. He glanced back to the tapestry again and moved closer to Franca at the same time.

Adamo stood, displaying none of his old man's weaknesses.

Hellboy grabbed Franca's upper arm and pulled her back, urging her behind him so that he was between her, the tapestry and the tunnel beyond. But when the fire wolf came, it was not from the tunnel.

It was from Adamo Esposito himself.

CHAPTER II

Amalfi

At first, Franca thought that the fire wolf had appeared behind Adamo and was burning him alive. She clasped Hellboy's arm, and was about to urge him to help when she saw Adamo's eyes explode into twin pools of fire . . . and the smile grew on his face.

He was not being burned by the fire wolf; he *was* the fire wolf.

Naked, the old man stood and let fire become him. He held his hands up in a crucifixion pose, head slightly back and mouth open. His skin bubbled and split, and where in a normal person the result would be a rush of blood, from Adamo there flowed fire. It languished around him to begin with, gentle, almost loving flames moving across and around his body like burning snakes, meeting each other, merging and flowing again. His legs changed into pillars of fire, and his body bent at the waist, lowering to the ground as his arms extended and thickened. His head was the recognizable human feature, and Franca could not tear her eyes from his terrible, vicious smile. It was all too human on this monstrous face, and she was certain he was staring at her with his fiery eyes.

"Back up!" Hellboy told her. He didn't seem surprised—ready for a fight, in fact, his face grim and hands fisting—and she wondered whether he'd already had an inkling of this.

Adamo is the fire wolf! Which means . . .

"You killed Carlotta!" she screamed, and the unfairness of it all struck home. "You bastard!"

The fire wolf roared. It was a sound she could not remember hearing from it before, on the two previous occasions when she had seen it, and in the confines of this small subterranean room, the noise was horrendous. It was the roar of flame amplified, an animal growl as hot as Hell. The thing rolled and shook its head, as if revelling in its true form again.

Hellboy put three bullets through its head, but if there had been a hope of stopping it that way—perhaps when part of it was still Adamo, still flesh and blood—he'd lost the opportunity. The slugs hit the wall behind it in melted splashes, and then it came for him.

Hellboy punched out at the fire wolf with his right hand, at the same time pushing Franca back with his left. She staggered and almost fell, keeping her balance by stumbling back against the few steps leading up into the previous room. But terrified though she was, she could not leave. Her skin stretched across her features, she smelled the acrid stench of singed hair, but she could not turn her back on this monster and let it scare her away.

And all the while, she was trying to come to terms with what this all meant for her, and what might be left of her family.

"Come on!" Hellboy roared, a wild war cry.

The fire wolf went at him. He fell beneath its assault, and Franca backed up three stone steps, crouched down so she could still observe.

Hellboy punched at the thing with his strange right hand, and it was driven sideways as his hand slipped through it, trailing flames behind like threads of treacle. It fell against the table and chair, and they immediately burst into flames. Franca wondered for a moment where that book had gone, and then she had an image of Adamo writing a name with a grin on his face. In her dreams, that name had been her own.

The fire wolf rolled across the burning furniture and fell against the wall. Hellboy advanced. *He's brave*, Franca thought, but there was more to it than that. This was not bravery in the true sense of the word. Hellboy *needed* to fight this thing, just as he needed to do the job he did. There was something inevitable about the way he entered into combat with the fire wolf, as if this was all his life had ever been. She vowed there and then to talk to him later, if she had the chance; find out who he really was; discover, perhaps, his calling.

The burning thing was still thrashing against the base of the wall when Hellboy fell upon it. Franca could see the bubble blisters raising across the red man's forearm and hand. His right hand was unaffected, and it was this that he thrust deep into the conflagration. He growled, then lifted, and the fire wolf rose from the floor.

It's weak, she thought, *maybe because it's only just changed.*

Hellboy battered the fire wolf against the second tapestry, the dried, old material bursting into flames.

Hurt it, she thought. *Hurt it for everyone it's killed, hurt it for Mother . . .*

Franca knew she should be running back through the rooms, searching the house for survivors and then escaping this place of death. She should be leading whatever was left of her family to safety. But what she was witnessing was compelling. Terrible, horrifying, unbelievably compelling. She was seeing things that no one else had ever seen, and her whole world view had been blown wide open over the past couple of days. *Run!* she thought, but she could only stand and watch.

The remains of the tapestry fell in a swathe across Hellboy's head, and he spluttered and blew the flames away from his mouth. The fire wolf curved blazing limbs around his neck, the fire brightening towards white, and Hellboy roared in pain.

He let go, wiping his right hand across his face and pressing it to his eyes.

The fire wolf fell to the floor and darted across the room. Before Franca could blink, the creature had passed into the narrow tunnel beyond, the roar of its flames even louder as it was channelled from there. It moved quickly away, the glare diminishing, noise lessening, and as it reached the end of that tunnel and the caves beyond, a surge of cool air blew back up.

"Damn it!" Hellboy said.

"You fought it off!" Franca said.

He shook his head, and flickers of flame came off like loose hair. "Too easy," he said. "Didn't put up a fight."

"Maybe because it had just changed from . . ." She could not even mutter the name.

"Adamo," Hellboy said, sneering. "That son of a bitch."

Franca could barely comprehend what she had just seen, and trying to understand what it meant to her family as a whole . . . that was way beyond her, for now. It was a land she had no wish to visit, so she did her best to concentrate on the here and now.

"Are we going to chase it?"

"Not we, no. *I* am. I told you, Franca, it let me grab it too easily, let go too gently. I could feel the strength there, but it didn't use any of it. It *wants* me to follow, and maybe it wants you to follow as well."

"Me?"

"Don't forget what this is about." He came closer, pulling a clump of burnt hair from his goatee. "Sacrifice," he breathed. "Carlotta escaped Adamo, so maybe he's turned his attention on you."

"But he's not even human!" she said, feeling a note of panic entering her voice.

"Which is another reason for you to go back up into the house. That's Adamo, who just went through there. Can't pretend to understand it all just yet . . . but I've got a pretty good idea."

"Back into the house?"

"And beyond. Franca, I hate to part ways with you. I think you're safer with me . . . but not here and now. He's luring me down there, for some reason, and knowing that gives him the advantage. You go back up. Find Mario and those others, tell them what's happened. Tell them to hide."

"What if he can sniff them out?" she asked, and the panic was really taking hold now, raising her voice and galloping away with her heart.

"I won't let him," Hellboy said, and he came even closer. "I've got a plan. Now . . . you go." He looked into her eyes, just a little too close and for a little too long.

Franca blinked and broke the contact. She could smell burning and fear, but beneath that was the scent that she only now identified as Hellboy's own. She had a terrible idea that she would never smell that again.

"Be careful," she said.

"Hey. If I had a last name, 'careful' would be my middle one." He checked his gun, smoothed his sideburns, and gave Franca a grin that lit her up. "See you soon."

"You will," she said, false confidence belying the terrible sense of doom that enveloped her. And before she could say any more, Hellboy had crawled into the tunnel mouth and was pushing his way inside.

She remained in that small room for a minute, listening to the sounds of Hellboy's scrabbling hooves, the scrape of his big hand pulling him through. And when she heard no more she turned and left.

La Casa Fredda was silent, and smelled of the dead.

So where are you leading me? Hellboy thought. *Something to show me? Or just a trap?*

Hellboy had the little flashlight out again, playing it around the cavern he had seen before. He clicked it off every few seconds to check whether the glow of the fire wolf would give it away, but he was in complete darkness.

Of course, now the rules had changed. For all he knew the thing could revert to Adamo in the blink of an eye. Damn thing wasn't only a fire wolf, it was a *were*-fire wolf.

The bats hung across the roof of the cavern, pinprick eyes flickering in the flashlight beam, the stink of their crap filling his nostrils and scouring his throat. They seemed calmed and relaxed, and he could hardly believe that a flaming creature had stormed through this cavern only minutes before. But just as he had seen a hundred places like this, so bats were known to Hellboy. Strange creatures, gentle and usually quiet, they often used unsettling silence to drive unwelcome visitors from their domains. Almost as if they knew the minds of people.

"Hi," he said, and his voice barely echoed against the layers of soft bodies swathing the ceiling.

Something moved. He froze, breathing out softly to see if he could feel it again. A subtle vibration came up through the ground, like a silent groan felt in his chest, and Hellboy heard the mutter of dust and grit falling across the cavern. He shone the flashlight around again but there was nothing to see. Even the bats were unmoved. *Vesuvius*, he thought, and feeling it from this far away could only be bad news.

The dark mouths of several tunnels tempted him on. He could not make out whether they were naturally formed, and there was no clue as to where they led. If his plan had any merit at all, he'd have to find out which one led all the way down to the sea.

He pulled his gun, aimed at the far wall and pulled the trigger. The explosion was immense, and he winced as the echoes roared back at him. A blink later the bats took flight, weaving and swerving around Hellboy's head. He stood motionless, knowing that none of them would collide with him, shining his light up at an angle so that the beam picked out the tornado of creatures. A few seconds later, they swirled down one of the tunnels, and in half a minute they were gone.

"Echo," Hellboy said, and this time his voice came back at him from the bare walls and ceiling.

He headed for the tunnel. Its mouth was quite small, and he had to squeeze inside, but once through it opened up into something resembling a corridor. This one was definitely man-made—he could see tool marks on the walls, and a power cable ran along the floor—though its entrance was disguised to look natural from the cavern. An escape route, for sure. But then what of the power cable?

He walked for a few minutes. The tunnel erred downwards, and here and there very rough stone steps dropped it a long way in a short distance. There was no sign of the bats, nor any indication that the fire wolf had even come this way. But when he breathed in deeply he could smell seawater, and there was a constant breeze running up through the tunnel.

This is the way I'll need to go, he thought. And then he turned around and retraced his steps.

Back in the larger cavern, Hellboy climbed around the wall and examined the mouths of the other three tunnels leading off. None of them gave any clues, but he chose the middle one. It was the smallest, and therefore the most likely to be used as an emergency hiding place.

As he crawled, flashlight gripped between his teeth, he untied the binding knot on the leather thong once more.

Ahhh, the spirit gasped.

"It's in the form of a human," Hellboy said.

Yes . . .

"Did it do that before?"

I never knew his name, the spirit said. *A young man, quite beautiful. The fire wolf entered him, became him, but it was naïve in the ways of our world, and inexperienced in the use of its own powers. I saw the man burn up before my eyes, melting, bubbling, and then the fire wolf was free, and—*

"Old guy it's in now, I saw it burn out of him. But he's fine. And it's done it many times before."

Then over the years, it has perfected its talent to disguise.

"But water hurts it."

In my time I saw it subdued by water, but never for long.

"Great," Hellboy said. "Anything else?"

Only that I doubt your ability to defeat it. And the girl, Hellboy . . . I sensed her mind, and knew her grief. If one sacrifice failed, there is another that can be made.

"I won't let that damn thing near her, ever again."

I was not talking of the fire wolf. Vesuvius rumbles, and you can sate it simply by—

"Okay, night-night time again." He started tying, wondering why he'd been fool enough to bring this deceitful old thing with him in the first place.

She is of the same blood, and—

"Can it." He pulled the knot tight, and his mind was all his own again.

You can sate it, she had said.

"No way," Hellboy muttered, and his words echoed back to haunt him.

Why had the fire wolf's failure to sacrifice Carlotta to Vesuvius driven it to do what it had done? The possibility existed that it was because Hellboy had come and unearthed some of the truth, but he abhorred that idea. That put blame onto him, however passive and indirect, and he remembered the kids he'd seen up in the house, all those burnt people . . .

"Bastard!" he growled, voice muffled in the low, narrow tunnel.

From ahead came an echo that sounded like nothing he had said.

Hellboy paused, striving for silence though he had been making noise before. He tilted his head slightly so that the torch shone straight along the tunnel. It curved slightly ahead of him, and the shadows around the corner seemed darker than they should.

Just his imagination.

He moved on, trying to shift more quietly than before. He debated whether to draw the gun, but favored keeping both hands free; it had not proved effective against the fire wolf up to now.

Rounding the corner, the tunnel opened up into a wide, short corridor that reminded him, for some reason, of a prison. There was a door set in each wall, both closed. And outside one door, footprints in the dust.

"Well I'll be . . ." he muttered. A hidey-hole for the Espositos? Maybe Adamo hadn't killed as many as he'd first feared.

As Hellboy took one step towards the door it opened, and a frightened, old face peered out. He recognized one of the Elders he'd tried talking to back in the house, and she obviously recognized him. Though her eyes went wide for a beat, she soon sighed and dipped back through the door, leaving it open in invitation.

Hellboy unholstered his gun. No need to take any unnecessary chances. Then he stepped forward and glanced through the doorway, finding a scene he never have anticipated.

The room was twenty feet square, and carved out of the rock by hand. It was beautifully furnished: hanging carpets; oil paintings; sofas and easy chairs. Several electric lights hung from cables suspended back and forth across the ceiling. The thick carpet was ridged here and there where the floorboards beneath showed through, and on a large table along the right wall sat several open bottles of wine, and an array of food on silver platters. Cold meats, cheeses and breads set Hellboy's stomach rumbling, and he tried to recall the last time he'd eaten. Pizza with Franca?

"Morning," he said. "Lovely day."

The Elders were all staring at him, and none of them were surprised. They seemed sad, if anything, and he wondered whether they knew exactly what had occurred up at the house this morning. It looked like they'd been down here for a while.

"Don't worry," he said, then frowned. Only the Elders?

"Worry?" one of the men asked.

"Yeah. I'll look after you." He glanced around quickly, but he'd been right the first time; there was no one here who looked younger than eighty.

The old man cackled, a wet sound like damp wood burning. "Thank you, truly, but . . ." And he pointed to the far corner of the room.

What Hellboy had taken to be a glass-faced cabinet was actually a hole in the wall.

And what he'd assumed to be lamp-light reflected from glass was actually the steady glow of fire.

• • •

Franca moved cautiously through the large hallway of La Casa Fredda. She could smell death on the air, and was desperate to leave. But there was something she needed to know. There had been a sensation just now that she did not like, and which she could not bear to associate with the thing Hellboy was pursuing deeper.

If the fire wolf had the power to shake the ground like that, there was no hope for any of them.

She passed through the dining room, looking away from the dead towards the open windows and the gorgeous view across Amalfi that they framed. All seemed normal out there; boats slashed the sea, and there was no sign of panic. If only the atmosphere in here could be so rosy.

The television room appeared untouched, and for that she was glad. She dashed to the window and glanced outside, looking across the garden towards where the main gates stood closed against the world. If Mario and the others were coming back, that's the way they would come. She would keep watch, and soon she would go and find them. Hopefully they had stayed out for breakfast, or to shop, or maybe something of what Hellboy had been trying to tell them had taken root, much as they had projected doubt.

If not, returning home this morning would be a shock for them all.

She flicked on the TV and picked up the remote control, but there was no need to channel surf. Every channel showed the same image: Vesuvius, breathing billowing white smoke at the sky. No lava flows yet, and the rumblings had been contained within the volcano's ragged sides thus far. But the emergency evacuation was fully underway, and surrounding areas had been warned to expect an influx of evacuees.

Franca turned off the TV and took in several deep breaths. She could not help wondering what was happening far below her feet, but Hellboy had sent her back up here for a reason. She placed the remote control very gently on a small table and looked around the room. She tried to conjure memories, but none came. *This is no longer the Esposito house*, she thought, and the idea pursued her back out through the hallway and to the big front doors. Opening them, she welcomed in the sunlight and started for the main gates.

That was when the shakes hit. Her knees turned weak, spilling her to the ground. She smelled roses and burnt meat, and her eyes blurred, not with tears, but with dizziness. *Stay away!* she thought, commanding her grief to swath her with its shocked numbness once again. There would be plenty of time to mourn, if she even got out of this with her life. Now . . . now was *not* the time. If she gave in to her emotions—

(*Mother, lying there dead, her outline burnt into the wall and it must have* held *her there while it*)—

—then she would crumple, and that would put Mario and the others in terrible danger. If she was able to salvage something from this terror—their lives, their escape, and the potential of their futures—that would be something.

If she curled up into a ball here and now, crying for what was passed, there would be no future for any of them.

Franca bit her lip. The pain drew her up and out of herself, and she started walking. Her knees felt stronger. The sun warmed her in a pleasant way, and when it touched the burn on her ankle, the tingling pain was good. It made her realize that she was still alive.

Her mother's pain was over.

So she walked, and the house brooded behind her. It seemed so silent, so peaceful in these gardens that she could scarcely believe what had happened inside, and what might still be happening in those caverns below. She glanced back up at Carlotta's bedroom window, and it seemed weeks ago that she had last been in there, not days.

"What are you still doing here?" a voice called, and Franca turned back towards the main gates. Mario stood there with the others gathered behind him. They were all carrying bags of food and drink, obviously having taken advantage of their early morning meeting to do some shopping before returning home. *Being away saved your lives*, she thought, but the impossibility of trying to explain what had happened struck her then.

Mario glanced over her shoulder at the house, and Franca suddenly feared something much worse.

I haven't been here for so long. What if some of them know?

"Where is *he*?" Mario asked.

"Mario, Hellboy came here to help, and . . ." But she could not finish. How terrible it would sound, relaying what had happened since Hellboy's arrival in Italy. How incriminating.

Mario looked past her again at the house, and she saw the exact moment when he perceived the change in things. His hands went limp and bags fell to the ground. He looked around briefly for the dogs, then back at La Casa Fredda.

"Franca," he said quietly, "what has happened?"

"It's Adamo," she said, unable to hold back the tears. "He's . . . changed. He's the thing that attacked Carlotta, Mario. And now he's changed again and gone mad, and there are—"

"Where's Hellboy?"

"Down in the basements, chasing him." She could see the uncertainty in Mario's eyes, and the others around him were suddenly unsettled.

"What's that smell?" one of the children said. "Is someone cooking breakfast?"

"We have to go," Franca said. "We have to all turn around and leave, go back down into town and hide until Hellboy comes for us."

"And we should believe you?" Mario asked.

"Yes! Because I love my family, and—"

"You *deserted* your family!"

"And because I wanted my own life, you see that as proof of my lack of love?"

Mario started walking, leaving his dropped bags behind. His uncertainty had changed to fear, but he was angry as well, and that was what drove him. Franca tried to halt him but he shrugged her off, pulling away as if she was poison.

"Mario, some of them are dead," she said quietly, hoping that none of the children would hear. He paused beside her, looking at the house but listening.

"Who?" he asked.

"My mother," she whispered, voice only breaking slightly. "Others. But they were dead when Hellboy and I reached here. Mario . . . they're too badly burnt to tell."

He did not move, did not flinch. *Does he know?* Franca wondered. *Am I the only truly ignorant one here.*

Mario looked at the house for a long time, and though there was nothing to see, the peace was unnatural, and the silence was the quiet of the dead. He turned to Franca at last, and it could have been hatred in his eyes.

"For the children," he said. "And for the others. But I'll be coming back as soon as I know they're safe."

Franca nodded. "And if Hellboy isn't back by then, I'll be coming with you."

He did not want her with him, that was clear. But Franca went to the children, smiling and touching heads and hands, and when they asked what was wrong, she said nothing. The other adults only stared at her.

As they all walked back through the gates and down the winding path into Amalfi, Franca realized just how much she and her family had grown apart.

CHAPTER 12

Amalfi

This did not look good. They might be a bunch of old folk hiding out belowground from the fate that had befallen their family and home . . . but their eyes said not. Their eyes spoke of complicity, and Hellboy had seen too much to be seduced by their frailty.

"So you know all about the old boy," he said. He kept the gun swinging by his side, his right hand fisted, and he did not take his eyes from the illuminated hole in the corner of the cavern. *Fighting to come*, he thought, but something was not quite right.

An old woman laughed and put her hands up to her cheeks. She was not looking directly at him, and he wondered whether she was blind.

"You know what that bastard's done upstairs?" he said, gritting his teeth. But it was a stupid question. Of course they knew. Why else would they be down here, and why else . . . ? *Sheltering the fire wolf?* he wondered. *Protecting it? But from what?*

An old man stood—the only one who'd yet spoken—and reached for a bottle on the table. He poured a generous amount of red wine into a goblet and took a drink, sighing in satisfaction, staring at the goblet as if it were the holy grail itself.

The other Elders were all watching him, eyes open as if coveting what he had.

The fire wolf emerged from its hole in the corner of the room. Its flames seemed lessened somewhat, their fury dampened by the presence of the Elders. But still the thing looked at Hellboy with its whitest of eyes.

He lifted his gun and pointed it between those eyes.

The old woman laughed again, a cackle that turned into a gentle, scorching roar. And when Hellboy looked at her, her eyes were alight, and her hair was shrivelling back to her taut scalp.

"Oh, this is *not* good," he muttered, swinging the gun around and blasting the old woman in the face. She flipped back in her chair, old lady's hands clawing at the air, and her laugh rose into a wail of rage. He fired again through the upturned chair, and at the sound of the second gunshot, the room erupted into chaos.

Fire seemed to leap from person to person, but it was not really leaping; it was igniting. The Elders were changing, their clothes burning away, skin blackening, eyes melting, hair shrivelling. The air in the room jumped ten degrees, then another ten, and Hellboy backed to the door, blasting away with his gun wherever he saw any hint of humanity left. The fire wolves twisted and writhed as they changed, and he knew that bullets were no good against their flames. His only hope was that he could kill them in their human form, like the old lady whose head he'd—

The old woman rose from behind her tipped seat, and the chair's upholstery caught on fire. She stretched and screeched, revelling in her natural form.

A whole damn family of fire wolves! Hellboy thought. *This is something that old ghost neglected to mention.*

But maybe she didn't even know. The time would come to ask her, but now—

He holstered his gun—the bullets had done no good, even against flesh and blood—and backed through the doorway.

The Adamo fire wolf was the center of the room, and the others waited around it, watching for some signal which Hellboy knew would inevitably come soon. He had fought this thing three times now, and the idea of taking on . . .

He counted quickly. *Twelve!*

"Hiding away like scared dogs?" he said, but he was not at all certain they could hear. The furnishing was all aflame now, carpet smoldering, and a wine bottle on the table burst, spewing warm wine across the room. A splash of it touched one of the fire wolves and it howled, flinching away and passing one fiery limb across the affected area. Flames flickered there again, but for a beat beforehand, Hellboy saw the unmistakeable glow of sweating flesh.

"So . . ." He drew his gun again, aimed at the Adamo fire wolf. The burning things hissed, and he supposed it could have been laughter. Then Hellboy turned quickly and shot at a rack of wine bottles on the table. Three of them smashed, and wine splashed. A fire wolf screeched as the fluid damped its flames, and Hellboy backed through the door and swung it closed behind him.

As he started running back along the corridor, he chuckled at the idea of closing a door on fire. Still, maybe it would give him a second or two, and for what he had planned he didn't want *too* much of a head-start.

This was all going to be about timing.

For a beat he fished around for the flashlight, but then the door behind him exploded open and shattered against the tunnel wall, and the glow of pursuing fire wolves threw his shadow before him and lit the way. They had him at a disadvantage; he assumed that they knew these tunnels, and the way that room had been furnished hinted that they maintained it as a hideaway should events call for it. And now, events had. Their latest sacrifice to Vesuvius, Carlotta, had taken her own life before they could do whatever they needed with her. The volcano was erupting, and they could fool it no longer.

But what exactly did they fear? Or did they even fear anything at all?

He ran, putting the thinking aside for later. Surviving was his prime concern right now, and he needed to come out of this with the upper hand. If all he did was escape, leaving these damned things to do as they wished, then he would have gained absolutely nothing, other than the knowledge that there was more than one.

Damn, I should have seen this coming!

A few questions had been answered, but a hundred more had been posed. Usually in a case like this he'd beat the truth out of the bad guy, but when the bad guy was mainly comprised of fire, that wasn't the easiest course of action. He'd been wounded enough over the past couple of days; he'd heal, but there was only so much he could take. No, standing and fighting was not the way to gain the advantage in this one.

Not yet.

Making them think he was running . . . feigning fear, leaving a hint of panic in the air behind him . . . *that* was the first step towards control. Besides, he'd sent Franca back into the house. The last place he wanted these things to go was back up there.

Emerging into the main cavern, Hellboy did not hesitate in plunging back into the tunnel down which the bats had fled. He breathed in deeply, picked up the scent of seawater, and heard the fire wolves coming after him.

The doubts began to crowed in within a minute of fleeing the room. There was no way he could tell how many fire wolves were pursuing; glancing back, he only saw a mass of flame coming his way. Sometimes the curves and angles of the tunnel hid the things from view, and he was left with their reflected glow. Other times, they filled the tunnel behind him completely. They burned air and more was sucked in from outside, drawing the briny smell of the sea up to him.

Run, Franca! he thought. They wanted her. Now that Carlotta was dead, they needed another young Esposito to fling into Vesuvius, a sacrifice to the erupting volcano. How the fire wolves were actually related to the Espositos he had yet to discover, but he suspected they were an old family that the creatures had adopted for their own. *But now they're* burning *their family . . .*

He stumbled, reaching out to the tunnel wall for balance. His hooves scraped across the stony floor and he winced at the sound. Fire raged louder than ever behind him, as if the fire wolves had seen his slip and were celebrating the fall of their quarry. He cursed and forged on, rebounding from the wall and using the momentum to carry him faster down the gently sloping tunnel.

At one point he sensed another tunnel opening on his left, and looking up he saw the vaguest hint of daylight filtering in through bends and clefts. This must have been the bats' way in and out, but it was not escape into open air he was seeking. He turned away from the light and headed downward.

The floor suddenly sloped down even more steeply, and the ceiling of the tunnel dropped so that he had to crawl. It was an unnatural stance for him, but the fire wolves took to it easily, gaining on him with every breath. He let his weight move him down, struggling to maintain balance so that his descent did not turn into a roll or fall. A spur of rock jarred him in the back and he grunted, left hand slipping from beneath him and sending him rolling.

Flame roared, unnatural mouths hissed in triumph.

The descent lasted for some time, and then the tunnel opened out again. But there was no floor.

Hellboy had a second to consider his options, and he realized quickly that there were none. He could feel the heat of the fire wolves behind him, and his own hesitant shadow was thrown against the opposite wall of the pit. He took in a deep breath, somehow hoping that would tell him how deep the pit might be. And he had time to smile at this foolishness before he rolled forward and tipped over the edge.

He started counting. One . . . two . . . three . . . As four began, he hit bottom.

He'd been expecting the impact of solid rock, and he'd wrapped his arms around his head and tucked in his knees in preparation. So when the cold bit in, and the water closed around him, it robbed his lungs of air and sent a shock deep into his bones. He gasped and sucked in a mouthful of water, gagging, fighting against the automatic reflex to spit it out and swallowing as much as he could instead. He let the weight of his clothes pull him down and turned onto his back, looking towards where he believed "up" to be.

Flames played across the water's surface. The fire wolves were down in the pit, crawling across the rocky walls like giant spiders. Part of one of them dipped into the water—accidentally or intentionally, Hellboy could not tell—and the flame immediately extinguished, replaced with a spur of gray flesh that might have been a fisted hand.

His lungs were burning. He felt the ebb and flow of the sea, as if in mockery of the breathing he could not perform. And the fire wolves were above him, steaming the water's surface, ready to burn him as soon as he surfaced.

Hellboy closed his eyes and tried to calm himself. He played the flashlight beam around him, using his heavy right hand to steer himself in a rapid circle . . . and then he saw the small tunnel. There was no way of knowing how long it was, or whether there were any air pockets in there at all . . . but he was sure it went the right way, out towards the sea. And the alternative was even worse. If he surfaced, he'd be treading water. Nowhere to run to, nowhere to hide, and the fire wolves would be on him in a beat, grabbing his head and arms and pulling him out, then taking turns to hold him against the side of the pit while the others came in and burnt away another part of him.

So he swam, clamping the torch in his teeth and using both hands to pull himself along the submerged tunnel. His lungs were burning, vision blurring. It was terrifying. Climbing down that narrow tunnel from La Casa Fredda to the caves beneath had been bad enough, but he knew that if he faced a dead end here, the chance of turning around and making it back to the pit was remote. He'd drown down here, and that would leave Franca back on the surface just waiting for these things to re-emerge, track her down, drag her to Vesuvius . . .

Anger bit in and gave him strength. He pulled with his hands, pushed with his feet, and then the sense of space grew around him. He surfaced and gasped in lungfuls of air, catching the flashlight as it dropped from his mouth and wading to the edge of the pool. This new cavern was large and contained a hundred shadowy areas, any one of which could have been the start of a new tunnel.

To his right, one of these shadows suddenly grew bright.

"Oh, gimme a break," he muttered, but he was already pulling himself from the water. His soaked clothes weighed him down, but adrenalin drove him on. By the time the first of the fire wolves entered the new cavern, Hellboy was entering another tunnel.

But he was never so far ahead that the fire wolves did not know which way he had gone.

The sea smell suddenly grew much stronger—the stench of brine, the rot of old seaweed and dead fish—and he knew that he was where he needed to be.

Allowing the fire wolves to remain close on his tail had not been difficult. In fact, he'd had little choice in the matter. They were fast, and for the last couple of minutes, Hellboy had felt their hot breaths on the back of his neck. Several times he'd suspected that they would bring him down before he reached his destination, but then another swelling and retreating pool was before him, and he knew that the open sea was close.

This was when timing meant everything.

As he stopped at the edge of the shifting pool of water, standing in a mass of rotten and rotting seaweed, he turned to face the approaching fire wolves. They swarmed into the wide, low cavern, spreading around him and closing off any possible escape route. He did a quick count and was pleased to see all twelve of those bastards down here with him. Good. At least that meant Franca might have a reasonable chance at escape.

But soon, he knew, the clock would be ticking for her once again.

"You run like crippled dogs," he panted, but he had no idea whether the things understood, or even heard what he was saying.

The Adamo wolf was easy to recognize. Not only was it the largest of them, it also stood at their center, the sun around which all the others orbited. Its star-bright eyes glared at Hellboy, and he hoped they were full of rage.

Hellboy casually pulled his gun and fired at the Adamo wolf three times. Little happened—ripples of flame sprang out from where the bullets passed right through—but the thing lifted its head and roared flame at the ceiling.

"Wimp," Hellboy said. He was acting casual, but each moment was judged, every second measured. He glanced around at the others. Yes, they were following the Adamo-wolf's lead. That was good.

"So you chase me all the way down here and can't even decide—"

The Adamo wolf came for him. He heard or sensed no instruction, but the other eleven all remained in place around the cavern as the fire wolf leaped through the air, fiery limbs extended, ready to burn him down.

Here we go! Hellboy thought, and he fell back, hands held up to warn off the attacking demon. Everything around him was fire. He squeezed his eyes shut and reached forward with his big right hand, spreading his fingers wide until he felt the white-hot heat give way to something slightly more solid.

Teeth of fire bit into his shoulder and left arm, and as he screamed his own breath caught fire.

He stumbled backwards, feeling the welcoming coolness of water closing around his legs as he entered the pool. Then he closed his right hand, took a deep breath and shoved backwards with every remaining ounce of strength he possessed.

As the flame teeth closed again, scorching into the flesh of his chest and neck, Hellboy felt the blessed relief of water swilling across every inch of his body. The fire stuttered out, replaced by pain. The fire wolf screeched, and clouds of steam rose around him, demonic shapes twisting within and through them as the other fire wolves scurried around the edges of the subterranean sea.

Then they were beneath the water together.

Hellboy kept his eyes open so that he could look into Adamo's face as it appeared once again.

The fire wolf struggled in his grasp, flames receding as flesh replaced them. Hellboy's fisted right hand was forced apart, but his fingers were still buried in the man's flesh, and the pain he saw in Adamo's eyes gave Hellboy reason to smile. Remaining beneath the water, held down by Hellboy, the old man's fires went out totally, and he was as gray as ash.

His eyes were now deep, dark pits, nothing human within them, and no flames. Hellboy wondered whether the man Adamo could every truly return after this.

He stood, dragging his new prisoner upright with him. Hellboy could feel the strong surge and fade of the sea around his thighs, and the open water beyond the caves called to him. But he needed one more deep breath before he undertook the last, long swim, and he also needed to know what was happening to the others.

Still aflame. He cursed. He'd been hoping that they were somehow connected to Adamo's state, but life was never so convenient.

Adamo steamed and spat in Hellboy's hand, and even in the few seconds they stood half out of the water, his skin began to glow, and flames licked across his throat and beneath his arms.

"Oh no you don't!" Hellboy said. He pushed Adamo back towards the water's surface, but with one final burst of strength, the old man—the fire wolf clothed in human flesh—let out an ear-splitting screech, clicks and whistles snapping at the air of the cavern.

Every one of the other eleven fire wolves froze in place, as if listening.

As Hellboy gathered in a huge breath and ducked down into the water once more, his last image of the other creatures was as they turned and started fleeing from the cavern.

This chase was not over, he knew. It had only just begun.

Chapter 13

Amalfi

Amalfi was abuzz with news of Vesuvius. People were excited more than scared, and Franca had never felt so removed from the place she had once called home. Now it was not only her differences with her family that repulsed her, but also the attitudes of the Amalfians themselves. With such terrible things happening in their midst, still they laughed and shouted to each other in the streets, and revelled in the sense of companionship that the vague danger of the volcano engendered in them.

They don't know what's been going on, she thought, but she could not make excuses for them. Amalfi had been sullied by Adamo, and for her, it could never be the same again.

She followed Mario and the others down the winding, steep paths from the hillside and into the bustle of the town's center. All the way down he talked with some of the others, letting the kids follow them, and Franca came on behind. She wished Mario had wanted to talk with her—ask her what had happened, find out exactly what she had seen back up at La Casa Fredda—but there was something about him that she recognized from looking at herself in the mirror that morning: he was scared. She had told him that people were dead and that the other Espositos were in danger, and now fear ruled his emotions. Every time he glanced back she tried to catch his eye, but he looked only at the children.

At least he knows his priorities, she thought.

They needed somewhere safe. Once Franca knew that they were shut away out of sight, she would take Mario back up the hillside to their family home, and there they would discover the full extent of what had happened.

And Hellboy? she wondered. *Will he be back by then? Will he have defeated Adamo?* She guessed not. She had little idea of what he had planned, but she was sure that at least part of it involved a trip back to the volcano. She could not help feeling that it would be too little, too late.

A rush of hatred came over her then. Her face hardened, and she looked at the children's backs before her, wondering how many of those they knew and loved were now dead. Adamo . . . that *bastard*! He had duped their family, nurturing them as a line of sacrificial victims to save his own . . . skin? No, not skin. He might have looked human for as long as she'd known him, but he was something far less, something more basic. Whatever arcane means he had employed to dress himself in human guise had been melted away by Hellboy's presence, and now he was naked once again. The fire wolf. The fire demon, as the shrivelled corpse of the ancient demon hunter in Pompeii had called him. Franca only hoped that what had begun two thousand years ago could be ended today.

Mario crossed the square before the cathedral and passed along one of the narrow walkways beside the wide, impressive steps. There were several small shops and a café down here, and Mario paused to talk to an incredibly old man sitting and smoking at one of the café tables. The others kept a respectful few steps away, and Franca also held back, struck by a shattering sense of nostalgia.

Here was old Orso, the man who had allegedly owned this café for sixty years. Franca had sat at the pavement tables many times with her friends, drinking espresso and smoking illicit cigarettes, eyeing the boys as they sped through the square on their scooters and sometimes edged their way towards the cafe, only to be chased away by Orso. The stench of their exhaust fumes spoiled his coffee, he would say, constant cigarette hanging from his lips. Even when Franca was a child, his face had been a mask of leather, browned and grizzled by the sun and cigarette smoke. But Orso had always borne a worn-in smile, and he had long been a friend to the true inhabitants of Amalfi. He charged tourists high so that he could charge people he knew low, and his café was a favorite among locals.

Mario spoke to him now, and Franca could perceive the deference in her cousin's manner. He never touched the old man, but his hands hovered close, expressing much of whatever he was saying with lively gesticulations. Orso nodded, expression unchanging, and halfway through Mario's talk, he lit a new cigarette.

Once, Mario looked down at the ground and held one hand across his mouth, obviously trying to compose himself. Orso glanced across at Franca, giving nothing away.

At last the young man smiled and nodded his thanks, grasping one of Orso's hands in both of his and shaking once. Then he turned back to the children and adults who had been waiting behind him. He spoke quickly to the adults, and as each child passed him by and entered into Orso's café, he touched their heads and whispered something encouraging.

But little encouragement was needed. "Ice cream!" Orso said, and his rugged laughter accompanied the children's excited chatter.

Mario came back to Franca. "It'll be safe here," he said.

"You're suggesting I stay?" Franca frowned.

"I don't think La Casa Fredda—"

"You have no idea what I've seen today," she said quietly, feeling Orso's eyes upon her. "You have no idea because you won't let me tell you, and now you want me to hide away while you put yourself in danger?"

"I believe you about the house. It looked wrong, lifeless, and I have to go and—"

"And you believed me about Adamo?"

Mario stared at Franca for a very long time. He blinked slowly, never taking his eyes from hers, and what scared her the most was that she could not read him. He was appraising her, but she had no idea what he saw.

"Orso has known Adamo forever," Mario said.

"That means nothing."

"Doesn't it?"

Franca frowned, because nothing was making sense.

"Franca, I'm sorry, but I need to get back to the house, and I don't want you with me."

"I don't give a shit what you want, Mario," she said, louder this time. Looking over her cousin's shoulder, she swore she could see a glitter of amusement in Orso's gaze. "I'm coming with you. I already know what you'll find at the house, but I need to know what happened with Hellboy."

"Why? That demon comes and—"

"I need to know because if he loses to Adamo, I'll be the next to die."

Mario sighed in frustration. "What is Hellboy to you?"

Franca did not answer, because truly, she did not know.

"Come on then," her cousin said. "But without the kids, I'm running. Make sure you keep up."

"I might just surprise you," Franca said, and Mario's slight smile lit her up inside.

Surprise him she did. In her years at university in Sorrento, Franca had been an enthusiastic member of the long distance running team. She'd already completed the Rome marathon, and she'd had plans to travel further afield—London, perhaps, or maybe even New York. Mario was fit as well, and by the time they were back across the square and climbing once again, she detected a definite air of competition in their energetic jog. It should have been vaguely amusing, but she could not find it in herself to smile.

There was almost a carnival atmosphere in Amalfi. Fifteen miles to the north, Vesuvius was venting, boiling steam and gases billowing miles into the sky. The eruption was not quite visible from here yet, but the promise of evacuees had the town buzzing. There would be people to accommodate, and more importantly, to feed and water. Restaurants were drafting in extra staff. Nobody expected the worst.

No one cares about Carlotta or my mother, Franca thought, a random idea that saddened her as she ran. Most people here probably weren't even aware that Carlotta was dead.

And after all this, when it was over one way or another, what would Amalfi make of the slaughter at La Casa Fredda? She had no wish to muse upon that. It was too horrible to contemplate, and until it was over the possible outcomes all felt bad.

She let Mario lead the way. The higher they went, and the closer they drew to the house, the more nervous Franca became. Her heart thumped from the exertion, but there was something else controlling her heartbeat, she knew. Fear. She had no idea what she would find upon arriving at the house, nor who or what would be waiting there for her.

Was she betraying Hellboy's trust by returning here now? He had sent her away to lead the others to safety, but she knew that he'd had her own safety at the forefront of his mind as well. Adamo was seeking another Esposito to sacrifice, and she was in grave danger—

—*(her dream, the book, and remembering it now it was Adamo burning her name onto the final page)*—

—but she could not just stand by and let things happen, hiding in that café with the others. She had seen and heard things that made no sense, and she had a duty to herself to discover what those things meant. Besides, she had left Amalfi and the Espositos years ago. She was her own woman.

"Mario!" she called. They were up out of the town now, skirting past the less frequent buildings on the steep hillside upon which La

Casa Fredda had stood for many centuries. They were almost there, and she had to make one last attempt to persuade Mario to turn back. He would know about the horrors in the house soon enough; the dead aunties, the burnt relatives. But danger might still stalk those silent rooms and corridors.

He paused, leaning on his knees and breathing in heavily. "What is it?"

"Go back," she said.

But Mario laughed, and she knew that he was strong.

"If you won't, then at least let me go first. And if you see anything . . . strange, promise me *then* you'll go back."

"I've always loved you, Franca," he said. "Even when you left I still loved you, like any good cousin loves another. But I won't listen to you now. If it's as bad as you say . . ." He trailed off and looked across Amalfi, the beautiful town that had been their home forever.

"It's worse than you can imagine," she said. "I saw—"

"Then I can't help blaming you," Mario cut in. "Come on." And he turned and continued running up the path.

Franca ran hard. Their vaguely competitive run became a race, and whenever she thought she was gaining on Mario, he put on a burst of speed, or blocked the narrow paths so that she could not squeeze past. By the time they reached La Casa Fredda's front gates they were both panting hard and sweating freely, and it was only the sight of the deserted house that brought them to a halt. They stood between the two gate columns, the heavy cast iron gates standing open as usual, and stared at the façade before them.

The garden was silent but for the occasional swish of a breeze from the sea. The house was still, other than the gently billowing curtains dancing in several open windows and doors. There was no one there.

Franca was desperate to see the telltale flash of red as Hellboy emerged from the house, but there was nothing.

"Are you coming in with me?" Mario asked. He looked at Franca sidelong. She could see for the first time just how scared he was, and she was glad. His shirt was plastered to his skin with sweat, heavy black hair pasted down across his forehead, and his eyes were wide and wary.

"If we see Adamo—" she began.

"Then I have questions for him myself!" Mario said harshly. But there was little belief in his eyes for anything Franca had said.

She ran. With the surprise lead on Mario, she was the first to reach the house's main doors. They were ajar, and as she pushed one of them all the way open, Mario cried out behind her, and she realized her mistake.

A trap! she thought, and spinning around she saw the three flaming shapes streaking towards them across the garden.

Three?

Mario caught her eyes. He was terrified.

"Run!" she shouted. "Get away from here!" And then she entered the house and sprinted for the staircase.

Mario screamed, and then the burning things crashed through the doors behind her.

Halfway up the wide staircase Franca looked up, and fire touched her eyes.

Hellboy swam. With his right hand fisted into the flesh of Adamo Esposito, he could only use his left to pull at the water, kicking hard with his booted hooves. So pull and kick he did, with the flashlight clenched once again in his teeth and providing minimal illumination against the murky water ahead. A few fish darted before him, and one or two floated dead, shoved down below the land by the vagaries of the tide. Seaweed drifted by, sometimes settling across his face like some gentle, insistent hand. He wiped it away and went on.

Adamo bobbed behind him, apparently lifeless. Hellboy knew he was still alive, however, because every now and then his fingers burned, and bubbles rose from the gray body. Naked and withered, the old man looked decidedly unthreatening. His skin was blistered here and there, his hair drifted around his head like the tendrils of rotting seaweed, and his eyes were open and sightless. But there was that intermittent heat, and the knowledge that he was something far more than a drifting, old corpse.

If and when we make it out of here and climb from the sea . . . But Hellboy cast the thought adrift. Whatever happened then, he'd *deal* with then. For now he had to swim, hold his breath, and stay alive.

The currents in the water grew stronger, and he angled his head upwards. The light splayed across foaming water, and Hellboy rose carefully, breaking surface in a small cavern barely higher than his head. He took in a few deep breaths, then ducked and started swimming again.

There was not a second to spare. He knew that those things would be on him as soon as they could, and as he swam he tried to imagine and time their journey. Back up through the caverns, into the basements, then the house, out through the gardens and down amongst the buildings of Amalfi, and what panic they would cause in the streets! Then to the harbor, and they would patrol the seafront and wait for him to emerge, dragging their leader with him.

His absolute priority was leaving the sea and getting out of Amalfi before the fire wolves even reached the harbor.

He kicked hard against the current, and then the sea grabbed hold of him and sucked them both out, spinning and dipping them deep so that the old man was dragged across the seabed. Hellboy did little to protect him, and a smear of blood followed them. *Great White sharks in the Med*, Hellboy thought, but he grinned around the torch. Even he couldn't have such bad luck . . . could he?

Helpless in the hand of the sea, Hellboy expended what little energy he had left avoiding collisions with spurs of rock. At last he looked up and saw daylight, and his lungs burst for contact. He kicked up. For a beat he thought Adamo was holding him back—dying in the water, perhaps, and determined to drag Hellboy back down here with him, embraced in death. But when he glanced down, the old man was merely caught in a swirl of current. His eyes seemed to reflect the sun, and Hellboy knew he had to prepare himself for when they broke surface.

Once out of the water, he had no idea how long it would take before Adamo Esposito became the fire wolf once again. But as soon as he had the chance, there was someone he could ask.

He surfaced, spluttering and sucking in a wheezing breath. He pulled Adamo behind him, lifting him so that his head broke surface as well. He looked dead, but those pulses of heat still beat into Hellboy's right hand, as if the old man had a heartbeat of fire thudding away somewhere deep within his deceptive flesh.

Looking around, trying to place exactly where those underground caverns had vented into the sea, he saw waves breaking against cliffs not a dozen feet away. The swell was carrying him very slowly in that direction, and unless he did something soon both he and the old man would be dashed against the rocks.

"Going to kick for me?" he asked, but the old man bobbing a breath away did not seem to hear. His eyes were still open, glittering with water but little else. If Adamo was still alive and conscious, then he was biding his time. "Thought not," Hellboy said. "So here I am, doing all the work again."

He swam them away from the cliffs, heading along the coast towards where he could see Amalfi's harbor wall stretching out into the sea. That would be a safer place to land; it would also be a good place for an ambush. But one thing at a time. Swimming took all of his strength, hauling the waterlogged fire wolf and kicking against the tide.

When he drew close to the harbor wall he trod water for a while, scanning the shore and harbor, squinting against the sun reflecting from the sea's surface. He was trying to discern any hints of fire anywhere across the face of Amalfi, but as far as he could make out there were none. *It'll never be that easy. They'll hide themselves away, revert to the Elders, however the hell that works*. But he was out of options. His right hand was almost frozen into place where it fisted into Adamo's body. He had to leave the water, find Franca, and then make his way to Vesuvius.

The volcano was eagerly ejecting rock and gas from its furious body. Here in his hand, Hellboy held something that belonged back inside.

In the end he dragged Adamo up onto the beach beside the harbor wall. It looked safer, was easier to approach, and if the Elders sprang an ambush he'd have a better chance of fighting back. Hellboy slumped in the sand, gasping, and as he caught his breath he maintained his grip on the old man. He still felt the occasional pulse of heat, but he was reasonably certain that the old bastard was still unconscious. Maybe as humans could be destroyed by fire, perhaps Hellboy had drowned this fire wolf with water? But it seemed unlikely. Hell, it seemed too easy.

An old woman was walking her dog on the beach. It was a little, yappy thing, making up for its lack of size and strength by barking incessantly at whoever dared invade its personal space. This dog's personal space seemed to extend along half the beach, because as soon as it saw Hellboy and Adamo it started, *yap yap yap*, and Hellboy actually shifted his left hand slightly towards his holster.

Damn, I'm tired, he thought. He raised his hand instead and waved at the woman, but she was already hastily dragging the dog up towards the road. But the dog's barking brought his attention back to Adamo, and he realized he faced another acute problem. Here he was soaked to the skin, with his huge right hand grasping a naked old man so tightly that the fingers were piercing his chest and side. There was no blood—weird—and the old man showed no exterior signs of life.

There was no way that Hellboy could let him go.

"Hmm." He sat up and tugged Adamo closer to him, checking his forehead for heat. Still cool. The man's eyes were open, but there was nothing even remotely human about them, nothing *living*. Yet Hellboy remained certain that he was not dead.

Untying the knotted thong around the bone once more, Hellboy retied it in a simpler knot and hung it around his neck again.

Thoughtful of you, the ghost said.

"It's got nothing to do with thoughtfulness. I've got the damned fire wolf and it feels dead, but—"

Fool! You can't kill it so easily. Water will temper its fire, but little more. Ahhh, I sense its mind . . . horrible, wretched! And afraid.

"Afraid?"

It is desperate. It has destroyed all that it built.

"Slaughtered. Yeah."

It will need to build again.

"But first . . ."

First it must appease Vesuvius, or the old god will rise and come in pursuit of it.

"Figures." Hellboy tried to imagine what that would entail, whatever ancient power existed at the heart of Vesuvius rising up to chase after Adamo and his clan. "That would be bad."

Vesuvius' fury will be greater than ever . . . it will know of the fire wolf's deceit, and you must put the creature back into the volcano still, alive, still raging—

"Newsflash, lady. Not 'it,' but 'them.' Twelve of them."

In his mind, Hellboy felt the ghost voice fall silent with shock.

"Yeah, well," he said, "stay quiet for a while. But don't tell me the odds."

He considered tying it away again, but thought better of it. There was a chase to come, and he might not find time to be untying knots. Unpleasant though it was, the old demon hunter would have a place in his mind for the foreseeable future.

He scanned the beach, and close to where the harbor mole stretched out into the sea, several young couples were playing an impromptu game of volleyball. They'd left their stuff on several blankets arrayed around a huge picnic hamper.

Hellboy stood and hefted Adamo up into both arms. That way he could carry him like a baby, keep an eye on the bastard's condition, and hopefully get away with what he had planned.

As he approached the kids they paused in their game, watching wide-eyed as he clomped along the beach. He'd long since discovered that hooves weren't the best type of feet for walking on sand, and his exhaustion was aggravated as he sank in several inches with each step.

One of the boys shouted in surprise, but tow of the girls rushed to their bags and brought out cameras.

"Hey!" Hellboy called. "My grandfather's ill! Can I borrow one of your blankets? Poor guy's cold."

One of the girls shouted something in Italian, looking around at her friends and throwing the ball down in disgust. She dashed forward, flicked a blanket free of sand and stepped hesitantly towards Hellboy.

He took the blanket and dropped it across Adamo's body, tucking it beneath his chin and making sure it covered where his fingers penetrated the flesh.

"Thanks," he said, nodding at the girl. She was beautiful, her skin caramel-brown, bikini a mere afterthought. "Grazie!"

The girl smiled and said something he couldn't follow, and then Hellboy turned and walked towards the road. It led along the harbor into town, and from there he'd begin his search for Franca.

Twelve?

"All the same."

They must have followed the first, after they realized its escape. I have to think.

"Think away." He approached the harbor's parking lot.

No sirens, no panic, no running and screaming and shouting, and that's a good start.

But a few minutes later, as he drew level with the road that led up through the town, the running and screaming and shouting began.

And somewhere in the cacophony, Hellboy heard his name.

CHAPTER 14

Amalfi

Halfway up the grand staircase, Franca lost hope, and felt the dregs of sanity threatening to leave her. In the hallway behind her milled the three fire wolves from outside. Above her on the second floor landing, several more were gathered at the head of the stairs, their flames combining to form an impregnable barrier. She could feel the dreadful heat of them before and behind, and when she edged to the banister and glanced over, down at the narrow walkway that led to the door to the basements, she saw another. It looked up at her with bright, unblinking eyes staring from a sea of fire. Those eyes were blank and timeless as the stars.

"Who are you all?" she cried, but their answer was to burn.

She turned slowly, afraid that any sudden movements would provoke a harsh response. Looking back towards the main doors she could see no sign of Mario, though one door had been smashed from its hinges and lay propped against the other. She could see into the gardens, and there were two definite tracks of burnt grass leading from far corners towards the entrance. No body.

Please be gone, she thought. *Please escape, Mario, and tell everyone what you've seen.*

The things seemed to be waiting, at the top of the stairs and at the bottom. So Franca waited in the middle.

"Who are you?" she shouted again, and this time an answer came. It revealed itself slowly, but with each heartbeat Franca realized that the truth had never been very far away.

One of the fire wolves below her in the hallway was the first to change. It slumped to the ground, its four legs splayed, head resting on its forepaws. The flames dancing along its back lessened, growing smaller and smaller before stuttering out in small patches. Beneath, she saw the unmistakeable shine of wet skin. The extinguished areas grew and joined, then shifted down the thing's legs and onto its head. The body beneath shook as if flicking the flames away. It was naked and hot and wet, the moisture lifting rapidly in geysers of steam when the flesh rippled. The thing turned onto its back and snapped arms and legs out straight, a crackling napping sound indicating the presence of bones once more.

It rolled again onto hands and knees, raised its head and howled.

Great-Aunt Sophia! Franca thought, but the surprise was less than it should have been. Sophia had been one of the Elders for as long as Franca could remember, and as she glanced around at the other fire wolves—and more of them were changing now, twisting and sometimes thrashing as their flames receded to flesh—she realized how easily she had ignored the truth.

Franca sat on the stairs and watched, because there was no way for her to escape. One fire wolf remained in the hallway and one at the head of the stairs, each of them threatening agonies she could not bear to imagine. The others changed, manifesting into old, naked people who were not human. They stood uncertainly and smiled at Franca, but there was nothing pleasant about their expressions. They were unconcerned at their nakedness.

And then Great-Aunt Sophia spoke.

"Franca," it said. "I never thought I'd see—"

"Shut up, monster!" Franca shouted, more afraid than angry. "You killed my *mother*!" The old woman looked briefly hurt, but then the smile returned.

"We don't need to talk," she said. "But there are a few things I need you to do. First, we all need clothes, so if you'd remain where you are while we dress . . . we won't be long . . . we don't want to miss the fun."

"The fun of watching Hellboy kick Adamo's ass?" she asked.

Sophia laughed as she started climbing the stairs. She said no more, but continued laughing, leading other Elders up towards the rooms they had occupied for countless years. They moved much faster than they should have, their ancient bodies still exuding the unnatural heat of their recent incarnations.

Countless questions buzzed Franca's head, but she would not give them the satisfaction.

So she waited on that staircase for several minutes, conscious of the fire wolves above and below her promising pain were she to attempt escape. She edged over slightly so that she could look down at the doorway to the basements. It was open, its painted metal face blistered by heat. However much she concentrated, Hellboy did not walk through that door.

"He's gone," Sophia said. The old woman descended and sat on the stair beside her. She was dressed, though she had taken no notice of what she had shrugged on. *Dressed to look human and nothing more*, Franca thought.

"So where's Adamo?" she asked.

"Gone too," Sophia said. "Taken Hellboy down, deep as he can, and there the demon will burn for a long time." She looked at Franca and her eyes were dark and bottomless, not the rheumy old eyes that Franca remembered.

"So now what?" Franca asked, but she had a good idea of what came next. She was terrified, and though she tried not to show it, there was a quaver in her voice and a shake in one hand.

"Now you do what Carlotta would not," Sophia said. She stood and shouted instructions at the other Elders.

Franca stood and ran down the stairs, faintness washing over her. *Hellboy!* she thought, but still he did not come. One of the still-blazing fire wolves flowed before her and raised itself on its hind legs, roaring at the ceiling and blistering the old paint there. Franca cried out unconsciously, lifting her hands to shield her eyes from the heat.

Hands grasped her arms, and old people who she had once known and loved marched her from La Casa Fredda.

Three of them went to fetch three of the big cars they kept in the house's extensive garage. The men holding Franca dug their fingers into her arms, and she had to bite her tongue to stop herself crying out at the pain. There was no sign of Mario, and for that she was glad, but she could not shake the feeling of abandonment.

First chance I get, she thought. *I'll be away from them the first chance I get.* She tried to calm herself, control her breathing, because she knew that time was not now. She had to let them think they had her, and had defeated her. Get in the car, curl up and cry, exude weakness just as they still bled heat. And when the time came, she would not hesitate for a second to kill them.

These were not the Elders she had known, if they had ever really existed at all.

These were monsters.

Hellboy stood by the buses and cars that were disgorging evacuees from closer to Vesuvius, listening to their excited chatter and wishing he could understand more Italian, and then Mario was rushing along the street towards him, his clothes singed, hair shrivelled by heat, and he was shouting.

"Hellboy! Franca! *Hellboy!*"

Startled people parted to let him pass, and with everything that was plastered on the news and rife in their minds, perhaps they made some link between this screaming man and the volcano to the north. *And they'd be right*, Hellboy thought, squeezing with his right hand but feeling no change in Adamo. The old man made no sound, seemed to feel no pain. Not good, but good to know.

"Hellboy, they have Franca, many of them, I hid and watched and they put her in a car—"

"The others?" Hellboy asked.

"Safe. I left them with—"

"Don't tell me!" he hissed. "Not here." He nodded down at Adamo, and Mario took a couple of steps back.

"But . . . ?" Franca's cousin said.

"Lots to tell," Hellboy said. "You okay?"

Mario was shaking his head, unable to take his eyes from the Esposito family patriarch.

"Mario!" Hellboy said. There were lots of people milling around now, and Hellboy knew that they'd be suspicious. To his right a policeman was guiding traffic in and trying to squeeze it all into the beach parking lot, but he had already glanced over a couple of times. *How the hell do I explain this?* Hellboy thought. "Mario, we need a car."

"A car," Mario said softly, and Hellboy didn't like the look in his eyes. Even after what Franca had told Mario and what he must have seen—and Hellboy would ask him about that soon enough—his gaze still contained a measure of respect, and a mindless love for Adamo Esposito.

"Mario, your past is over," Hellboy said quietly, hoping that the man could detect the intonation in the English.

Mario blinked a few times and looked at Hellboy, his face hard and shocked. Then he sighed and slumped, nodding his head. "I know," he said. "But the past . . ."

"Is dangerous," Hellboy finished for him. "Believe me, I know. Bad place to dwell. Do-gooders and touchy-feely types will tell you to live for the present, but I need you to help me save the future of what's left of your family. Think you can do that?"

"Let's walk," Mario said, glancing around at the curious onlookers. "We're attracting too much attention." And that was when Hellboy knew that Mario would help.

They walked in the direction from which Mario had run, most passers-by paying more attention to Hellboy than what he carried.

"Are you hurt?" Hellboy asked quietly, and the thing in his arms shifted.

"It's not too bad," Mario said. "I ran, one came at me by the gates, but I got away."

"No," Hellboy said. He paused, looking down at Adamo's calm, deceptive face. *Had he really moved?* He bore a very slight smile, but the heat Hellboy could detect with his fingers was no greater than when they'd been beneath the sea. "You didn't escape. They let you."

"But I ran." He looked at Adamo's face, and there was anger there at last. "What has he done?"

"'He' is an 'it'."

Mario paused in the square before the cathedral, looking up at the magnificent façade with tears in his eyes.

"Mario, we need a car," Hellboy said again. "Can you get us one without having to go back up there?" He nodded back at the hillside, towards where La Casa Fredda stood dead and empty. He'd spent enough time there, seen enough bad things, and they didn't have the time to climb that hill one more time.

"Yes, I can get a car," Mario said. "My girlfriend lives not far from here. But where are we going? And where are those things taking Franca?"

"Vesuvius," Hellboy said, and a shiver passed through the body in his arms. Perhaps it was fear. That pleased Hellboy.

A few people around them glanced his way when he spoke the volcano's name, and Mario frowned, shaking his head in confusion.

"Plenty of time to talk in the car," Hellboy said. "While you're driving, I've got some questions to ask this son of a bitch. First, though, there's somebody else I need to talk to. Lead the way, and don't get all freaked out if it seems like I'm talking to myself."

Mario frowned but nodded, and Hellboy followed him into a side street.

"I need to keep Adamo weak," Hellboy whispered. "How long will he be like this?"

Water might keep him down, the old ghost said. She sounded hollow, shocked into hopelessness.

"Hey, wake up. I can do this," Hellboy said.

You can do what I could not? she asked, anger tainting her voice.

"With your help. You were on your own, weren't you? Back then in Pompeii, there was only you."

And no one would believe.

"Well, I believe. But I need to know what you know."

Such life, the ghost said, and there it was, the familiar shade of jealousy that Hellboy heard in any ghost's voice.

"Lady, yours ended two thousand years ago."

Mario glanced back, frowning, and Hellboy smiled and nodded, indicating that they should move on. The man looked down at Adamo. Behind the confusion in his eyes there lay hatred, and Hellboy knew that could serve them both well.

Water, the ghost said. *As much as you can, that will keep it subdued. It has merged with a man, and in the human form it knows a man's weaknesses. Ahh, weaknesses . . . .*

"That's it? A little water's gonna keep his fire out?"

Weak as he already is, yes. But not forever.

"We need to talk more soon." The ghost was silent. "Hey. Soon?" Still no response.

Just what I need, Hellboy thought. *A petulant spirit advisor.*

They walked up through the town, and outside a grocer's Hellboy waited while Mario went in and bought as many bottles of water as he could carry in a plastic bag. He asked Hellboy what they needed it for, but Hellboy shook his head and said, "In the car."

Soon after the shop Mario took them right, into a narrow gap between buildings that Hellboy had to negotiate sideways. Stuck between those two walls, Adamo began to shake in his arms, steam rising from his mouth and heat pulsing from him in several huge waves.

"Water bottle!" Hellboy said, and when Mario came with one Hellboy said, "In his mouth, all of it!" Mario poured, and steam billowed around them as soon as the water touched the insides of the old man's mouth. The last few glugs from the bottle spilled down his cheeks and chin, and Hellboy saw his throat flex as he swallowed. The heat faded, the man stilled.

"Good," Hellboy said. "It works. Now you know why we needed the water."

Mario looked stunned, but Hellboy recognized the expression: this was so far beyond his experience that his mind was not yet fully comprehending what he saw. For now, that was good, because it meant he could still function.

"Get the car, Mario. And if you don't have a phone, get your girlfriend's. I need to call a friend."

"Who?"

"Someone alive."

Mario drove, using one hand while he applied salve to burns on his neck and forearm with the other. He had been curiously quiet since leaving his girlfriend's place, and Hellboy was happy to give him time.

Hellboy sat in the back, with Adamo's unresponsive body strapped into the corner of the rear seat. The seatbelt would do little were he to change, but it meant that Hellboy had his hands free to use the phone. He only hoped it could make international calls.

He sat there for a while, frowning, doing his best to remember Liz Sherman's cell phone number. He cursed when he couldn't. Damn technology, you didn't need to remember numbers when you had speed dial, but then when your phone took a swim and died . . .

So he dialled B.P.R.D. headquarters instead, and they patched him through to Liz. She was still in Seattle, and when she answered he could immediately hear the strain in her voice.

"Hey, Liz," he said, "how're the ghoulies on that yacht?"

"Hey, H.B! Huh. Sometimes people just set out to piss you off, and then they try to go even further. What is it about humans that makes us so deceitful?"

"Don't ask me," he said, chuckling at the old joke. But Liz seemed beyond humor.

"No one knows anyone, isn't that the truth? We're mysterious to all but ourselves, and even that . . . well, we both know where the weirdest stuff is."

"Closer to home," Hellboy said.

"Yeah."

Hellboy saw Mario glance at him in the rearview mirror, and he offered a comforting smile. Mario did not return it. Hellboy could hardly blame him.

"So the yacht's not haunted," Hellboy said.

"I'm more sure every hour I spend here that it is," Liz said. "That's the thing. The woman who called us up here is suddenly denying she even made the call. She can't refute ownership of the yacht, but she says she hardly uses it. She won't let me on board, but I'm staying close by. Sat on the jetty yesterday evening for a few hours, and I saw some very weird things."

"So the woman's happy with a ghost ship, leave her to it."

"I should, shouldn't I?" she asked, and for a beat the old Liz was there.

"Any nasty stuff going on?"

"That's just it, H.B. I'm sure there is. I think this woman's being tortured somehow, and how can I just let that go?"

"Hmm." Hellboy looked across at Adamo, feeling the old man's forehead to make sure he wasn't too hot. A brief, tiny trickle of flame flowed from the old man's nose and broke across his lip, fading to the air like a breath of smoke. "Hang on, Liz," he said. He propped the phone in the door handle, opened a bottle of water and poured it into Adamo's throat.

The steam came again, and the old body shook and convulsed. But once again, by the time the bottle was half empty, the water simply filled Adamo's mouth and poured out over his chin.

"Gotta keep an eye on this one," Hellboy muttered to no one.

"What's happening?" Mario asked.

"Sorry, I'll warn you next time." Hellboy picked up the phone.

"That sounded interesting," Liz said.

"That's one word for it. Another word is 'screwed'. It's all gone bad here, Liz. Really bad. Wish I'd taken you up on that offer to come over."

"I still can."

"Too late."

"Vesuvius?"

"Oh, you've seen that."

"You're kidding? It's all over the news. Half a dozen really bad Pompeii films are probably on right now, if I could be bothered to surf the channels."

"Yeah. Well. There's more than one fire wolf. A dozen at least, but I've got their head honcho with me right now."

"How did you manage that?"

"Lots of water. The Mediterranean."

"What form's he in?"

"Human." Hellboy looked Adamo over; gray skin, sallow flesh covered with the beach blanket, those blank eyes. "Ish."

"Wow," Liz said.

"It's from the volcano," Hellboy said. "Got something else with me as well, something that remembers. I think it'll help. It was there when the first fire wolf came up out of Vesuvius just before Pompeii was destroyed, and as far as I can figure, it's been out ever since. The others . . . maybe they followed after they realized this one had escaped. But this is the main man."

"So let me guess: you're heading back to the volcano to throw it back in."

"That's the plan."

"You think that will end it all?"

"No," Hellboy said without pause, and he experienced a depressing, sinking feeling in his gut. "Not for good, at least. But maybe for now, yeah."

"So the family that called you over?"

"He was their patriarch. And every now and then, he arranged for one of them to be sacrificed to the volcano."

"And that prevented Vesuvius from erupting?"

"Seems that way."

"So you stopped the sacrifice and started the eruption."

"Thank you, Liz," Hellboy said. He'd already realized the truth of things himself, and Liz was anything but subtle. There was no blame in her voice, nor condemnation, just a statement of fact.

"Just saying," she said.

"So you're getting on that yacht tonight, Liz?" Hellboy asked.

Liz did not answer for a while, and he heard the gentle hush of fire as she lit a cigarette. It made him crave one. "Yeah," she said. "On the yacht tonight."

"Have you got anything?"

"The charm knot you gave me from Spain. And the vial of Belladonna extract and horse blood."

"That wasn't horse blood."

"I know, Hellboy. I just don't like to think about what it really is."

"Well . . ." he said, trailing off.

"You take care, H.B.," she said, her voice suddenly very soft. "I know you're a big tough guy and punch before asking questions, but . . ."

"Yeah. But this is a volcano."

"I mean it. Take care."

"You too."

Liz inhaled sharply, and he could imagine her laughing silently in a haze of cigarette smoke. "Pah! It's a ghost, Hellboy. On a boat. Dream job."

"Speak to you soon, Liz."

"Betcha." And Liz broke the connection.

Hellboy glanced at Adamo and rested his head back against the seat, staring up at the car's ceiling and yearning for a smoke. His had been soaked, and he'd not seen Mario smoking. Franca entered his mind once again, and he wondered where she was now, what they were doing to her.

She'll be safe in the car, he thought. *They need her, so they'll keep her safe.*

He only hoped that were true.

They were being nice to her. Exposed now, they did not attempt to play on familial concerns or their supposed humanity. But they made sure she was comfortable in the back of the car, offered her food and bottled water, and generally fawned over her.

And she wanted to kill them all.

For the first few minutes in the car, Franca had pulled away from the Elders, hugging herself in the rear seat, pressed against the door and regarding them only with terror. One of the men drove, another sat in the front seat, and beside her sat her Great Aunt Sophia. The old woman smiled and purred at Franca, and every now and then fire glittered in her dark eyes, lighting up their unnatural blackness and depths with fearful conflagrations. Sophia whispered, and her voice hissed like burning paper. When she breathed, smoke left her mouth. And when she reached out to placate Franca, her hand was hot, skin bubbled with weeping blisters.

Franca tried the door handle yet again, but the driver controlled the master lock.

"Even if you did open it and jump," Sophia said, sounding far from human, "you'd die on the road."

"Better than die in the volcano."

"Whatever gave you the idea that we wish that for you?" Sophia said. But her expression could not be read.

"I'm not stupid!" Franca said. "And I won't be easy. I'll do everything I can to make Vesuvius rage at all of you."

"And in doing so, you'll doom thousands to death," Sophia said.

"Jump in yourself, bitch."

Sophia blanched and turned away, her skin growing pale and her eyes watering. For a few beats she looked utterly terrified, and Franca would have given an arm to know what Sophia was thinking right then. But then the fire dog in old woman's clothing turned to her again, and smiled, and said nothing in response.

Franca glanced behind them. Another car followed close containing more Elders, and ahead of them was the third car. A convoy, though they drove with other cars between them sometimes, trying not to give the impression that they were all together.

With every mile that passed beneath their wheels, she felt Hellboy growing farther away. Even now he could be dead, burnt to death by Adamo.

Perhaps she would never know.

She closed her eyes and reinforced the promise she had made herself a dozen times already: *they won't get me.*

If it meant killing herself to take from them what they needed, then so be it.

She tried the door handle yet again, looked across at Sophia's smile, and flicked the old lady the finger.

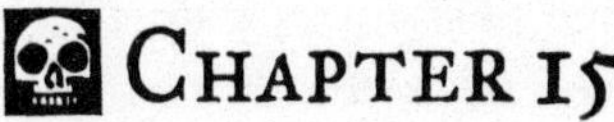

The Road to Vesuvius

Adamo woke up as they left the outskirts of Amalfi. Hellboy waited with a bottle of water, but the man's eyes opened without any sign of fire. He looked around, fixed on Hellboy, and when he sighed and adjusted his position he looked just like a human being.

"Be warned," Hellboy said, tipping a splash of water onto the man's face. Adamo winced back, but there was no steam, and no sizzle. Hellboy reached out and touched his face, and he was merely warm.

Adamo smiled. It twisted his face up, wrinkling the already leathery skin.

"I've got plenty of questions for you," Hellboy said.

Adamo glanced at the driver. "You're consorting with demons now, Mario?" He spoke in English so that Hellboy could understand, but Mario did not respond.

Good boy, Hellboy thought. *Don't let him suck you in*. He had met a hundred demons—though none quite like this—and however cruel, however twisted, they all had a weakness for the sound of their own voices.

Hellboy splashed more water over Adamo's face. The old man winced again, closing his eyes and breathing deeply as if to calm himself. "Leave him alone," Hellboy said. "He knows what *you* are."

"He might think he knows."

"And he knows what you've done at La Casa Fredda."

Adamo looked from the window, a strange smile on his face. He seemed almost sad.

"So we're off to Vesuvius to give you back," Hellboy said.

Adamo turned to him, trying to feign puzzlement with a face that was no longer quite human. "What makes you think I have anything to do with Vesuvius?"

"The volcano fires up, and so do you. You and all your pets."

Adamo shrugged, shaking his head. "Strange way to think, Demon."

"My name's Hellboy. And I have someone here who's been waiting to meet you again."

Monster! the ghost hissed.

Adamo frowned, glanced at the bone tied around Hellboy's neck. "You actually found the old bitch?"

This time, monster, the spirit whispered, and Hellboy wondered if Adamo heard her words.

"She knows plenty," Hellboy said. "And now she's got muscle."

"And that is meant to concern me?" Adamo laughed.

"You killed Carlotta," Mario said. His voice was soft, deferential. Hellboy knew that there was still danger here.

"I remember the day she was born," Adamo said, sounding genuinely nostalgic. He looked from the window as if seeing into the past, and Hellboy wished he could observe the bastard's expression. "A time for celebration for the whole Esposito family, as any new child is. Or was." He glanced at Mario in the mirror. Mario kept driving.

"So how soon after birth did you write her name in your book?" Hellboy asked.

"Book?" Mario said. The car's speed dropped, and Hellboy tapped the back of the driver's seat.

"Keep going," he said.

"You have no idea," Adamo said, and Hellboy hated the way the fire wolf was looking at him.

"I've seen more than you can know," he said, leaning close to Adamo and breathing in his smoky breath. "You? You don't scare me. I've had worse than you for breakfast, then taken the rest of the day off."

Adamo shrugged—an incredibly human gesture—and then he coughed a blast of fire from his mouth.

Hellboy pressed the fire wolf's face against the window so that the fire did not touch Mario. The passenger seat's head rest melted in a cloud of stinging smoke.

"Drive!" Hellboy said, emptying a bottle of water across Adamo's head. Adamo hissed, the fire retreated, and Hellboy snatched up another water bottle. Without relieving the pressure on Adamo's head, he crushed the bottle in his right hand and let another litre pour into the fire wolf's mouth.

Adamo swallowed, and Hellboy felt the fight go out for him for a while.

"Mario," Hellboy said, "break the speed limit. If they're driving fast, we need to go faster."

"We'll be on the 366 soon. We'll move quicker then."

Hellboy nodded.

"What book, Hellboy?"

"Your patriarch here kept a list of the Espositos he'd sacrificed to Vesuvius."

"This isn't happening," Mario whispered. He shook his head, knocking down a gear to negotiate a sharp bend. The road was winding up from the coast now, zig-zagging up the steep hillside, and when Hellboy did not reply, Mario fell silent.

He and all his monsters, the ghost said. *I understand, now. They always knew that Vesuvius would need satiating. Merging with humans must have been essential for them to survive, and it was a way to make offspring with fire wolf essence. And that offspring would be . . .*

"Sacrificial objects," Hellboy said. "Just enough of the bloodline to fool the old god, or whatever's really down there under the volcano."

Adamo rested his head against the window. The blanket splayed across him had been scorched by his fiery outburst, but he seemed unconcerned at covering this human form. He blinked slowly, calmly, and Hellboy could not decide whether it was complacency or resignation.

Hellboy kept a bottle of water in his right hand, his left holding the unholstered gun. If Adamo tried anything funny again he'd blast his head apart first, then shove the water bottle down his throat and squeeze. That should give them more time.

And he was very conscious that they only had four bottles left.

"Don't take me there," Adamo whispered.

"What was that?" Hellboy asked. He'd heard well enough, but this was the first instance of Adamo sounding weak. Hellboy wanted to hear it again, and needed to make sure that Mario also heard. The boy was still too much in thrall to the patriarch, and that could be dangerous if there was trouble.

"Don't take me to Vesuvius," the old man said.

"Why not?"

"Vesuvius is pain."

Hah! the spirit laughed.

"And you?" Mario asked. "Just what the hell are you?"

"I'm *nothing!* Vesuvius is torture, agony, fury and *damnation!*"

Hellboy shrugged casually. "I've met worse."

Adamo glared at him, and Hellboy thought he was going to go again. And deep down, that was when Hellboy realized that they would never make it as far as the volcano. The fire wolf was recovering from its long soaking in the sea, the water bottles were only effective for so long, and soon it would change again, killing Mario and exploding the car.

It's so strong, the voice Hellboy carried with him said. *Stronger than ever before. And I can sense its determination, and its fear.*

"It's your fear that will kill you," Hellboy said. Adamo only smiled, and steam came from his mouth. "Faster," Hellboy said to Mario. "Go faster."

The car revved, their speed increased.

And then Adamo sat up straight, sniffed at the air like a wolf seeking its pack. And grinned.

Sophia continued trying to talk with her, but Franca turned away, staring from the window at the real world outside. Inside the vehicle was a world of pain that she had no wish to dwell upon; the reality of her family, and the doom that had been visited upon it. There was so much that she did not understand, but she refused to lessen herself by asking.

Outside, people continued with their lives in blissful ignorance of the terrible things among them.

"I'll tell you," Sophia said.

Franca shrugged.

"You must want to know. Don't you? We're not bad. Not evil. We're only trying to survive, and that's not wrong, is it?"

It is if you kill to do it, Franca thought, but she would not be lured into conversation with this thing.

"Adamo was the first," Sophia said, and Franca closed her eyes, hating herself for wanting to know more. But she could not prevent herself from hearing. *I'll never feel sorry for them*, she thought. *I'll never believe they're anything other than evil.*

"He was the first to escape, up out of Vesuvius like the volcano's own breath, but it didn't *know!* And when he didn't come back, we others went after him. He was the savior, the rescuer, the founder of our new lives. And we *liked* what we found. Bound together forever by fire, cursed to live in flame and molten rock forever, we *liked* the coolness of our escape, the sea, the air . . . and we liked living beneath the skin of humanity."

Franca glanced at her, questions burning. But she cooled them and looked away. "You think I give a shit?"

"We took the flesh of the family that would become Esposito," Sophia continued. "Esposito was great because of us. A powerful family, but not too powerful. A strong family, but not so strong that it would draw attention. Each generation, we moved from one dying elder to one with many years left. Our fire, buried in your flesh. Simple. And not evil."

"You're killers!" Franca shouted, turning and lunging for Sophia. Her nails caught the old woman across the face and drew blood, and in that red trickle were tiny, quivering flames.

Sophia put a hand to her face and looked at the blood. "We're *survivors*," she whispered.

"You won't survive Hellboy!" Franca said, grinning, trying to project a confidence she no longer felt. "He'll kill Adamo, hunt you down one by one, and send you back to where you belong."

"Hellboy?" Sophia said, still looking at the blood on her fingertips. She smiled. "He'll bleed too, Franca."

Franca glanced forward at the car ahead of them, and one of the Elders was looking back. Then she turned in her seat . . . and the Elders' car that had been following was no longer in sight.

"*He will bleed*," Sophia growled, and fire danced across her teeth. There was a tone in her voice that denied everything she had been trying to convey.

Right then, she sounded pure evil.

The car came from out of nowhere.

It struck them side-on, sending their vehicle skewing across the road, over the rough curb and sideways down an embankment. Mario shouted as the steering wheel spun in his hands, twisting his arms and jarring his shoulders. Hellboy grabbed Adamo and crushed a water bottle across his head, shattered glass from the side windows mixing in with the water, speckling his face and ricocheting around the car's interior. And the fire wolf roared.

The car came to rest at the base of the embankment. Its windows were smashed, steam hissed from the crushed radiator, and Hellboy could smell leaking fuel.

Oh hell, that's not good!

"Can't I just shoot this thing until—"

Fool, idiot, I told you it has to go back in alive!

"Fine!" He kicked out at Adamo, pressing him against his buckled door, and reached across the front seats for Mario. He felt movement, and that was enough.

"Okay," Hellboy shouted, "Mario, get out and *run*!"

He must have been shaken, and he was repeating something rapidly in Italian, forgetting in his panic that Hellboy would not understand. But through all that he listened: Mario kicked his rumpled door open, took one look up the gentle slope at the front of the Elders' car stopped up there, and ran.

"Good!" Hellboy said, and he broke another bottle of water.

Adamo flamed. Wherever the water touched, the hint of flesh appeared again, but the fire quickly took control once more. He seemed to expand as he changed, fiery limbs stretching to fill the car, head jarring against the roof and blackening the lining. His eyes bore into Hellboy, and flame teeth scorched the air when he opened his mouth in a wide grin.

Hellboy snapped up the final bottle of water and threw it at the fire wolf. Its plastic skin melted and water flowed, but this time there was not even the hint of flesh where the water touched. However weakened it had become after its submersion in the sea, it's strength was now back.

Hellboy pushed backwards with both legs, knocking his door open and falling onto the embankment above the car. He kicked the door closed again, still smelling spilled fuel, scrabbling up the bank on hands and knees. *Behind me!* he thought, and he turned just in time to see three Elders appearing over the head of the embankment. Pistol still gripped in his left hand, he twisted and fired, letting off several shots in the hope that they would be confused. But even though one of them went down with a hole in her chest—and fire licking around the hole, like animated blood—the other two skidded down the slope, changing as they came.

He could hear other cars passing by on the road above, but none of them stopped to see what was happening.

The car behind him exploded. Adamo's fire wolf must have opened the door and ignited the spilled fuel, and the resultant explosion consumed the vehicle, a billowing ball of fire and smoke rising above the crash site.

Someone's got *to stop now*, he thought. A Samaritan could do no good, but at least it might distract—

One of the Elders—the one he'd shot in the chest—loped along the bank after Mario. She was completely transformed now, rippling fire fur throwing glowing sparks at the stony ground as her flame feet burnt dark patches in the scrub.

"Run, Mario!" Hellboy shouted. He could see the figure farther along the base of the bank, and Mario turned to look at the fire wolf bearing down upon him.

Below Hellboy, the Adamo fire wolf emerged from the conflagration that had taken the car, stretching upright on its legs and waving its burning arms at the sky. It roared a throaty laugh. And then it fell on all fours again and shook, shrinking, going from lighter to darker as flames flickered out all across its body.

Adamo appeared from the flames, naked and shrunken and grinning at Hellboy like a madman.

Hellboy lifted his gun and shot Adamo in the face. He knew it would have no effect, but it was out of frustration and anger. And spite, perhaps. "Son of a bitch!" Hellboy whispered when he realized his gun was now empty. *He must be changing back to say something to me.*

Adamo shook his head, flames licking out from his wound and sending tendrils across his bald scalp. His shattered cheekbone and ruptured eye filled in and healed, as if sutured with threads of fire.

"Run, Mario!" Adamo mimicked, and Hellboy looked along the bank once more.

The fire wolf was worrying at a small pool, dipping in, jerking back, exposed damp flesh quickly bursting into flame once again. *He's down in there*, Hellboy thought, seeing clouds of steam rise around the fire wolf. *How long can he hold his breath?*

Adamo advanced up the bank on all fours, as though regressing to a more primitive state in his human form. Sparks dropped from him, and fire emerged from his nose when he breathed. "You do seem to think—" he began.

"I've had more than enough of this," Hellboy said. He put every shred of strength he could muster into the punch, his right hand rising from where he'd propped himself against the bank, swinging in an arc to gain momentum and then connecting with the side of Adamo's head.

The old man's head broke. His body flipped to the side and his skull came apart, spewing gray wet insides that burst alight even before they spattered across the ground.

Hellboy was on his feet and running, not bothering to look back at Adamo. If he was lucky, he might have inconvenienced the bastard for a few moments, but that was all. Flesh was a vessel to them, and it seemed they'd had many centuries to master its form and control.

Hellboy hated shapeshifters. Give him a frog monster or dream witch any day.

He heard the other two fire wolves coming after him, but he did not look back. That would only slow him down, and from what he could observe, Mario's life might depend upon Hellboy reaching him in the next few seconds.

The fire wolf trying to get at Mario was becoming more and more frustrated, its flames spurting out into the air and licking at the ground. The small pool Mario had taken shelter in was clogged with weeds and refuse, but he must have gone deep, clinging to something to hold himself down there even while natural buoyancy would be doing its best to lift him to the surface.

If did break surface, the fire wolf would take him into its grasp, and he would be another Esposito statistic.

"Hey, ugly!" Hellboy shouted. The fire wolf spun around and he hit it at full speed, digging his right hand inside and grasping at its semi-solid innards. He squeezed his eyes shut and pushed the fire wolf down ahead of him, and as they tipped into the small pool with Hellboy on top, he hoped Mario could see what was coming.

Steam hissed and water boiled, and when Hellboy opened his eyes, there was an old woman thrashing beneath him. Her mouth was open, and the flickering of flames in there gave way to bubbles. Her eyes went wide, hands scrabbling at his face, but a few scratches didn't faze him. He bore down on her, glancing left and right in the murky water but unable to see Mario.

The old bitch seemed to be weakening.

Then Hellboy had an idea.

He stood quickly in the center of the pool, gasping in a big breath and stomping down on the old woman's head. There was little strength to her continuing struggles.

The other two fire wolves stood just out of reach, and by the burning car, Adamo was firing up again.

"Come and get her," he said to the two flaming demons.

Something broke surface behind him, and Hellboy crouched and turned, not shifting his feet from the old woman. Mario gasped, spitting water and looking around with wide eyes.

Something changed in the pool. All movement ceased, and Hellboy frowned as he felt something rise around him, leaving the pool with a steamy gasp. It was like a heat-haze, and behind it reality shimmered like the thin veil it was. Mario fell quiet, the pool grew still, and the two fire wolves drew back from its edge, their flames lessening almost to the point of being extinguished.

And Hellboy was chilled, because the heat haze was cold as the void.

"Oh," he said, and he reached down into the pool. Grabbing the corpse of the old woman, dragging it upright, he stared into her face, lifting her eyelids and seeing nothing remotely alive. "That's it for you," he muttered, and then he lifted the corpse to show the other fire wolves. "One down!" he shouted. "So decide amongst you who's next."

She was a weak one, the ghost voice said. *Not the prime fire wolf.* It was useful knowledge, and it gave him a spark of hope.

Adamo was aflame again, shaking his head and blazing rage.

A couple of cars pulled up next to the Elders' car, and when several people jumped out Adamo screamed, sending arcs of fire up the slope and bubbling paintwork on the vehicles. The people leapt back into the cars, and wheels span as they made their getaway.

Hellboy knew that he had only a shaky advantage at best. The two fire wolves close to the pool seemed hesitant and shocked, their flames laid low like a cowed dog's ears. But there was still Adamo, and he thought that old wolf would have fewer qualms about what must happen next.

As the head wolf charged, it changed back into a human once again. But now Adamo's head was misshapen, and he walked with the uncertain gait of an old man who'd misplaced his walker.

"I got to him," Hellboy said.

"Is that one dead?" Mario asked.

"Dead."

"She used to cut my hair when I was a little boy."

Hellboy glanced back at the terrified man. "Grow it long."

Adamo was there then, crouched beside the pool, hissing and clicking sounds at the fire wolves that sounded distinctly alien coming from a human-shaped mouth and throat. The two others ran back to their car, changing as they went.

"You've been noticed," Hellboy said. "You've been seen." He held up the old woman's sad corpse, so light that it felt like little more than a suit of skin. "And now I know you can die."

"And when the emergency services come, they'll find you holding a dead old woman," Adamo sneered. "You're a fool, Hellboy. You're trying to *stop* us from preventing the volcano's eruption? Who'll thank you for that?"

"You've spent two thousand years fooling Vesuvius. Sacrificing Espositos. Why?"

Adamo stared at him. "If it erupts, its full fury is unleashed. It'll find us and draw us back in. And after what we've tasted in the human world, we can never return *there*." He shuddered and looked away, ashamed of showing his weakness. "Never."

"I'm going to put you back, Adamo. Either that, or I'll kill you all."

"No," the old man said, and his confidence was chilling. "But you!" he pointed at Mario.

The young man, still in the pool, stepped back, almost tripping and going under again.

"I'll be seeing *you*," Adamo hissed.

Then he turned and went back up to their car, a naked, worn old man whose legs were too thin and whose head still bore an impact-mark from Hellboy's fist.

"That's it?" Mario asked, watching the car start and pull away. It disappeared back over the lip of the embankment, and they heard gravel spit and wheels spin as it powered away. "It's over?"

"Nowhere near," Hellboy said. He dropped the old woman's body back in the pool, and as it sank away, Hellboy felt his confidence and fight sinking away with it. A great weight pushed down on him, and he staggered to the edge of the pool before it crushed him down.

There is the alternative, the voice whispered. *Let them put her in, the volcano will be appeased, and then you can chase them down. You know them now, and I have marked them. We will find them together!*

"Shut the hell up, lady!" Hellboy said. Mario glanced at him, unnerved, but as Hellboy was about to say something more, a booming echo rolled across the landscape from the north.

The ground moved.

Chapter 16

The Road to Vesuvius

Franca rested her head against the window and watched the columns of humanity fleeing Vesuvius. The closer they drew to Castellammare, the heavier the traffic on the opposite side of the road. They were not the only vehicles going north, but they were among the few, while the southbound lanes were clogged with cars, trucks, trailers, and all types of vehicles towing laden trailers. Naples would evacuate northward, but all the coastal towns south of Vesuvius would come south, aiming for the Amalfi coast and placing the high mountains between them and the volcano. It was a massive, unprecedented movement of people, but mostly it seemed to be occurring with good cheer and few problems. She saw an occasional vehicle broken down beside the road, but more often than not the occupants were not present, probably already picked up by someone else. Some of the faces she caught sight of were smiling and excited, and a few cars even fluttered various scarves and flags from their windows and aerials.

I'm going to stop your fun, she thought, and were she not so exhausted, she would have laughed. Franca felt jealous of these people; they were saving their families. Hers was already beyond saving, and its remnants had been revealed as monsters.

"You'll be helping," Sophia said. "You'll be saving many lives."

"Is that what all the other Espositos you've sacrificed over the years have done?" she asked, too tired to turn angry now. Too resigned.

"Yes," Sophia said. She sounded very sure of herself.

"But if you all step back in, the volcano will go to sleep?"

Sophia looked at her, as if she was examining a creature in a cage. "Wouldn't you do anything to survive?" she asked.

"No," Franca said, pleased at the speed and conviction of her answer. "Not anything, no. Not what you've done. I'd rather give myself back than have to murder. All those *murders*!"

Sophia frowned, as if perturbed at Franca's answer. "Your chance is coming," she said.

Franca nodded against the window. "I'm ready." They slowed behind a military wagon, and across the road she saw a car packed with children. One of them saw her and waved, and Franca waved back.

"How sweet," Sophia said, and she sounded like she had all the years Franca had known her; an Elder, caring and experienced.

Franca hated her right then. She hated all of them. But with Hellboy nowhere to be seen, she knew that they were driving her towards an inevitable outcome, and one which she could not fight against.

Franca closed her eyes and tried to consider how her death would feel.

The car was still burning, and soon the police would arrive. Adamo and the other two elders were escaping. And somewhere north of them, Franca was being driven towards the hungry maw of Vesuvius.

"Hellboy!" Mario called again. He was circling where Hellboy sat, helpless and desperate. Hellboy could sense the hopelessness in the young man. "We can't just wait here. The police will come, and what do we tell them?"

"We tell them we crashed." He looked down at the ground between his knees. He could still see the folds of soil where he'd grabbed at the ground, and through which he had felt one of the largest explosions yet from Vesuvius. There was still nothing visible to the north, but whatever was happening there was still sheltered by the folds in the land and the haze of distance.

He wondered whether Franca could see the eruption yet.

"*I'm* not just waiting!" Mario said.

"Then you're brave, and you'll die."

"What the hell is this?" The young man still circled, never coming closer than six feet. Hellboy liked that just fine.

He was thinking of what the ghost had said, and how fighting against the inevitable would actually be putting lives at risk. He was also dwelling on defeat . . . and though he hated himself for thinking this way, it was that more than the eruption that plagued his thoughts.

If the fire wolves won, there was a good chance the volcano would go back to sleep. If he succeeded in stealing Franca away from their grasp, then Vesuvius would remain enraged, and the eruption would kill innocents. There was no way a million people could be moved in time, and some would not *wish* to be moved. In his arrogance, he would have doomed many to death. And perhaps the fire wolves would be drawn back into Vesuvius by the eruption, returned to their rightful place forever . . . or perhaps not. There was the possibility that some of them would survive, melting away into the land, ready to merge their fire with the flesh of another family for their survival.

One to save many, he thought, and Franca's face appeared in his mind, smiling uncertainly and offering him a coy glance. Had there ever been anything there, really? He liked to think there had been, certainly in his mind, and perhaps in hers as well.

"And I'm going to let her die?" he whispered.

Goooood . . . the ghost voice soothed.

"No!" Mario said. He was gasping with frustration, feet slipping across the gravely ground, and then he fell silent.

The moment was a held breath.

"No!" Mario shouted, "you are *not*!" He was on Hellboy then, shoving him over onto his side and straddling his right forearm, raining blows down on his shoulder and chest. "You are not letting her die, because I won't *let* you!" He struck Hellboy in the face, one small fisted hand glancing from his cheek and across his nose.

"Ow!" Hellboy said, but surprise had stolen his strength. Mario pummelled him, then stood and kicked him in the ribs. "*Ow!*" Hellboy shouted. He stood and grabbed Mario's shirt, lifting him from his feet and swinging him above the ground.

Mario kept punching, his fists now connecting only with fresh air. But he was so furious that he could not see.

"Hey," Hellboy said. "Hey."

Mario stopped punching and hung limp from Hellboy's hand. Their eyes locked, and Mario's were angry and determined.

Hellboy felt a rush of something bracing and positive, as if hope had been injected like a drug. It galvanized his muscles and drove away the aches, and even the burns on his skin felt lively instead of painful.

"You're right," he said, "I'm not letting her die. However much that might change things that have gone bad, it's just wrong. And I won't have those things beat me."

Mario grinned as Hellboy dropped him. The man staggered a little, and then started up towards the road.

"Where are you going?" Hellboy asked.

Mario glanced at the burning wreck along the embankment from them. "We're going to need another car."

Hellboy pulled the pistol from its holster. "Allow me."

They walked along the road, trying to distance themselves from the burning wreck and the questions it would inevitably attract. As they climbed the hillside, they heard a siren behind them, and knew that the emergency services had arrived at last. Hellboy hoped they did not look too far; the dead old woman needed to stay lost in the pool, for now.

"This one?" Mario asked. A big four-wheel drive approached them, but Hellboy shook his head.

"Needs to be faster."

They walked on, Hellboy holding the pistol within the folds of his coat. He would not be surprised if Adamo sent a couple of fire wolves back to make sure he and Mario did not pursue too quickly, and while the pistol had little effect against them, it would still put holes in a car.

"This one," Mario said, sounding more sure of himself. A big Mazda swept around the corner behind them.

"Faster," Hellboy said. The car passed them, and he caught the driver's curious glance. As the Mazda disappeared up the incline, Hellboy tried rearranging his burnt coat so that it hung better, brushing creases from the sleeves.

The road curved around the side of the steep hill, switching back on itself and climbing higher. The traffic coming from the other direction was growing heavier, and he could see that many people were bringing as much as they could with them. They obviously expected the volcano to blow, and he could almost taste the excitement they left in the air after passing by. Kids waved at him, and he wondered what they thought he was. He waved back and their smiles did not falter. At least that made him feel good.

Mario's attack . . . that had done something to Hellboy. For a while, maybe he'd even been wallowing in self pity, and there were only a few things he hated more.

Fire wolves. That was one.

He heard a sound behind him, like the purr of a tiger amplified a thousand times, and he turned around.

"Oh," he said, "that one." A bright red Ferrari turned a corner below them and powered up the incline, seeming to glide on ice. Hellboy stepped into the road and raised his gun, finger resting across the trigger guard.

"Have you ever been in one of those?" Mario said. "They're *small* inside. You'll be crushed, even if you manage to fit. You're too heavy for it."

The driver's mouth fell open as he slammed on the brakes.

"Yeah," Hellboy said, "but it's my color."

• • •

Moving again, the Ferrari eating up the road, Mario at the wheel, Hellboy had time to consider what might come next. And his imaginings were not good.

Mario had been right—the car was more cramped than he'd expected. Once inside, he could not move his legs, and his right arm was pressed up against the door, motionless and dead-looking. He flexed the fingers and watched them move, and it was as if they belonged to someone else.

But the car was *fast*. Mario drove as if the Devil himself was on their tail, and never once did Hellboy have to suggest that they speed up. The man knew what was at stake here . . . but Hellboy wondered whether he had considered the "alternative," as the ghost had called it.

Mario threw the car around another hairpin bend, apparently unconcerned at the amount of traffic coming from the opposite direction. Wheels spun, tires screamed against the hot road, and he bit his lip, concentrating on not swerving them off the road. He was sweating, and Hellboy could see the concentration on his face. Perhaps Mario had been waiting to drive a car like this all his life, but there was not an ounce of enjoyment in his expression right now. He was deadly serious, and Hellboy did not want to do anything to distract him.

"Here we are," Mario said. The road ahead curved up slowly to the right, and when Hellboy looked from his window he saw the sea so far below and behind them that it seemed like a memory. They were leaving the long, climbing, twisting coastal road at last. "All good fast roads from here to Vesuvius," Mario said. "Thirty miles. And most of the traffic is coming this way, not going towards the volcano."

"Which is why we'll likely be stopped when we get closer," Hellboy said.

"If there are roadblocks, the fire wolves will go straight through, won't they?"

"Hope so. That way we'll be able to track their route."

Mario nursed the car into the center of the two northbound lanes, only edging towards the side to pass a slower vehicle.

"So do you have a plan?" Mario asked quietly.

"Of sorts. You sure they'll be coming this way?"

"It's the fastest way to Vesuvius. And their priority is getting there fast, yes?"

"Hope so." Hellboy shifted in his seat, feeling pins and needles cutting into his legs. Ferraris were obviously not designed for hooves.

"So?" Mario asked.

"It's Adamo and the other two we'll likely catch up with first. We need Adamo. I need to take him down, get him to Vesuvius and give him back to the volcano."

"You're sure that will stop the others?"

"Hey, you. Will it?" Hellboy asked.

I've been considering that, the ghost said. *I think it will do more than stop them. Once the ancient thing in the volcano has Adamo, it will know the truth of how it has been deceived over the millennia, and it will drag the others in after him.*

"You know this, or you're guessing?"

I feel it.

"Who do you keep talking to?" Mario asked.

"Kid, you don't wanna know. But yeah, I think it'll stop them. Adamo's the key . . . he always has been."

Hellboy sighed, played with some dashboard buttons, distracted. The wiper fluid squirted.

"But?"

"It's tight. They get there with Franca before we do . . . ."

"Oh," Mario said.

"Yeah, oh."

"No, I mean . . . look." He slowed slightly, dropping just below a hundred miles per hour. Ahead of them a big, black car rode the centerline, a trail of steam hanging in the air behind it. "Broke their radiator when they shoved us from the road."

"Ram them," Hellboy said.

"But we're going—"

"It's not as if we can just wave them over," Hellboy said. "Ram them off the road, and then help me."

"Help you how?"

"Find some water."

Mario eased back on the gas some more, dropping further behind the car. "About two miles," he said.

"Right." Hellboy did not ask what was two miles away, but he took the couple of minutes it took them to travel that distance to prepare himself. No more doubts. No more giving in.

No alternative.

"Hold on," Mario said.

"I'm not going anywhere."

Mario pressed down on the gas, taking the Ferrari out into the fast lane and swishing past the several cars that had overtaken them in the past couple of minutes. It seemed that people felt good overtaking a Ferrari, and Hellboy could not help but smile at the annoyed expressions he saw as they powered along the road.

"It's a canal," Mario said. "It runs beneath the road. If I hit them exactly right . . ."

Hellboy realized how hard Mario was concentrating. His hands were fisted around the wheel, sweat beaded on his forehead despite the air conditioning, and he frowned hard as he focused on the road ahead.

It was only at the last moment that the car ahead of them veered across the road. Mario had brought them up so quickly that the driver hadn't had a chance to spot them, and the automatic reaction was to veer towards the edge of the road . . . which was just what Mario intended.

As the cars connected, Hellboy looked at Adamo in the rear of the other car and gave him the finger.

It was only a gentle touch, but the impact speed was huge. The Ferrari skewed across the road into the central barrier, and though Mario fought with the steering wheel it jumped from his hands, jarring as the wheels took over. The car went into a spin.

Hellboy closed his eyes and tried to hold down his vomit. He hated being thrown around like this; much nicer to walk everywhere.

It was over in seconds. Even before the car came to a stop and levelled on its suspension, Hellboy was shouldering the door open.

"Mario?"

"Go, I'm fine!"

Where am I? I feel sick.

"Shut it, you." Hellboy ran back towards the bridge, trailing clouds of dust that had risen beside the road to track the course of the fire wolves' car. Other cars skidded to a stop beyond the bridge, and Hellboy held up his hand, fingers splayed, hoping that they'd pay attention.

He reached the bridge and looked over . . . and he could have laughed out loud. There was very little of the car visible. It had left the road, smashed through a metal barrier, taken down several fences, crushed a wandering goat against a wall, leaving a smear of blood and pelt, and then ended up nose-first in the canal that Mario had remembered so accurately. Steam drifted above the car, and bubbles broke the water's still-violent surface.

Hellboy didn't want to waste any time. He balanced on the parapet and then jumped, landing with feet wide on the car's slightly-sloping roof.

Someone was trying to force a door open. Hellboy shoved it closed.

The windscreen smashed and arms reached out. Hellboy stamped on them.

When two doors opened at once he lay flat on the roof, kicking down with his hooves and feeling them strike something soft, and smashed down on the other door with his right hand. He felt something give way, and he hoped that one was Adamo.

Mario appeared on the bridge above him, and Hellboy nodded.

It only took a couple of minutes. With the car almost completely submerged, the struggles were frantic and brutal, and Hellboy felt every impact transmitted up through the car roof and into his chest and stomach. He enjoyed the sensations, knowing that they marked the end for two of the fire wolves, at least.

From above, Mario started shouting at people in Italian. Hellboy hoped he was telling them to stay away. Anyone looking down and seeing this big red man forcing three old people to remain in the car to drown . . . well, he had no liking of where that could take them.

"Come on, come *on*!" he muttered.

At last the struggling seemed to end, and Hellboy slowly knelt on the car's roof. He glanced up for Mario, but he was out of sight, hopefully keeping the crowds back.

"They can drown," he said.

Good . . . . good . . . but not him. He *will only die in the flames of Vesuvius.*

A car door started opening. It moved slowly against the water, and the thin, gray arm that pushed it looked ready to be washed away by the water.

Hellboy leaned over and grabbed the arm. It was cold, bearing not a trace of heat. He pulled, and Adamo drifted from the car, his eyes dull, mouth hanging slack in a vacant expression he could not possible feign.

"Hi," Hellboy said. The old man did not respond. He dragged Adamo onto the car roof and knelt on his back, then leaned over and dipped his head into the water. His vision was blurred and the water silty, but he could just make out the other two shapes in the car, arms held wide, floating in complete unity with the water. No more struggles, no more fighting from these old fire wolves.

He knelt up again, shaking the water from his face. Beneath him, Adamo groaned.

"Two more down," Hellboy growled into the old man's ear. "You old bastard, you're going to feed a hungry volcano."

I almost have you, the ghost whispered to itself.

"Hellboy!" Mario called down.

Hellboy looked up, shading his eyes against the sun. "It's all good down here!" he said.

"We really need to leave," Mario said.

"Trouble?"

"Come up and look."

Hellboy stepped from the car's submerged hood onto the canal's concrete edging, dragging Adamo after him. The old man felt dead, but Hellboy had seen the flicker of an eyelid, felt the pulse of warmth deep within his chest. Even hurting this bad, the old patriarch was sly.

Mario met him at the top of the bank, glancing at Adamo and then nodding over Hellboy's shoulder.

Hellboy looked north. Above the horizon, driving up through the clouds, a billowing column of smoke rose high into the air. Lightning played around its head. And at its base, behind the horizon but illuminating the clouds, fire.

CHAPTER 17

The Road to Vesuvius

The fire wolves were terrified. The closer they drove to Vesuvius, the quieter they became, and when they saw the billowing clouds of smoke and gas illuminated from within by fire and lightning, Sophia caught her breath.

Franca tried her best not to look as if she was examining them, but she was certain. They were petrified. Fire trickled from Sophia's tear ducts, and her skin looked pale and cool. Her eyes were wide. They reflected nothing.

Franca turned her head casually and looked from her window again. She could see the column of smoke and dust in the distance, but also the rows of cars and trucks fleeing from the volcano. The mood here did not seem quite so light; fewer people smiled, and she could hear the impatient, useless screams of horns as the traffic stopped and started. A few people faced her way, obviously wondering at these two big cars driving towards the volcano, not away from it. For a beat Franca thought of looking for a police car, and then bashing the window and screaming for help, hoping that the policemen would be looking at just the right time to see her. But even if they did see, and did manage to catch up, she knew what the results of such an action would be. This close to salvation, she was certain that the fire wolves would not hesitate in exposing themselves to the public.

"We'll start meeting roadblocks soon," the driver said. That was Uncle Calvo, an old man who had once walked Franca down to Amalfi beach and helped her dig for crabs. They had found three, and he had insisted that they be given back to the water. *They're too young to eat*, he had said. *It's best to wait until they're older and more mature*. So they had let the crabs go and watched them scampering down the beach, seeking the water now that their underground hiding places had been discovered. She wondered whether Calvo had been the one to kill her mother.

"The others will deal with them," Sophia said, nodding at the car ahead of them.

"Right," Franca said. "You've killed your family, what are a few police added to that?"

"They had to die," Sophia said. "It's a shame, but a necessity now that we're found out."

"They're not all dead," she said gleefully.

"I know. But the days are long, Franca, and the nights are longer. The others will be found."

Franca caught her breath, trying not to cry out at her foolishness. She'd been nurturing thoughts of self-sacrifice, but whatever she did—fight or submit—the others would still be doomed. Wherever Mario had hidden them all away would be found by the fire wolves, especially in the confusion that would be rife in Amalfi with hundreds, perhaps thousands of evacuees staying there.

"You can let them go," she said. "Once the volcano has me, you can flee."

"From Vesuvius? We can never go far, girl. Why do you think we live so close even after two thousand years?" Sophia sighed, and it sounded almost pleasurable. "The best thing about escape is living beneath our former jailer's nose."

"But they don't have to die!" she said, turning to face Sophia.

"If they don't know of us, they know Adamo, and that's enough," Sophia said, and Franca realized how pointless it was trying to appeal to this woman. *She's not human*, she thought. *She's a monster that for now just happens to be wearing her human skin.*

Perhaps it was time to go another route.

"It looks hungry for you all," she said, leaning between the front seats. Uncle Calvo glanced back at her, but the woman in the front passenger seat—Franca had always known her as Eve—seemed enrapt by the incredible sky before them. Almost the whole horizon was now swallowed by the eruption.

"You don't know what you're talking about," Sophia said unconvincingly.

"You think you can go so close without Vesuvius knowing you're here?" she said. "Fools."

Sophia grabbed her hair and jerked her back. The sudden violence startled Franca, and she let out a brief, high squeal. The older woman pushed her back against the seat and then leaned over before her, face only inches away from hers. Franca could feel the unnatural heat of her breath.

"Don't think we can't burn you a little before we get there," Sophia said. She held up her hand and nursed a tongue of fire in her palm. It seemed to grow and shrink in time with her breathing.

"Why would you do that?" Franca asked. She was pressing her head back into the seat, yet still she could feel the heat against her face.

Sophia was breathing heavier now, and for the first time Franca had a true appreciation of the fire beneath the flesh. The old woman seemed uncomfortable in her false clothing. And now that the need to hide away was not so urgent, it would take little for her to strip it away and reveal her true self.

"You told me you weren't evil," Franca whispered.

"Sophia," Calvo said. His voice was flat, but still the old woman eased back and let Franca sit up.

"Don't test me," Sophia said. "You have no control here, Franca. You have no advantage. So you can see our fear? Good. The fear makes us strong. It feeds us, and gives us edge. So . . . don't test me."

Franca slid across next to the window again, and in the queues on the other carriageway she saw several police cars. She watched them flit by, and a couple of faces watched her as well. She did not quite manage a smile, but neither did she give any sign of alarm.

I'm lost, she thought, struggling to prevent the tears. But she *could* sense the fire wolves' fear, and though it might give them edge, it also meant that there was something for them to be afraid of.

So long as the fire wolves were scared, she still had hope.

Where are you, Hellboy? Don't abandon me, don't leave me.

Hellboy stood on the bridge over the canal. Several people who had stopped after seeing the accident cheered when he climbed up with Adamo, and Hellboy nodded and held the old man close to him. But then a couple of bystanders looked down into the canal, frowning at the roof of the car drowned down there, and when they glanced up again there was suspicion in their eyes.

Mario had been talking with a young woman for a couple of minutes, trying to persuade her to lend them her car. They conversed rapidly in Italian, Mario's pleas accompanied by expansive gestures, his voice raised. He pointed ahead of them at the volcano, then turned and waved his hands towards where they had come from. Traffic on the other side of the road slowed but did not stop, and Hellboy was keeping his eyes open for police or army. There was no time now to deal with them.

Adamo stirred, and Hellboy felt a flush of warmth radiating from the old man.

"Mario," he said.

Eyebrows raised, Mario glanced back. He looked at Adamo, turned back to the woman, and then nodded at Hellboy's gun.

"Oh crap," Hellboy said. He stepped forward and pulled the gun, keeping it aimed down at his foot. At a word from Mario, the woman looked at the gun and backed away. She threw Mario her keys, muttered something, ducked into her car, and pulled out her handbag. She kept backing away, and not once did she take her eyes from Hellboy.

"What did you tell her?" Hellboy asked.

"Does it matter? We have a car."

"Yeah. You drive." Hellboy opened the back door, easing Adamo inside and climbing in after him. "I don't think we have long," he said as Mario dropped into the driver's seat.

"The police will be after us now," Mario said.

"Least of our problems."

"The other two are dead?"

"Very."

Mario started the car, shoving it angrily into gear and hitting the gas.

"Mario?" He glanced at Hellboy in the rearview mirror. "We need to get there in one piece to make this work."

"All my family are dying, Hellboy," he said.

Hellboy wrapped the seatbelt around Adamo, clicking it tight and resting his hand on the old man's chest. The first flush of heat, the first sign of fire, and Hellboy would shoot until his head was gone. Perhaps that would slow the fire wolf change down, perhaps not, but right now it was all he had.

"The fire wolves stole the skin and flesh of your Esposito ancestors, Mario. But that doesn't make *them* Espositos. You should still be proud of your family, and you're fighting for those left alive."

Mario nodded once, concentrating on the road ahead.

Kid's amazing, Hellboy thought. Since leaving Amalfi, the man had barely paused to question what was happening. He saw an end, a solution, and he worked towards that.

"I'm going to stop this blight on your family," Hellboy said. "I am."

"And what will be left?" Mario asked. But then he shrugged, and offered Hellboy a weak smile in the rearview mirror.

A few minutes later, over a rise in the land, they saw Vesuvius.

Adamo whined in his sleep. The ghost sighed. Hellboy smiled. *Almost there.*

"How close do we need to get?" Mario asked.

"No idea. This is my first time too." Hellboy looked at Adamo, but the old man offered no easy answers. He was stirring a little more now, mumbling, eyes rolling behind closed eyelids. Having nightmares. "Our priority's finding Franca."

Mario sighed, slowing the car slightly.

"What?"

"That's just . . ." Mario shook his head, sighing heavily again.

"*What?*"

"One more level of difficulty. Hellboy, how many times can we be lucky? If I hadn't clipped their car just right, nudged it into that canal . . . that was pure chance. How long will he stay like that? If he turns into the fire wolf again, he'll kill me and maybe you, and it'll all be over. We have to get to the volcano and put him in, if we can, and putting Franca between us and that—"

"If they put Franca in first, the eruption stops and they go to ground. We lose them."

No, the ghost said. *Let them put her in, then we track them!*

"I can't allow any of that."

Mario seemed to be fighting with his doubts and fears, but the car kept moving. The vehicle picked up speed again.

"So how the hell do we find her?" Mario asked.

"Hmm," Hellboy said. He looked at Adamo, twitching more and more beneath the tight seatbelt. He leaned forward and looked up at the cloud rising from the cradle of Vesuvius. "Dunno."

"Excellent."

Ten minutes later, however, they found the beginnings of the trail they would follow.

A trail of the dead.

• • •

Franca cried as the soldiers burned.

The roadblock was there to help people, to keep the curious and the stupid away from the slopes of Vesuvius, and now the fire wolves were killing the soldiers who manned it. Franca had heard a few shots, the reaction of shocked, terrified men. But the gunfire had soon ended, and by the time the fire wolves had extinguished back into human form and returned to the lead car, the stench of burning meat was everywhere. Calvo drove them through the roadblock, and Franca recoiled as she saw the greasy, spitting fires eating what had so recently been people.

"Quiet," Sophia said. "Please."

"Screw you!" Franca yelled. She struck out at the old woman but Sophia was ready this time, catching her hand and squeezing her wrist, then sending a pulse of heat into her flesh. Franca squealed and snatched her hand back, looking at the reddened skin and the shrivelled heads of burnt hairs.

"They'd die anyway," Sophia said. "If we didn't do this, they would die, and many more with them."

Sophia turned away, sickened by the old woman's attempt to explain, to justify. She bit back the tears and closed her eyes. They were past the roadblock now, and she could feel the road starting to climb. The lower slopes of Vesuvius were gentle, and they were on their way up.

"It'll take you," Franca said, because she could think of no way of striking back at Sophia and the others. "It'll smell you and eat you, and somehow it'll get you."

"Never has before," Sophia said mildly.

Franca's head rattled against the window as Uncle Calvo steered the car from a paved road and onto a rougher track. She caught the first whiff of something wrong with the air, and she heard Sophia gasp.

One of the army trucks had caught fire, and it was blazing brightly as they passed by. The other wagon had not yet ignited, but several smaller fires were scattered between them. Hellboy recognized the smell of burning people.

"Drive on," he said.

Mario did so without speaking.

Minutes later they caught their first smell of the gases thrown up by the volcano. It was a rotten, sulphurous stench, and it made Hellboy gag.

Adamo shivered and came awake. His eyes were wide, his hands rising to the belt across his chest, and he looked around as if unaware of where he was. A word tumbled from his mouth, a language that Hellboy had never heard before. Perhaps it was a name.

"Almost home," Hellboy said, pressing the muzzle of his gun against Adamo's head.

The old man was still shaking. He glanced at Hellboy, the fear in his eyes genuine.

"There!" Mario said. He pointed uphill to his left, and Hellboy looked. He could just make out a ball of flame rising from something further up the slope, billowing up and out from a recent explosion. "That's them!"

"How can you be sure?" Hellboy asked.

"I can't. But it's the right direction."

He turned off the main road into the mouth of a rougher trail, knocking down a couple of gears and then flooring the pedal again.

Adamo continued muttering in the unknown language.

"What's he saying?" Mario asked.

"Not a clue. Hey you, what's he saying?"

A language I heard so long ago, the ghost said. *Demon whispers. Rumors from the dark. But rumors of things I have never known.*

"Yeah, well, you've been dead a long time."

Hellboy leaned forward and looked through the windscreen up at the mountain before them. The great, wide column of smoke and dust rose from the shattered mouth of Vesuvius like an extension of the mountain itself, so huge that its movement was as imperceptible as that of an hour hand on a clock. Lightning played high up in the sky, jagged arcs that danced across and through the clouds, and lower down was the unmistakeable glow of fire.

"Can't see any lava," Hellboy said.

"It's the pyroclastic flow that'll get us first," Mario said.

"Comforting." It was awe-inspiring, and Hellboy could not help watching in wonder. It was rare that an eruption such as this happened anywhere, and he suspected there would be helicopters buzzing the slopes higher up. What would they think of this car and its foolish occupants, climbing the gentle slopes towards Vesuvius's deadly mouth? He knew what *he'd* think.

He glanced back at Adamo, and the old man had started smoking from his mouth. No, not smoking . . . *steaming*. He coughed up filthy canal water and it hissed into the atmosphere.

"We don't have long," Hellboy said.

"I'm going as fast as—"

"I mean it, Mario."

They passed another burnt out army truck, several more bodies scattered around, and at least they knew they were on the right road.

"Hold on," Mario said. He dropped a gear and floored it, and the engine started to scream. The car shot forward, protesting at the misuse, but still it carried them higher.

No way we can get close to the crater, Hellboy thought. *We'll suffocate long before we get there*. But minutes later, after the road had given way to little more than a rough trail, and the car kicked stones and dust behind them as it struggled to maintain a grip, they came to the first vent.

It was a fresh wound in the land, ragged and sharp-edged, with the debris of its birth scattered all around, from gravel to boulders almost as large as the car. Smoke rose from the hole as if forced under pressure, and from a distance they could see the unmistakeable glow of immense heat inside.

"Lava channel?" Mario asked, and Hellboy could hear the hope in his voice.

"Maybe. But we can't just put him in here."

"Why not?" He stopped the car. Motionless and with the engine idling, they could hear the sounds from outside. Roaring, whistling, cracking, and the fine rattle of dust pattering down across the car's bodywork.

"Franca first," Hellboy said. "Besides, the lava down there is flowing *away* from the volcano, and that might not work. We might need to put him right inside."

No way to tell, the spirit said. *No way, and we cannot risk—*

"Okay, okay."

"The crater?" Mario gasped. "We'll suffocate—"

"I've thought about that," Hellboy said, nodding. "Just get us closer, and higher."

"What about him?" Mario asked.

Hellboy looked at Adamo, and he was wondering the same thing. But the old man seemed to be dreaming, still affected by his dunking in the canal.

Hellboy hoped they were nightmares.

Chapter 18

Vesuvius

Uncle Calvo continued driving even though he screamed. The woman in the seat next to him had curled up into a shivering ball, and Sophia had dug her fingers into the car's upholstery, head pressed back, tendons standing out on her neck.

The car ahead of them slewed back and forth across the road, as if steered by a child.

They're trying to get me right to the crater! Franca thought. They were terrified, and she hoped it was all to do with coming home.

She took her chance. Moving as quickly as she could she reached across Sophia and around Uncle Calvo's shoulder, flipping up the door lock on his door that mastered the rest of the car. Then she fell back into her seat and plucked at the door handle, pushing against it as it opened, rolling out of the car and bringing her arms up to protect her face as she fell. She hadn't taken time to judge the speed they were travelling, nor the terrain, and she struck the rough ground with a staggering impact. Her arms were both smacked against her face and she tasted blood. She rolled twice and came to a halt, and the car continued on without her much further than she could have hoped.

They hardly know I've gone, she thought, and then the brake lights blinked at her.

Standing, she could only look in wonder for a couple of seconds. Without the car restricting her view, the whole wonder of the eruption was before her, and it was like another world. Further up the hillside, past the second car, was another open vent, gases hissing out in an opaque curtain. Above that she could see great cracks in the shoulders of the land.

I can end all this right now, she thought, looking at the vent and imagining tumbling inside. It wouldn't be too painful, surely? A moment of heat, and she'd be dead the instant she struck the lava. But dead how? Would her heart explode from the shock. Would her brains boil? Or would the intense heat melt the flesh from her bones, giving her just that brief instant of measureless agony before reaching inside and snuffing out her existence?

The two cars exploded almost simultaneously. She saw the flames of the fire wolves, enraged by her escape, erupting seconds before the explosions, and she knew her time had come. But like anyone with any sort of life, she craved a final few impossible seconds, and as death faced her, she realized that she would do anything she could to grab them.

So she turned and ran downhill. Metal clanged behind her as car doors came off, and then, above the continuous roar of the volcano, she heard a different whisper of fire, and saw her own shadow thrown before her. It started long, but quickly shrank as the fire wolves closed in.

When she tripped, Franca knew that was the end of her. But at least she'd tried.

And then a car veered around a ridge below, spitting gravel as it roared uphill towards her, and in the driver's seat sat Mario.

Behind him, in the back of the car, flames.

There was little warning when Adamo went hot. One second he seemed to be unconscious, mumbling slightly in that old, unknown language, and the next—with the ghost suddenly screaming in Hellboy's head and the mountain spewing fire and gas around them—he was on fire.

The fire wolf went for Mario, not Hellboy. It reached out and closed its flame claws around the driver's seat, but Mario leaned far forward, and only the headrest caught fire.

Hellboy reached into the heart of the thing with his right hand and clung on, pulling hard against its flexible innards, leaning into the corner of the back seat to drag it as far from Mario as he could. With his other hand, he scrabbled at the door lever.

"Franca!" Mario shouted, and the fire wolf hissed.

Hellboy looked between the front seats, and what he saw froze his breath. Franca was running, and she tripped just as she saw them, sliding on her chest and belly down the gravel slope. Behind her, eight fire wolves were streaking down the slope away from two burning cars. They were gaining on her rapidly, and the first was seconds away.

"Go," Mario said, gripping the wheel and pressing his face against it. "Hellboy, go."

Hellboy knew instantly what Mario meant. Beyond the burning cars there was another rent in the land, gas and smoke hissing upward under tremendous pressure.

"Mario—"

"No choice." His voice was calm now, quiet, and even when the Adamo-wolf lashed out and burnt a weal across his scalp, he did not let out a sound. He was determined, and Hellboy knew that talking would do no good.

As they approached Franca, speeding up rather than slowing down, Mario tweaked the steering to aim at the fire wolves.

Hellboy spat at Adamo's fire wolf struggling beneath and around his clasping right hand, and he heard a sizzle as the spit struck. Then the fingers of his left hand caught the door catch and he pulled.

As he fell, he opened his right hand and freed the fire wolf.

But the demon was not finished with him yet. Hellboy felt a searing pain in his left leg as he tumbled from the car, an internal fire that seemed to settle in his bones and travel through his entire body. It hurt so much that he forgot to break his fall, and his head thumped at the ground, his body rolling and shoulders twisting as the momentum scraped him uphill.

It's still with us! Into the flames, Hellboy, throw yourself in now and take it—

"Shut up!"

The fire wolf growled and opened its black-mawed mouth, snapping for Hellboy's face. He brought his arm up just in time and fire-teeth pierced, settling in the bone and joining the fire from his leg.

Franca struggled to her feet just as the car struck the first fire wolf pursuing her. Mario must have missed her by inches, and the vehicle flung the burning thing high into the air, careering into the others and spilling them across the hillside. They hissed and roared, unhurt but angered. Some of them streaked after the car, but four converged on Franca . . . and surrounded her. She stepped this way and that, but the things prevented her escape, careful not to burn her but determined never to let her go.

The car skidded across the rough road, spinning on the gravel, wheels smoking as they sought purchase, and it fishtailed as Mario drove it hard back down the hillside. Three fire wolves clasped onto the bodywork, their flames streaked back by the wind force, but another seemed to have smashed its way into the car.

Mario's hair was on fire.

"No . . ." Hellboy muttered, and the Adamo fire wolf burning into his arm opened its mouth to utter a rumbling laugh.

"Funny, is it?" Hellboy asked. He punched at it with his right hand. "*Funny?*" He punched again, growling, bitter, angry and hurting.

"Mario!" Franca screamed, because she had seen what was becoming of her cousin.

Hellboy saw too, and in the young man's blazing hair and melting face, he perceived such a grimace of determination—and hatred—that he knew he had to do everything he could to help

Mario go through with his final heroic, desperate act. So he punched the fire wolf again, and grabbed hold of its insubstantial insides, and as the car roared downhill he leapt into its path.

Hellboy knew that this was going to hurt.

But they were all out of time.

Franca stepped this way and that, trying to gain a better view. The fire wolves remained close, but not so close that they burned her. And they too were watching.

The car struck Hellboy and the fire wolf head-on. The sound of the impact was sickening, and she saw a confused blur of red and yellow—flesh and flame—bouncing onto the hood and shattering through the windscreen. The car continued careering down the hillside, leaving the trail and slamming into rocks, jumping left and right, and all the while its insides were aflame. Windows shattered and fire burst out, and then the rear window misted and disintegrated, and Hellboy struck the ground behind the car. He rolled and stood unsteadily, glancing back uphill at Franca, then down again at the car that continued on without him.

There was something in his stance that Franca did not like. At first she thought it was pain, because much of his body was scorched black, and he was holding his left arm awkwardly across his chest. But then she realized that Hellboy stood like a held breath, a moment between blinks, and she knew that this was the end.

One way or another, this was the end.

The car struck a large boulder and tipped onto its side, sliding across the rough ground and throwing up sparks as it went, fire wolves still grasping its sides. And then it tipped forward, nose disappearing into the first gas-and-smoke-spewing crevasse they had passed so recently. It seemed to balance there, the exploding front tires audible even at this distance.

The Adamo fire wolf appeared at the smashed rear window, flame arms raised, and the things around Franca hissed what might have been relief.

And then the car tipped forward and disappeared completely.

"Oh, Mario," she said, but her face was too hot for tears.

The car's fuel tank exploded, throwing a shower of metal and upholstery high above the landscape . . . and writhing in that cloud of debris, the twisting shape of Adamo's fire wolf.

Behind them, high up the mountainside, a staggering explosion stirred the clouds and shook the land.

Adamo landed beside the crevasse, stretching and twisting in triumph. Franca saw Hellboy's shoulders slump. And when he glanced back at her she saw his face, and knew he had given everything he had.

The fire wolves surrounding her faded back to flesh, and Sophia grinned as she grabbed Franca's arms.

Something came out of the crevasse. It looked like a massive spurt of blood, but it rose high, maintaining its solidity and shivering the air with heat haze: an eruption of lava, the width of the car it had swallowed and the height of twenty men.

That rising wave of lava slapped down onto Adamo faster than mere gravity would have taken it, as if the deep muscles of the land had flexed and brought it down. It crushed the fire wolf flat and swallowed his flames, dragging him back across the ground and disappearing into the crevasse with an earsplitting hiss.

Hellboy turned and glared uphill at Franca. And then he started to run.

Franca!

With Mario dead, and the Adamo fire wolf taken back into the heat and fury of Vesuvius, she was his only concern. Because he had no idea what would happen next. He started running towards her and the fire wolves that still surrounded her . . . but his concern was unfounded.

It's done . . . it's done . . . the ghost whispered, and Hellboy had never heard such relief, and such tiredness.

The fire wolves were screaming. In the guise of old people, they gripped at the ground, but there was no purchase to be had there. Pulled inexorably downward, they shouted at Hellboy, at Franca, flaming again as their true natures came to the fore once more. But no one and nothing listened to their screams. Only Vesuvius, drawing back what had been taken from it so long ago, and still furious as ever at their deception.

They disappeared into the rent in the land, the only sign of their passing a sigh of flames.

By the time he reached Franca, she was kneeling, holding her face in her hands and crying tears of relief and pain, joy and grief. Sweeping her up into his arms he kissed her forehead and hugged her tight, and even though it hurt them both to do so, she hugged him back.

"Come on," Hellboy said. "We need to go."

"Would Mario have been enough?" Franca asked through her tears. "He was an Esposito . . . would he have been enough?"

Always women, the ghost whispered. *Always the life-bearers.*

"Not on his own," Hellboy said. And it felt like a betrayal, because for a while the ghost had made him consider the benefits of Franca's own demise. "But because he took Adamo with him . . . that means he'll definitely be the last."

"I can't believe . . ."

"Brave kid. Braver than I gave him credit for." He winced, looked at the dreadful wounds on his arm. He was going to be sore in the morning. "Let's get out of here."

Chapter 19

Amalfi

Amalfi was alight with celebration.

It had taken Hellboy and Franca eight hours to make it back to the city, and by then it was midnight, and the glow to the north had faded away. The eruption of Vesuvius had faded and passed, perplexing the myriad volcanologists who offered their opinions on TV and the radio, but delighting everyone else. The evacuees in Amalfi had joined with the town's inhabitants to rejoice in the danger's passing, and the massive street party that snaked through the city seemed set to continue long into the night.

Hellboy was exhausted. And with every step he took closer to La Casa Fredda, he wondered more and more about what his intentions had been up on Vesuvius. The ghost had fallen silent for now, but he could not forget her sly suggestion that Franca should be left to her fate. However much Hellboy had denied that alternative, there had always been a part of him that . . .

But there were deep parts of him that bore many such doubts, where suspicions and fears made their home. Sometimes when he was asleep, the doors to that place were opened, and he had nightmares. And sometimes even when awake, he stood outside, rifling through those dark things he tried to keep small, and quiet. This was just one more to add to that collection.

Franca was alive, with him now, and approaching her devastated family home once again. He could spend ages thinking about what could have been, but he decided to revel in what was.

By the time they reached the big house Hellboy was barely able to walk. The burns he'd received in his various tussles with Adamo's fire wolf needed attention, and some of them—those on his left arm and right ankle especially—seemed to have planted a seed of fire in his bones that still burned. But more than anything, he needed sleep.

They found the survivors of the Esposito family in the house, huddled in one room and mourning their dreadful loss. They had left Orso's café and come home. The police had not yet been called, because Espositos were used to handling problems on their own. But Hellboy knew that tomorrow would be a harsh day for them all. The bodies needed removing, police would shut down the house as a crime scene, and an investigation would begin. He promised as much help as the B.P.R.D. could give them, but he felt detached from the conversations, distanced from their tears and loss.

Franca told them all that Hellboy had saved them, but he made sure they knew the truth. It had been Mario. Hellboy had just been the muscle, and in the end, it was Mario who'd had the guts to end things.

The bed in Carlotta's room was comfortable and luxurious, and Hellboy and Franca lay there together. She fell asleep almost immediately, but enervated though he was, it took Hellboy a while to drift away. He tried to cast his mind through the land and into the roiling, boiling guts of Vesuvius, imagining what was happening down there right now, but he realized quickly that it was beyond his understanding. Something asleep had been woken, and now it slept again. For now, that was all that mattered. What the future might bring . . . ?

As with his doubts concerning his intentions with Franca, Hellboy decided it best to live with what was, not what might have been.

"I'll take you back tomorrow," he whispered.

No need, the ghost replied, and its voice was so very far away. *I can find my own way.*

At last, sleep found him. Cool, calm sleep.

And when he woke in the morning, all he had around his neck was an old, chipped bone. Before Franca stirred, he sat up and dropped the bone into one of his belt pouches. Then he lay there and watched the dawn.

"Hey, Liz."

"H.B! So I see from the news things have calmed down over there."

"You could say that. Yeah." He trailed off, not really sure why he'd called Liz. He'd be back with her by the evening. He looked out over the gardens of La Casa Fredda and beyond, and dawn seemed to wash Amalfi clean.

"Bad one," she said. They knew each other so well that she recognized his silences.

"Yeah. A lot of good people . . ." He glanced at the bed where Franca still slept. "Lot of good people died."

"But the fire wolves are down?"

"All of them." Hellboy sighed and stretched, wincing at the pains that sparked across his body, and the heat that still seemed embedded in his bones. It would go, he knew, given time. He hoped his next assignment would be to somewhere *cold*. "So, tell me about that boat."

Liz got the message. She told him about the haunted boat, and her night on board, and what had happened to her and the others who came to see what the ruckus was all about. He listened and nodded, grunting here and there, chuckling when she told him about the poltergeist's almost unnatural interest in her shoes. And for a while, Liz Sherman's voice took him away from the pain and the recent past, and also diverted him from the awkward moments he knew were yet to come.

For a while.

• • •

Franca drove him to the airport. Commercial flights were cancelled for the day because of the dangerous build-up of dust and ash on the runways, but the B.P.R.D. had arranged for a private jet to fly him back to Connecticut. Tom Manning wanted a rapid debriefing, and while Hellboy felt frustration at the man's overzealousness, the thought of being back home felt good.

They remained quiet on the drive, and Hellboy felt the weight of unsaid things hanging between them.

"Are you going home?" he asked at last.

"Yes. Back to Amalfi. Are you surprised?"

"Not at all," Hellboy said, though he was a little. "I think it'll be good for the family to—"

"What's left of it."

"Yeah. What's left. So, your boyfriend? What was his name, Alex?"

Franca shrugged, frowned. "After what happened . . . I don't know. He feels so distant. So . . . innocent of the reality of things."

"Hey, that's no way to think," Hellboy said. "Don't let what happened here make you think normal's lost its value, somehow. Normal is *good*, Franca. It's where most people live. It gives them peace, and something to build their lives on. I mainly live outside it, and take a look at me."

Franca did look at him, but her smile was pained. "Maybe," she said. "Maybe I'll call him, in time."

"You do that," he said, and he leaned back and closed his eyes. They travelled in silence for a while, but it was a loaded silence, not a comfortable one. He knew that the airport was a long way yet.

"Hellboy . . ." Franca said at last, and he thought, *Here it comes. This is what she's been waiting to say.*

"What's on your mind?"

She gripped the wheel, sighed, and he saw the trickle of a tear mark her cheek.

"Hey." He reached out and touched her shoulder, and Franca drifted their car to a halt beside the road.

"There are some things that don't need saying!" Franca said. She sounded angry, but he saw the desperation beneath that. "There's going to be investigations, and your organization will liaise with the Italian authorities, but no one here needs to know about our bloodline, do they? The fact that we've got fire wolf blood in our veins?"

Hellboy imagined the results of that. The subtle tests to begin with; keeping the family under observation, testing their motor skills and psychological functions. But then after that, if examinations weren't conclusive, he knew where things could go. Genetic tests to track aging of cells. Blood make-up. Aversion to water.

There were few enough Espositos left as it was.

"Some things don't need to go outside B.P.R.D.," he said.

"But even there—"

"That's my home," Hellboy said. "It's who I am, and they're my friends. We're good at keeping secrets."

"Really?"

Hellboy chuckled. "Really. Believe me. The things I could tell you."

Franca laughed, and he could see the terrible weight lifting from her shoulders. "Thank you," she said, "but I think I've had enough of that for a while."

Approaching Naples, Hellboy saw Vesuvius to the northeast, nothing but a gentle finger of smoke trailing from the crater now. He noticed that Franca kept her eyes fixed on the road, and he wondered whether she'd look at the volcano on the way back to Amalfi. He thought not. He *hoped* not.

He was going home. He was glad, but with every mile they drew closer to the airport, he felt a strange loneliness growing. He guessed he was going to miss Franca more than he'd believed.

• • •

At the airport she accompanied him onto the runway, waiting at the bottom of the steps leading up into the private jet. "Thank you," she said. She moved into his embrace. They both had wounds, and she would have scars, but the worst ones would always be inside.

As Hellboy hugged her, she felt his hand press flat against her back, and sensed his held breath. *Is he feeling for heat?* she thought. She pulled back and looked up at him, and his smile could not have been more relaxed. Good. He didn't find any.

"You've always got a holiday home in Amalfi," she said.

"I've always wanted to come to Italy." He kissed her on the forehead, then turned and started up the steps.

"Hellboy." He looked back. "I'd have put myself in," she said. "I was ready for that. If all else failed, I'd have jumped."

He nodded. "Then we should *both* give thanks for Mario."

Franca walked back to the terminal and watched the jet take off. She waited until it was out of sight, and then waited some more. She had to drive past Vesuvius to get back home. There was no rush.

TIM LEBBON is a *New York Times* bestselling author of over a dozen novels—including *Hellboy: Unnatural Selection, Dusk, Fallen* and *The Map of Moments* (with Christopher Golden)—several collections, and over a hundred short stories and novellas. He has won three British Fantasy Awards and a Bram Stoker Award, as well as being shortlisted for many more. Several of his novels and novellas are in development as movies on both sides of the Atlantic. Find updates at www.timlebbon.net.

In a London funeral parlor, the dead rise and walk again. On a train in the London Underground, a young couple is terrorized by a demon. In a suburb, a poltergeist forces a family to flee their home. Called in to investigate these supernatural events, B.P.R.D. agents Abe Sapien and Liz Sherman discover a wellspring of black magic under the London streets. Hellboy descends into the dark underworld of London, encountering demons that prophesy the coming of plague and the opening of an Eye to the otherworld, bringing forth death and destruction upon the land.

ISBN 978-1-59582-204-8 | $12.95